D1343739

And So It Began

Owen Mullen

007068501 0

Copyright © 2017 Owen Mullen

The right of Owen Mullen to be identified as the Author of the Work has been asserted by him in accordance Copyright, Designs and Patents Act 1988.

First published in 2017 by Bloodhound Books

Apart from any use permitted under UK copyright law, this publication may only be reproduced, stored, or transmitted, in any form, or by any means, with prior permission in writing of the publisher or, in the case of reprographic production, in accordance with the terms of licences issued by the Copyright Licensing Agency.

All characters in this publication are fictitious and any resemblance to real persons, living or dead, is purely coincidental.

www.bloodhoundbooks.com

Print ISBN 978-1-912175-55-0

This Copy is For Press Review Only.

Also By Owen Mullen

PI Charlie Cameron Series:-

Games People Play

Old Friends New Enemies

Before The Devil Knows You're Dead

Praise for Games People Play

Longlisted for the Bloody Scotland McIlvanney Award 2017

"Owen Mullen sucks the air out of your lungs in the opening pages of his novel and the standard of his writing that he has set here simply continues throughout the book."

Susan Hampson - Books from Dusk Till Dawn book blog

"Games People Play is an easy to read, fast paced thrilling page turner that is bound to capture your attention."

Gemma Gaskarth - Between The Pages Book Club

"The book is very well written and it kept me gripped right through to the end, its fast paced and compelling with enough twists to keep you engaged and guessing."

Donna Maguire - Donnas Book Blog

Praise for Old Friends And New Enemies

"The tension was more palpable, the storyline was grittier, and the stakes were higher as Charlie faced some serious betrayals."

Amy Sullivan - Novelgossip

"This is the second book to feature PI Charlie Cameron, I loved the first book so had high hopes for this one it delivered. Bucket loads."

David Baird - David's Book Blurb

"The mix of thrills, tension, suspense and a touch of humour worked really well, as did the interactions and relationships between the characters."

Mark Tilbury - Author

Praise for Before The Devil Knows You're Dead

"Before The Devil Knows You're Dead gives you a tightly knit and enthralling plot, with Glaswegian grit and gallows humour thrown in; Owen has an uncanny knack of creating solid and multi-dimensional characters that will draw you in and leave you wanting more… it will keep you engrossed until the very last page and shouting for book number four!"

Sharon Bairden - Chapter In My Life book blog

"If you like your books fast paced, gritty and multilayered, then grab this book, and if you haven't read the others grab them too."

Alfred Nobile - Goodreads

"The author manages to keep me guessing and keeps his cards close to his chest so that I never know what quite to expect. This is sure to be a hit with fans of the series, new and old."

Sarah Hardy - By The Letter Book Reviews

To
Catherine Mullen: a friend when friends were few.
And Devon and Harrison: The Carney boys.
I think about you every day.

Prologue

The Little Louisiana Pageant, Whitfield Centre, Baton Rouge

Timmy Donald waited to be introduced; he wasn't nervous. Timmy was a round-faced cherub, kiss-curled and confident. A tiny robot programmed to perform, and at five, already a veteran.

The MC gave him a big build-up. 'From East Baton Rouge, a homeboy paying his tribute to one of the greatest entertainers of all time … Timmy Donald!'

The red velvet curtain parted, leaving Charlie Chaplin in the spotlight – lost, unsure and vulnerable. Timmy played it to a T, cocking his head to one side, leaning both hands on his stick. The face of a comic genius gazed out of the golden light. A single note gave him his key, and the spot followed the diminutive performer through a show of stagecraft beyond his years.

A piano track, played without finesse, tinkled in the background. Timmy brought the walking stick into action in vintage Chaplinesque. He scrunched his shoulders and tipped his bowler, letting it run down his arm, a weak smile revealing the courage of the little tramp beset by cruel misfortune. He sang "Smile," and the audience loved him.

At the end of the song, he twirled, walked his "Charlie" walk and shuffled towards the back of the stage. The spotlight died, the curtains closed, the lights came up.

Timmy's father was pleased. All the hard work, the day after day rehearsals, had paid off. That trick with the hat had taken months to get right. Worth it, though.

'You can't put it out if you don't put it in,' Tom Donald reminded his son every chance he got. The old jazz musicians' maxim about the value of practice appealed to him. Timmy's performance shouted its truth.

He was the winner for sure. Everybody said so.

* * *

'We can't find him.'

Claudine Charlton couldn't believe it. It had been going so well. A good crowd. No hiccups. No tantrums. Even one or two who might have something. Not as good as the Chaplin kid but not bad. She watched Alec Adams giving out instructions. He'd been with her for years, from the very first contest, and she would be first to admit that when it came to stage-management, there was nobody better. They had been married once, a very long time ago. Claudine never let herself forget that he was a snake.

Alec shook his head. 'No sign.'

'Did you ask his parents?'

'His father thought we had him.'

In a room off to the side, the judges sat round a beat-up table, drinking coffee. Claudine didn't knock. The interruption took them by surprise.

'We have the final result, Claudine.'

'Who won?'

'The little boy.'

'Forget it. He's out of the running. We need another decision and fast. Bump everybody on a place; that'll give us a new winner. Stick any of them in third, it doesn't matter. The cowgirl, the crowd liked her, she'll do. OK? Two minutes.'

'But she was awful.'

'No.' Claudine stared the objector down. 'She was third.'

Alec met her behind the stage. 'Cops are here. And the father. Somebody needs to speak to him.'

'What? Oh, yeah.' She ran a hand through her hair in quiet desperation. 'What do I tell him? What can I say?'

'Reassure him.'

'You do it. You speak to him.'

'It's your show, and I'm busy. You're the boss, remember?'

She hurried towards a guy in an ill-fitting suit – had to be a cop – talking to Timmy's father. Uniforms covered the stage door; the front was already closed.

'Mr Donald, Claudine Charlton.'

Timmy's father was too upset to reply. She placed a comforting hand on his arm and spoke to the policeman. 'I'm in charge. What do you need to know?'

'When did you notice the kid was missing?'

The policeman glanced at Tom Donald and walked-back his tactless question. 'I mean, when did you notice Timmy was missing?'

'Twenty minutes ago. He was one of the last to go on. Once they've done their thing, the contestants stay in the dressing rooms. No wandering around until we announce the winners.'

'Sounds fine. So how come he's gone?'

'Wish I knew.'

The detective gave an order to a sergeant. 'Start interviewing. We need ID, names and addresses. It's going to be a long night.'

Claudine said, 'Is there anything I can do?'

'Start looking.'

'What about the show?'

He didn't answer her.

'Shouldn't we go with the final ceremony? Keep it normal'

'Good idea. Finish the thing. Nobody's going home for a while.'

* * *

One hour later, a locked store cupboard in a back room was the only place that hadn't been searched. The detective wasn't prepared to wait for a key; he barked his instructions. 'Break it open.'

Two uniforms forced the door. The wood frame cracked and splintered and gave under the pressure. In his career, the cop had come across plenty of bad stuff; that didn't make it easier. The colour drained from his face, and he knew he'd been doing this shit for too many years: time to take the pension, kick back and go fishing. But for now, he was the officer in charge, so he made himself look at the horror guaranteed to keep him awake at night long after he'd turned in his gun and badge.

Stuffed in at the back, on top of paint pots and dustsheets, was a broken Charlie Chaplin doll that used to be Timmy Donald.

And so, it began.

Part One

Summer in the City

One

Julian Boutte threw his cards on the table face down so the FBI agents didn't see his winning hand. 'Beats me,' he said. 'I'm out.'

He yawned, scratched the heavy stubble on his jaw and stood. The agents ignored him and concentrated on the game. They'd been in the safe house since before the start of the trial – now ten days in – and were battling boredom. Their level of alertness had fallen; the prisoner was becoming part of the furniture. They called him Juli, talked football, and showed him photographs of their kids, while he faked interest and lost at Blackjack to keep them happy. Occasionally, they baited him because they could, and Boutte acted uptight, as if the consequences of testifying against his former boss, Beppe "Little Man" Giordano, the head of one of the oldest crime families in the South, made him nervous.

It didn't.

Boutte and Giordano hadn't seen each other in seven years, not since Boutte was convicted and sent to Angola. But the thick-set felon was a ghost from the past, the last man the accused would want in court: Julian knew where the bodies were buried – literally – he'd put some of them in the ground himself. If he took the stand, it was all over for "Little Man." With Boutte's testimony, the FBI would close down his operation and give him a one-way ticket to the Farm. As for Julian Boutte, he would be handed back to the U.S. Marshals and swallowed by the Witness Protection Program. In a month, a guy who looked a lot like him would be pumping gas in Oregon, or somewhere far from Louisiana.

That was the deal. Boutte had been removed from the penitentiary for his own protection, and it was common knowledge Giordano's men were searching for him. The Mafia boss should've known he had nothing to worry about from his former employee.

Boutte paced the floor. Over at the window, he fingered the blind.

Sammy – the fat Fed – remembered he had a job to do and spoke without taking his eyes off the two aces he was preparing to split. 'You know the rules, Juli. Sit down and chill.'

The agents had seemed distracted, but the admonishment meant they hadn't switched off completely.

Boutte stayed in character. 'Yeah? Easier said.'

The other agent, a bald guy called Maurice, enjoyed himself at his expense. 'What's the matter? Can't wait to be washing those cars? Shine'em up good now, y'hear?'

'He's scared his pal Beppe's coming 'round to cool him out.'

The agents sniggered into their cards. Boutte pretended to be irritated and slumped into an armchair. He turned the television on and listlessly began surfing the early-evening channels.

Fat Boy wasn't done. 'Stick with the cartoons, all right. Stay away from the news, Juli. Your ugly mug'll be on every channel between here and the Gulf soon enough.'

Maurice tossed in his two cents. 'Don't blame you for being nervous. Giordano's gonna be awful pissed when you start blabbing. Introducing him to The Electrician at Angola won't go down well. Might not speak to you again.'

The agents laughed and dealt a fresh hand. Their coats hung on the chairs behind them, and their sleeves were rolled up. Holstered weapons rested against crumpled shirts. Underneath the table, Maurice had his shoes off and was whistling out of tune: for all the world, just buddies at the regular Tuesday night meet, instead of law enforcement officers guarding the prosecution's star turn. Boutte let them have their fun. The more relaxed they were the easier it would be.

He complained on cue. 'When's dinner? I'm hungry.'

'Too soon. Have some potato chips.'

'Sick of potato chips.'

'Then suit yourself.'

The split aces delivered. Fatso grinned and pulled his winnings towards him. He pitched a dollar across to Boutte. It landed on the carpet between them.

'A contribution towards your new life, Julian, or whatever you're gonna call yourself.'

'Shove it up your ass.'

Fat Boy was better at dishing it out than taking it. 'You're an ungrateful fucker, d'you realise that, Juli? With what you've done, they should've thrown the key away. Instead, you're sailin' free.'

'Is that what I'm doing?'

'Too right. Free and clear.'

Julian imagined the wall behind Fatso, splashed with blood and bone, after he blew a hole in the bastard's skull.

Boom! Boom! Boom!

At seven, a knock on the door and an exchange of passwords meant the food had arrived. The game was abandoned. The agents opened the boxes.

'Pizza again. Doesn't the budget run to anything else?' Boutte complained.

'Maybe somebody doesn't share your sense of importance? Eat it or don't eat it. Your choice.'

'I'm just saying. Does it always have to be junk? It gives me stomach ache.'

Maurice shook his bald head at his partner. 'And they told us this was a tough guy.'

They ate in silence, tearing off pieces of red dough and stuffing them into their mouths until the boxes were empty. Boutte didn't join in. Maurice wiped his hands on his pants and went to the kitchen to make coffee. From what he'd seen so far, Boutte was a loser; a low-energy nobody with an undeserved reputation. Riding him never got old.

Fat Sam rubbed his belly and spoke, spraying grated Parmesan across at his prisoner. 'Gotta eat, man. Keep up your strength for when Beppe's thugs come bursting through that door and drag you away.'

Boutte tapped out a Gitanes and lit it.

The fat man said, 'Heard something once – way down the line – 'bout what Giordano did to a traitor.'

Maurice came back with the coffee. 'Don't tell him, Sammy. He'll go running back to Angola.'

Sammy smiled. 'Too late. Option's off the table. Wouldn't last a day.'

Maurice agreed. 'Lucky if he lasted an hour.'

Boutte drew on his smoke and stared at the floor. It was eight o'clock.

Almost time.

The overweight agent studied him. 'Nah. Best Juli realises where it's at. Anyway, the guy's name was Foy. Narcisse Foy. Ever heard of him?'

Boutte ignored the question.

'Took him into the bayou, stripped him naked, and tied him to a big old Spanish Oak. Then, they got to work on him. According to the story, one of Giordano's men had trained as a chef. He showed the others what was what.'

Sammy savoured the details.

'Started at his toes and worked their way up. Didn't stop until it was done. Skinned him alive then dumped him in the water for the 'gators.'

He paused and pointed. 'That's who you're about to fuck with.'

The ash on Julian Boutte's cigarette was a tiny grey finger. His hand was steady. As steady as it had been in the bayou fifteen years ago after he'd given up on the idea of becoming the next Emeril Lagasse. And Fatso had it wrong; they'd taken the hide off Narcisse Foy in two long sessions, though on the second, he hadn't known much about it. Boutte wondered what had happened to the knife; it would be perfect for trimming the fat on this moron.

He flicked the ash on the carpet and followed it to the floor with his eyes. 'It's a myth.'

The agent hooked his thumbs inside his belt and let his chins settle on his chest. 'Maybe so. Maybe so. But what if it isn't, Juli? You ready to die that hard? Oh, and just so we're straight. If they come for you, I won't stand in their way.'

Boutte got out of his chair. 'Anymore scary tales? No? I'm gonna shake hands with an old friend.'

Alone, he revisited the plan. The next shift would arrive at seven a.m. Ten hours; more than enough time to cover the eighty miles to New Orleans.

When he came back into the room, the agents were watching a quiz show on television. They paid no attention to their charge. Boutte walked up behind Maurice. He reached over the man's shoulder, grabbed his gun from the holster and shot him in the neck, severing his spinal cord. His partner struggled to get his bulky frame out of the seat, fumbling for his weapon. A bullet in the knee ended his attempt.

He howled and cried like a baby. 'This is a mistake, Juli!'

'Think so?'

A second bullet destroyed the fat man's other knee, and he roared.

'Talking of mistakes, Sammy, what Narcisse got wasn't Beppe's idea.'

Through the pain, the agent's face twisted in disbelief. 'You? You were there?'

'Shame you never got to try my blackened cod. Some reckoned it was as good as the plate at the Commander's Palace.'

The third shot shattered the FBI agent's collarbone. Boutte ignored the screams and took aim; he'd saved his head 'til last.

'Could be I'm in the wrong business. For sure one of us is.'

Two

It rained during the night. Hard rain that cut the stifling air and drummed on the roof, then stopped as suddenly as it had started. But by that time, along with half of New Orleans, I was awake.

Lowell sensed I was in the land of the living and padded through. 'Good morning, mutt. When you gonna learn how to make coffee? That would be a trick I could use.'

Some people had kids to save their relationship. I'd bought my fiancée, Ellen Ames, a dog: a tan mongrel with white paws and the deep eyes of an old soul. He was in a pet shop window in Basin when I saw him, and while his brothers and sisters rolled all over each other, he sat at the back – aloof and apart. His expression said he was too fucking cool for any of that shit. Unfortunately, the relationship didn't work out, and when we split, Lowell wound up with me.

Even as a pup, he was a creature of habit, starting every day the same, with porridge – no sugar, no milk. If it had been down to me, I would've fed him from a tin, like a regular dog. He had other ideas. I sipped black coffee, ate a bagel, and watched him lick the bowl clean, then he picked up my harmonica up in his teeth and dropped it at my feet – his way of saying he wanted us to cycle into the city.

With me vamping on a harmonica on a holder round my neck and Lowell running along beside me and wagging his tail, I guess we were quite a sight. If I hit a bum note, he gave me a look; he's got a good ear for this stuff. My sister Catherine swears I'm eccentric. I disagree, although a six-foot guy riding a bike and blowing the blues for a music-loving hound isn't something you see very often.

In the Quarter, shopkeepers were already setting-up for the next wave of tourists. Outside a café, a black cook with a cheroot hanging from his mouth leaned on the frame of the door. He smiled as we passed him, wiped a hand on his whites and shouted his appreciation. 'Yeah! I hear you, brother!'

At Dauphine, I chained the bike to the railing at the bottom of the wooden stairs and climbed to my one-room office. As usual, the paperboy had used the *Times-Picayune* to improve his throwing action; the newspaper lay at the door where it had landed. Inside, Lowell headed for his basket. First up, I phoned Stella. Usually, we spent the weekend together, but on Sunday night, a friend had needed her.

'Hi, baby. Missed you last night. How's your friend?'

'Better. Hates every man born. Who can blame her?'

'You don't mean that.'

'Lucky for you.'

We chatted for a while, then I made coffee and scanned the paper. Two copies of the *Times-Picayune* – one for home and one for the office – was overkill. But I like what I like.

The news had moved on from the five-year-old kid abducted and murdered at a pageant up in Baton Rouge. At the time, details were scarce. I hadn't read them, and I didn't envy the detectives working on the case. That kind of stuff was one good reason for getting out of the NOPD.

The start of the football season was still weeks away. I settled down with my current obsession: The Word Jumble. Today's puzzle was a beauty. I read the letters aloud to Lowell.

'REPDHAOTI. Any ideas?'

He thought about it.

'REPDHAOTI.'

Lowell was better at this than me, but I preferred to get there by myself.

Around ten-thirty, a call from Harry Love, a defence lawyer who hired me to do work for him from time to time, interrupted our attempts to crack it. Harry was a lawyer and a liar by trade, who tossed work my way – mostly uncovering information that wouldn't appear in the usual background checks. He was a man of few words, who made a point of ending every conversation first, to let people know that in his world time was money; in mine, it was only time. Most of our talking was done over the phone. Harry knew as much about me as I did about him, which suited both of us.

'How's your dance card, Delaney?'

'It could stand a little filling-in. What do you want?'

'Just checking you're still in business.'

'Still am, Harry.'

'Good to know. I'll be in touch.'

And he was gone.

I went back to the Word Jumble, scribbling one failed attempt after another in the margin and crossing them out. Lowell stared from the comfort of his basket, telling me in his quiet way he thought I should be, at least, trying to keep the wolves from the door. Overreacting. We hadn't died a winter yet, and I was doing what I was born to do: not very much.

Three hours went by, before the phone rang a second time: Danny Fitzpatrick. Fitzy was a detective with the NOPD and played bass in our band. He didn't bother with small talk.

'An old friend of yours is back on the street.'

'Yeah, who?'

'Julian Boutte.'

'Impossible. He's in Angola.'

'Not anymore. Made a deal in exchange for calling time on his old boss.'

The trial had been front-page news for a week and a half. I hadn't read it. As far as I was concerned, it was nothing to do with me. I was done.

'You said back on the street.'

'That's right. They were keeping him in a safe house in Baton Rouge until he was needed. Never got that far. Boutte killed two Feds and busted out. What a shit storm that's caused. Everybody's been pulled in.'

'When was this?'

'Last night. He's here, and we both know why. Juli Boutte's a Class-A bad guy with a grudge against the whole world, especially you. He's a psycho. He'll have obsessed about what you did to him every day he's been inside. Testifying against his boss was a ploy to get to you.'

I sighed, and Danny snapped at me. 'Take this seriously, Delaney.'

'I am taking it seriously. But worrying never changed anything, did it?'

'Says who? You're the guy who put this nut's brother in the ground, in case you've forgotten.'

Fitzy faded. The voice in my head belonged to an old detective and the speech he'd made at his retirement party. "Sometimes, the line between good shit and bad shit is invisible. Can't know which side you're on until the game plays out."

I've always remembered that. And I hadn't forgotten Julian Boutte, either.

* * *

Seven Years Earlier

On that sunny afternoon, the bad shit showed up first.

My shift had finished, and I'd already dropped Danny off when the radio crackled an APB about a 2002 tan Oldsmobile with a broken headlight and three occupants – two African American males and a female. Suspected abduction. A minute later the Olds passed me heading towards the river. I called it in, made a U-turn and followed it all the way to Algiers and Behrman, north of Tall Timbers. For a while, I lost it then found it again, parked behind a shotgun shack on a patch of ratty grass that doubled as a garbage dump.

From inside the house, a high-pitched laugh that didn't make it past a giggle squeezed through the clapboard to where I crouched underneath the window. Across the yard, a barefoot kid, no more than five or six, dressed in washed-out overalls, stared at me with big, round almond eyes. I put a finger to my lips, hoping he was in the mood to play along, and took a look over the frame.

In the middle of the room, tied to a chair, a woman who was probably in her mid-twenties – dark-skinned and stick-thin – glared terror at her kidnappers from sunken eyes strung-out on crystal meth. She was gagged, and her head had been crudely shaved. Clumps of hair lay on the floor, and the yellow shirt she'd been wearing hung from her waist, exposing sagging breasts that may have been beautiful before fear of losing her buzz became more important than eating. Two black men in jeans and vests drank beer from the bottle, one of them balancing a knife by the tip in the palm of his hand and smiling a glassy smile at his skill, while his bro boogied to hip-hop coming from a radio. They passed a joint between them big enough to choke a horse, clearly enjoying the groove, easy about what they were gonna do.

Until that moment, I didn't know Cedric and Julian Boutte from a hole in the wall.

How much better if it had stayed that way.

The guy with the knife moved towards the woman, gently taking her face in his hands, studying her like the lover he'd been or had wanted to be, then traced her cheek with the blade, drawing a thin red line from ear to jaw. Light glanced off the steel. He turned his attention to the other side and did the same. She trembled but didn't cry out. I admired her courage.

Cedric, the dancer, spoke. 'Do her slow, Juli. Slooow.'

He dragged the word to make his point and went into a moonwalk that wouldn't have disgraced Michael Jackson. When he pivoted, I saw the gunmetal handle of the piece tucked into the back of his belt and realised it was going to go down hard. Over my shoulder, the street kid was still there. Before he got much older, those big eyes would see plenty of things no child should see.

I pressed myself against the wall and listened for a police car in the distance, hearing instead the sound of a zillion insects carried on the warm air. In the house, the woman finally broke her silence. She screamed. The kid's expression didn't change, which told me all I needed to know about his life. The smart thing would be to wait for back-up. By that time, the woman would have a new face, and it wouldn't matter anymore. Whatever she'd done, she didn't deserve this.

The door broke easily against my weight. I rolled on the bare board floor and came to a halt with my arms outstretched and my gun drawn.

'Hands in the air! Now!'

Dulled by the dope, Julian Boutte's brow furrowed at the unexpected interruption. Boogie Man reacted faster. He reached behind his back for his weapon, and I fired a shot that blew a hole in his heart. Cedric had boogied his last boogie; he was dead when he hit the ground. His brother put his surprise aside long enough to topple the chair, with the woman in it, on top of me. Our heads cracked. Boutte took a step towards me and kicked my gun across the room.

I got to my feet. There was no feeling in my hand; maybe my wrist was broken. Joy crept slowly across Boutte's ugly mug. Somebody was going to die today; the woman had been his first pick, but he'd settle for me.

The blade shimmered and flashed, missing my throat by inches. Boutte passed it from hand to hand, grinning like a maniac, and brought it in an arc that was intended to distract rather than find a target. Suddenly, he altered the direction and lunged forward. I stepped away. At first, I thought he'd missed, then I felt the back of my neck wet and the faint smell of metal told me he'd found his mark.

Boutte's expression hardened; he moved in to finish me off. The siren saved my life. Confusion twisted his features as he weighed his desire to kill me against escape. Self-preservation got the vote. Juli ran to the kitchen, dived through the glass into the afternoon sun and disappeared into Algiers.

The uniforms arrived. Cordite hung in the shotgun, and I was cradling the woman's head in my arms, whispering the usual BS about how it was going to be all right while she bled out all over my coat. Boutte had sliced her windpipe as the chair was going down. She was barely breathing when the medics took over.

Outside, the street was crawling with cops. An ambulance, with its engine running and the back doors open, waited to take Boutte's victim to hospital. I massaged my hand and saw the kid; he hadn't moved. This was the world he lived in. Nothing in it was news to him.

For the record, the woman didn't make it.

* * *

The impatience in Danny's voice brought me back into the now.

'Are you even listening? Don't underestimate this guy. In Boutte's crazy head, you fucked his life up.'

'It was the other way 'round.'

'He doesn't see it that way. Until we get him, I'm putting a couple of men on you.'

'Think you're overreacting.'

Fitz quit trying to convince me and went quiet. When he spoke again, he was closer to the truth than I wanted to admit. 'You seem less than surprised. Like you've been expecting him to come after you.'

'Sooner or later, the circle gets squared.'

Metaphysics didn't impress him.

'Get that from Deepak Chopra? It's total bullshit. Juli Boutte has carried a grudge against you for seven years.'

'Yeah? He can join the club.'

His frustration boiled over. 'Do the right thing. Do right, Delaney.'

'Ever known me do anything else?'

That was when line went dead.

Three

The car park filled from early Saturday morning. Harassed parents streamed from stationary vehicles trailing nervous performers, lugging bags, costumes on hangers protected by cellophane, and the rest of their brood. The event itself was a local affair. Overhead, clear skies promised a fine summer day, the oppressive humidity of recent weeks gone for now. Katie Renaldi lifted herself up onto the back seat between her mom and her gran. Both women held on to her; neither tried to stop her climb. This was a big day for her. It was unrealistic to expect her to sit quietly when she could see children making their way to the venue.

North of Burgundy Street in the St Claude district, the community centre looked exactly like a hundred others. Constructed in the 1970s, it was difficult to believe the architect had billed anyone for his services. Functional described it kindly, rectangular, more accurately. It was a giant, sub-divided shoebox with a pitch roof. The windows, whenever they disturbed the charmless character of the structure, were small, square and barred. An occasional graffiti scrawl of misspelled obscenity brought some relief to the blandness of the design. Katie's dad slowed to manoeuvre past uptight parents and hyper kids. Here and there, a man trailed along, dragged into the vortex by the force of female will. Bob Renaldi saw none of this. He had his own uptight-parent thing going on and silently asked God to let Katie have a good one.

When the car stopped, everybody got out. Gran Russell's exit was a good deal more deliberate than her granddaughter's. Katie jumped on the spot, all energy and anticipation. Bob opened the trunk and removed the paraphernalia of pageantry and waited on his own set of instructions from Eadie.

Katie said, 'We're here, Gran.'

Her grandmother straightened, patted her clothes and looked clear-eyed at the ugly building, outdated and old before its time. Her reply was a 'Well' that dripped doubt but dropped short of articulating the deep misgivings she'd had when Eadie had told her about Katie and the pageants.

'Come on, Mama.'

Eadie was terse. She felt under pressure – from her mother who lived to disapprove, and from herself for ever suggesting the goddamned thing in the first place. To put the tin lid on it, her period was two days late. Just something else to chew at her this morning. Fuck! Why did she ever think this was a good idea?

Katie skipped and ran ahead. The grown-ups followed at a more sluggish pace, slowed by the lethargy of conflicting emotions. They entered through glass doors lined with metal wire under a sign saying, "Community Centre." Bob Renaldi looked round the multi-purpose facility, tried to stay positive and saw the kind of activity they'd expected: adults and children, some as young as three, milled around an open door.

A blonde woman about forty, in black jeans and a white T-shirt, balanced reading glasses on the end of her nose. A long thin white-on-black name tag gave her status as "Registration Secretary." She smiled when Eadie Renaldi approached her.

'Hi, honey. Have you booked a place in the competition?'

'No, I only heard it was happening a few days ago.'

The woman nodded and smiled at Katie holding her father's hand, half-hidden behind her gran. 'No problem. Can I have your name?'

'Renaldi.'

Bob left public Q and A exchanges to his wife; that way, it got done how Eadie liked it.

The blonde passed a form to his wife. 'Fill this in please.' She looked Katie up and down. 'How old is she?'

'I'm six.' The little girl peeked out to answer for herself then hid, overwhelmed by self-consciousness.

'Six?' The woman sounded impressed; she knew how the game was played. 'OK, Katie, you're six, so you'll be in the six-to-eight-years-old section.' She peered over the specs. 'Tough group. Lotsa cute.' Her look softened. 'You'll be all right.'

Katie kept her face turned away.

The woman spoke to her mother. 'Down the corridor, second on the right. The show's in the main hall at the end. Your first pageant?'

'Yes, it is.'

'Each group has its own changing room. Valuables are left at your own risk. Someone will come 'round, collect your CD and give you timings. Approximate, of course. This is just an itty-bitty thing to give the kids some practice, see if they take to it.'

Katie still lurked behind her gran. 'See if you take to it.'

She spoke to Eadie. 'It's best to get her ready then go in and watch the others 'til about an hour before performance time.' Her forefinger counted them. 'One entrant and three spectators. Fifty dollars, please.'

Bob counted out the bills and handed them across the table. The blonde woman unzipped a bum-bag on her waist and placed them inside. Emily Russell noted how full the bag was. Whatever was "itty-bitty" about the pageant, it wasn't the money.

'Have a good day. Enjoy yourselves. Go get 'em, honey.'

Katie held her gran's hand until they reached the room.

'I'll take Katie in,' Eadie said. 'Get her sorted out. You go to the show. We'll catch up with you.'

'Right.' Bob glanced into the changing room, realising it was no place for him. He bent down on one knee and took his daughter's small hands in his. 'See you soon, baby. You're gonna be great.'

Her reply was a nervous whisper. 'Ok, Daddy.'

Emily Russell's features were cut from granite; she didn't speak. Bob Renaldi looked at his wife, and Eadie wondered for the hundredth time what she'd started.

* * *

Bob and Mama found seats towards the front, in an oasis free from children climbing on parents and chairs. Neither spoke. It was going to be a long day.

Eadie was too preoccupied to think about whether or not she was enjoying herself, or about Bob or Mama. Where she was held enough challenges. Low benches, the kind used in training sessions, were laid out in lines. Competitors left whatever they weren't wearing onstage in little bundles.

Valuables are left at your own risk.

Katie was very quiet now. Her mother unpacked. A woman, another blonde, the sister of the one at the main door, moved between the chicane of over-excited bodies being marshalled by all-business moms.

'Name?'

'Renaldi. Katie Renaldi.'

The blonde didn't try to connect with the owner, preferring to address the parent. Her hand scribbled on the paper held tight by the clipboard.

'Right,' she said, 'the first stage for this group is eleven o'clock. Mr Darlington'll come 'round an hour before to talk about the sequence and collect your music. Up until then,' she looked at her watch, 'you can stay here or go watch the show. Just don't get lost. If you miss the sequencing, you're out of the competition. Understood?'

'What happens after that?'

Blondie eyed Katie. 'If you're still in, you'll go through to the final.'

Her face said she didn't think they needed to worry overmuch about that.

When Eadie joined Bob and her mother, the first group was coming to the end of its time. She shuffled along the row with Katie in front. Her husband pulled a sour face. Eadie's heart sank; had the hostilities that had threatened all morning arrived? No, Bob and Mama were all right. Not communicating, but fine. The problem was something else. On stage a child, no more than a baby, was trying to sing. The audience ignored the tuneless din. Eadie leaned across to her husband, while Katie studied the infant competitor.

Bob patted his wife's hand. 'Everything's fine. Enjoy the show.'

She smiled at his joke; there was nothing else to do. The amateur nature of the event was demonstrated by every contestant for another thirty minutes. Before the judging got underway the MC, a bald man, ridiculous in a shiny gold jacket, asked the entrants in the six to eight-year-old section to go back to their dressing area.

Eadie took her daughter's hand. 'Come on, baby.'

'Good luck, honey.'

Bob's eyes were on his wife, his words meant for all of them.

Emily Russell looked at her granddaughter and her eyes softened. 'I'm here, Katie. Just do your best and have fun.'

A knife of resentment stabbed Eadie.

You're here? Fine! Good! But she's my daughter. I'm her mom, and I'm here!

Angry thoughts thundered in her head. When they got to the changing room, it was busy with women dressing unresisting children, fussing over details nobody but them would ever notice: talking non-stop.

'Listen up! Listen up, folks!'

A man in a red polo shirt and dark-blue trousers clapped his hands for attention. His face was unremarkable until he smiled. He used his hands and arms to include everyone.

'My name's Arthur Darlington. Artie. My job is to get us in shape to go out there and give it our best shot. It's ten-ten now. In fifteen minutes, we need to be ready to leave.'

Artie's words provoked a ripple of anxiety. It was always the same. These women were already strung high; their precious babies were about to perform, and worse, be judged by a group of strangers.

He smiled his big smile. 'In a minute, we'll do a roll call. Performers will go on in alphabetical first-name order, which means anybody called Abby is up first and Wanda – if you're out there – you can bet you're going on last. I'm gonna come 'round and collect your CD. If your music isn't on CD, tell your dad to join the 21st century because he's embarrassing you.'

Artie waved a thick pen. 'One more thing. Parents aren't allowed in the backstage area. There just isn't enough room, folks, so take your seats out front and enjoy the show.'

A few mothers looked uncertain. What had happened in Baton Rouge was in their minds.

Darlington reassured them. 'And don't worry; we'll be watching them every minute.'

He clapped his hands to signal everyone could go back to fretting and fixing. The last part wasn't true; there was room, but it made for an easier life and a smoother day if the kids were separated from their parents for a little while.

Katie stepped out of her street clothes. Her costume wasn't really a costume at all, just a shirt with the sleeves rolled up, and an overall, cut short and altered to fit. Bob and Eadie had decided to test the water first, before committing themselves to unnecessary expense.

Eadie put some black eye-shadow on her hand, dipped her forefinger in it and smudged it on to her daughter's cheeks. She could see lipstick and gloss being applied to innocent features changing them into something else – something not entirely wholesome or proper. Eadie understood part of her mother's concern and, without admitting it even to herself, didn't disagree. She knotted the headscarf held in place with two carefully positioned pins, finished with a final dab of black on the end of the waif's button nose and stood back to admire her work.

Orphan Annie looked back at her.

Tough group. Lotsa cute.

Well, how cute was that?

She allowed herself one last second to appreciate the effect then took the towel and the rag in one hand and Katie's hand in the other.

'Ok, baby? Show time.'

Four

The last contestant in the three-to-five-year-old section was a little blonde thing with curly hair. No make-up or fancy costumes for her, only a plain white dress. She folded her hands and sang unaccompanied. Before she uttered a note, she had the audience's attention. Her tiny frame and angelic face drew the crowd.

For the first time that day, people listened. Bob opened his eyes. Gran Russell's body language relaxed as Eadie slipped in beside them.

The singer kept them with her all the way to the end. When she finished, she got the cheer of the morning. Molly Lothian smiled at her parents out in the crowd. Ray and Catherine grinned, and there were tears in Catherine's eyes.

'Well,' Ray said, 'she doesn't get it from me.'

* * *

Gran Russell said, 'Now that's a performance.'

No one could claim that about Katie's routine. Except for a flawless entrance, when she timed her arrival and her actions to the opening chorus, it all unravelled; more than once she forgot the words. The fun of being there turned to panic. By the end, the child was a red-faced wreck. Her father watched the arrangement dismantle in slow motion, and Eadie bit her lip, ashamed. Her husband understood; he felt the same. Neither had the courage to face Mama.

Bob saw his daughter on the opposite side of the room, chin on her chest, following the child in front of her through the hall.

His heart sank lower; she looked so small and hurt. His face flushed.

What had they done to her?

* * *

Eadie was waiting in the changing room. The children arrived, led by Artie Darlington. Katie walked to her mother, head low, eyes down.

Eadie gathered her in a hug that said, "I understand, honey," and held her tight. She dropped to one knee, her face inches from her daughter. 'Hey!'

Katie didn't reply.

Eadie had decided not to go overboard, not to rehash the mess and let the whole deal get out of proportion. Her mind was made up not to lie. Well, not to lie very much.

'I forgot, Mommy. I forgot the words.'

'It doesn't matter, Katie. Really it doesn't.'

'But I forgot.' She was on the edge of tears.

Eadie pulled her close. 'That's all right, baby, everybody forgets things. Look at Daddy. How often does he forget where he put his car keys? Gran says he'd forget his head if it wasn't sewed on.'

'I need to go to the bathroom.'

'OK, you know where it is. Down the hall but be quick. Hurry up.'

Eadie finished packing and took a last look round. She would never be back. Her mother had been right for the wrong reasons; this was no place for them.

In the hallway, someone watched the child head for the toilets alone. Why did parents make it so easy? Didn't they ever learn?

No one was around. A risk because there were still plenty of people in the building. But it was always a risk, wasn't it? That was part of the thrill, a big part of it. A minute passed, going on two. Decision time.

The door opened. The figure moved towards her, just eight steps away, when a voice called, 'Katie! Where's your mother?'

An older lady walked past, her irritation and anger unconcealed.

'In there, Gran. I needed the bathroom.'

'I'll take you. You shouldn't be on your own.'

When Katie and her gran came through the door, Eadie could see her daughter was brightening up. Her grandmother's expression was fierce. The journey home was going to be fun.

They paid no mind to the person in the hall. There was nothing out of the ordinary to draw their attention.

Katie. Wasn't that what her grandmother called her?

Nice name.

Beautiful.

Well, Katie, I do hope we meet again. Don't be discouraged because you didn't win. Don't let it put you off. Things like that can be sorted. Work on it. Work hard and come back, and when you do, I'll be here waiting. Waiting for Katie.

* * *

For Ray and Catherine, the day passed pleasantly enough, buoyed by Molly's showing in the first round. That surprising success helped sustain them through hours of less accomplished stuff. Sometime after mid-day, they adjourned to the car for the sandwiches and Coke Catherine had brought. The little girl sucked her drink through a straw giving it all her attention, making rude noises just because she could, light years from the inspirational seraph who silenced the crowd.

Ray spoke through a mouthful of rye bread. 'Where did you learn to sing like that, honey?'

'She's always been a good singer, haven't you, Molly? And we practised. We practised a lot. Really hard,' Catherine said.

Molly answered her father's question through gulps of the secret recipe fizzy water. 'Delaney.'

'Vince?' Surprise mixed with pique in her mother's voice. 'When?'

Slurping noises came from the carton in Molly's hands. 'All the time. We sing all the time.'

Ray and Catherine looked at each other. They'd heard singing now and again coming from the garden but thought nothing of it.

'Delaney's teaching me. He says I might be a soul-singer when I grow up.'

'And I thought it was all me.' Catherine shook her head. 'I might have known.'

They finished their food in silence until it was time to go back. Around one in the afternoon, the finals began. Molly repeated her performance and won first prize. Her smile was as wide as any lottery winner.

'I'll go and collect our star,' Catherine said, beaming. 'Meet you outside.'

Her fingers brushed her husband's shoulder in a secret sign of togetherness.

'Yeah, and get the money off her, we can use it.'

'I won! I won!'

Catherine fielded her daughter and scooped her up. 'You did, didn't you?'

'Look, Mommy.' Molly held her poor-quality photocopy for inspection.

'Wow! Check this out.' Catherine read out loud. 'This is to certify that Molly Lothian achieved first place in the three-to-five-year-old section of the Stars of Tomorrow show. Wow!'

The small face glowed. Catherine lowered her daughter to the floor. 'Okay. Let's go get Dad.'

'Excuse me.'

Catherine turned to meet the voice. A woman with auburn hair was smiling at her. Laughter lines played around green eyes above an open smile, and her voice was a comfortable drawl. 'Can I just say how wonderful your little girl performed? I swear, I was in tears. Both times.'

'Well, thank you for that. We were surprised. And Molly loved it. It's her first show. She's over the moon.'

'And so she should be; that was real talent out there. She can afford to go up a class, maybe try her out at Mini-National level. Competition's tougher, but she'll do all right.' The woman divided her attention between adult and child.

'It's all about timin', honey,' she said to Molly then turned back to Catherine. 'Is the whole family here?'

'My brother isn't. He doesn't know anything about it. He's a little old-fashioned about this sort of thing.'

The stranger easily dismissed the fault. 'Nothin' wrong with old-fashioned. I'm kinda that way myself. Took me a long time to come to terms with the whole "pageant thing." My husband Peter spent an age tryin' to persuade me, but now, I'm glad he did. Our daughter Labelle competes all the time. Loves it. Your brother'll come 'round. We all do. In the end.'

'You think? What with the little boy in Baton Rouge, I didn't tell him.'

The woman put a hand to her mouth. 'That was so sad, wasn't it? Poor kid.'

'But we think it's important to teach Molly not to give in to fear.'

'I'm with you on that one, sugar. We make sure there's always one of us with Labelle. I mean, it's up to the parents to take care of their children. Anyway, what's his name, this big bad brother of yours?'

'Delaney. Vincent Delaney.'

'And he's here in the city?'

Catherine nodded. 'Yes. He's a PI. Thanks for the kind words. Maybe we'll see you again?'

'Well, I sure hope so.' She put an emphasis on the last word that was very southern and very sincere. 'Bye, bye, honey. You were great. Nice meetin' you and good luck.'

'You too.' Catherine was attracted by the woman's easy personality.

'And tell that brother of yours to lighten-up once in a while. Lightnin' don't strike twice, so they say. Oh, and since we're both "pageant people," guess we better get properly introduced.'

'Of course. I'm Catherine Lothian. This is my daughter, Molly.'

The hand that shook hers was cool and firm. 'Roy. Reba Roy.'

Five

It was Monday and felt like it – hot and already muggy. The weekend hadn't amounted to much. Our band didn't have a gig, and I'd decided to give Catherine and Ray a break by not spending Sunday with them for a change. They'd tried to persuade me, but their hearts weren't in it. Instead, I drove with Stella and Lowell to Audubon Park – beautiful in the afternoon sunshine – and lay on the grass, eating double-fried chicken with lemon and jalapenos, and roasted tomato salsa. Against her blonde hair, the golden rays gave her the aura of a goddess. Not so far from the truth. And she sure could cook.

Stella noticed how distracted I was, and at one point, she said, 'Penny for them.'

'What?'

'Something on your mind?'

'Just tired, I guess.'

The lie came easily. Truth was, I'd brought Danny Fitzpatrick's concern with me.

We strolled among the old live oaks, holding hands, while Lowell chased birds, and great egrets flew from their nests on Ochsner Island and back against the setting sun. It should've been perfect, except I was unsettled and decided to spend the evening alone at my place. Stella kept her surprise to herself.

Fitz's concern about Juli Boutte wasn't the overreaction I'd claimed. My low-key response was a crock, and we both realised it. A "Class-A bad guy," Danny had called him; he wasn't wrong. Boutte's crimes were sometimes random and unprovoked, sometimes planned and carried out on behalf of Beppe "Little Man" Giordano. But always violent. Yet, it might have gone a different route because, by all accounts, Juli was a talented chef who had drawn praise from the likes of John Folse and Frank Brigtsen.

Men like Julian Boutte were cut from a different bale. In his diseased mind, I'd murdered his brother; taking me down was a duty – his version of squaring the circle and not so far from my own. It didn't matter that it had been two against one, and I was defending myself. Boutte knew what he knew and that was enough.

At ten-thirty, the phone on my desk burst into life, and Danny Fitzpatrick said something I hadn't expected to hear ever again.

'Captain wants to talk to you.'

I felt myself tense. 'Bout what?'

'He'll tell you himself. How soon can you get here?'

Working for Anthony Delaup had been an experience, all right. It wouldn't be fair to say he was the only reason I had left the force, but he certainly was one of them. And now, after seven years, he was asking to speak to me. I should have been curious and maybe I was a little bit, though not enough to put a run on.

'Caught me at a bad time. Busy day. A lot on.'

Fitzpatrick's tone gave him away, and I realised he wasn't alone. 'So, when?'

'Tomorrow do?'

'No, it won't.'

'All right. Five o'clock this afternoon.'

The tension in Fitzy voice came down the line. 'I think you should come earlier, Delaney. I really think you should.'

It wasn't happening. Not for Delaup.

'Five's the best I've got. See you.' I hung up.

Harry Love would have approved.

* * *

Lowell wasn't pleased to be left at the house. I'd live with his disapproval because where I was going wasn't for him. He sulked his way into his basket, closed his eyes and pretended to be tired.

I'd told him my history with the department and how it ended; he hadn't been impressed and wanted to be with me. Appreciated.

'Doing you a favour, boy, believe me.'

The elevator stopped on the third floor. I knocked on the office door and went inside. Nobody rushed to greet me. Delaup was behind his big desk, chewing on one of those antacid tablets that tasted like chalk and left white residue at the corners of his mouth. His hair was greyer; at a guess, he'd gained twenty-five pounds. Sweat marks on his blue shirt told me he was faking relaxed for somebody. There wasn't a snowball's chance in hell he was doing it for my benefit.

He struggled to his feet and stuck a handful of pudgy fingers out for me to shake. 'Delaney. We've missed you around here.'

Convincing, if you didn't know him like I did.

Two men standing against the wall turned expressionless faces towards me; their haircuts and suits gave them away: FBI. The people the Captain was trying to impress.

Fitzy was by the window, eyes fixed on something in the street. I took the chair he had probably been in when he called. Unlike Delaup, he hadn't changed much from the dark-haired, sharp-eyed young black guy in his twenties who had nodded to me across a cold gymnasium one February morning.

Delaup said, 'How're things? Still playing your guitar?' He pronounced it "gee-tar" and spoke to the room. 'The music business lost a talent when Delaney became a cop.'

Bullshit. His speciality. He hadn't heard me. And he wouldn't know the difference even if he had.

'Can make that thing talk.'

Embarrassing. I blanched. Was he gonna pretend we were friends?

'Hear you're an uncle now, how's that working out?'

'Good.'

'Let me introduce you. These gentlemen are from the Bureau, Agents Rutherford and McLaren. Vince Delaney.' He explained me to them. 'Delaney got tired of the system and decided to try life as a civilian.'

Not exactly the truth.

They kept their admiration under control; they already knew who I was.

'Yes sir, best detective I ever worked with.'

For some reason, Delaup was trying awful hard to be nice. I wished he wouldn't.

'Ok. Agent Rutherford, would you bring everyone up to speed?'

Rutherford cleared his throat and read from an invisible script. Public speaking was never going to be his thing. 'Attacks on children are growing faster than any other crime in the USA. The Internet has brought perverts out from the rocks they've been hiding under. Porn sites exist in their thousands.'

Everyone in the room knew where this was going, except me. I'd been expecting something to do with Boutte.

'Paedophilia is king of vice. The people involved are prepared and planned and very careful. Today, we dismantle one of *these organisations, tomorrow, another takes its place. It's a battle we aren't going to win. Doesn't stop us trying.* Now and again, we discover something that forces us to think and act differently. That's why we're here.'

He was talking to me, I just didn't know why.

'The fastest-expanding business sector in America is pageantry, and in there, growing with the rest, are pageants for children.'

Agent Rutherford could have survived the Titanic and made it sound dull. But he had my attention.

'In the main, they pass without incident, and, whether you agree with them or not, they're really just a day out for the family, cheering on little Tania or Bobby Junior or whomever.' He paused. 'Until recently.'

Across the room, Danny seemed ill at ease and wouldn't meet my eyes.

'About seventeen months back, a child was abducted from a pageant in Panama City Beach, Florida. The body of seven-year-old Lucy Gilmour was never found. Last time anyone saw her alive, she was talking to an unidentified man. Then, they both disappeared. Best guess is Lucy's out in the mangroves, Lord help her. Twelve months ago, in Birmingham, Alabama, Dorothy Dulles went missing shortly after a pageant she was entered in ended. Her body was left in a parking lot a block from the venue. She was five. Four months later, Billy Cunningham turned up. Billy had just become the Supreme Mini National King in his age division. They lost track of him between the staging area and the dressing rooms.'

Fitzy spoke for the first time. 'Where was that, again?'

'Little Rock, Arkansas.'

Delaup said, 'We've got a serial.'

Rutherford walked to a water cooler in the corner and poured himself a cup. 'For a while, it went quiet, until March when Pamela White was found behind a movie house next to the hall where a local pageant was taking place in Fort Worth. She wasn't a contestant; her sister Donna was. Pamela was nine. We believe she was taken when her mother went to collect Donna after her performance.'

He sipped the water.

'Three weeks ago, in Baton Rouge, five-year-old Timmy Donald was murdered while competing in the Little Louisiana pageant. As Captain Delaup rightly says, we've got ourselves a serial killer.'

The agent sat down to let McLaren take over. Like everybody, I was shocked. Rutherford had given few details; the reports would make painful reading. I knew about Timmy from the news and had forced myself not to think about it too much.

McLaren said, 'Before we continue, any questions?'

I had a couple. 'When did you realise this was a serial killer? And how come no media frenzy?'

His reply was frank and unflattering to the Bureau. 'After Timmy – too long, I know. Billy Cunningham threw us off track: a boy. First two victims were girls. Nobody realised it was the same guy.'

He searched for the words to make us understand.

'Bear the facts in mind. The first killing was committed in Florida, the second in Alabama, then Arkansas, Texas, and lastly in Louisiana. The victims were from both genders. Harder than you think to find a pattern, unless you know you're looking for one. But when we connected the dots, it all fit. Exactly the same MO for each kid. Strangulation. As for the media, they missed it. Plain and simple. Now, they're baying for blood. Our blood. They're blaming us, although they weren't so cute at spotting the link themselves. Too busy with politics.'

McLaren was blowing off steam, and I understood why.

'The first child was never found. The second didn't suggest a link. The third one was Billy, a male. The next was another female. Same MO, sure, but hundreds of miles apart …'

He made a what-you-gonna-do face.

'Fourth was an older kid out with her sister and mother. It was only when Timmy Donald was dumped in a cupboard at the venue that some bright spark asked the right question. Forget age. Forget gender. What were these kids doing? Answer: attending a pageant. From there, we started to make connections, and all of a sudden, we were staring at a madman. Roaming across the southern states undetected, in spite of the overt nature of the crimes. It's impossible to imagine the terror these children must have felt. No sign of drugs, yet no one heard any of them scream. We guess they must have trusted him.'

Agent McLaren allowed what he'd told us to sink in.

'For all we know, that's just the tip of the iceberg. It's what we have so far. And catching this bastard won't be easy.'

He counted on his fingers. 'One: the crimes straddle five states. An awful big killing field. Two: all the victims have some kind of involvement in pageants. Great, until you realise how many take place every year in this country. Three: both sexes seem to be legitimate targets for him. So far, we know about two boys and three girls. Again, the waters are muddy. Four – and this is hard to believe – forensics has given up nothing.'

The atmosphere in the office had changed. I said, 'This is a horror show for the families of those kids, but why tell me? I left the NOPD years ago.'

A train was coming towards me and was going to hit, unless I could get out of the way. Rutherford knew what he was doing. He looked me in the eye and left nowhere for me to go.

'That's just it, Mr Delaney. You're in a unique position. We want you with us.'

Six

I rated Danny Fitzpatrick higher than most people on the planet. We had joined the force on the same intake, did our training together, partied and paid our dues; for years, he was my partner, someone I would trust with my life and had done plenty of times.

But we were different. He could see the road ahead. After the whole Boutte fiasco with the PIB, I couldn't, so I quit. Fitzpatrick stayed, and he was still a believer. No matter how many dead-ends he came up against, corrupt officials, red tape or senile judges who let criminals back out on the street, Fitzy stayed completely committed to catching the bad guys. The case he was working, whatever it was, was the only thing that mattered.

That attitude had cost him two marriages. Fitzpatrick was a top cop and a first-class human being, yet a couple of broken-hearted women would tell you he wasn't a great husband. But he was my best friend. Today wasn't the best day that friendship had ever had.

Once they'd sprung their little surprise, they waited for my reaction. They were disappointed. I didn't have a reaction, unless you counted staring.

Agent McLaren gave way to Delaup. 'Not full-time. Not card-punching. The rules allow me to create special officers in situations of specific need. Where someone is able to bring a particular talent to the party, they're sworn in and remain active for as long as the need lasts.'

McLaren explained. 'The Bureau sees it like this. We have two choices. Follow up on leads, if we can find any, interview people 'til the cows come home, hoping somebody saw something, anything, and wait for the killer to make a mistake. Meantime, children are likely to die while we chase after our tail. Or …'

His eyes willed me to understand.

'… admit we could use some help. That's what we're asking you for, Delaney, your help in nailing this bastard.'

Delaup pushed me to say yes. 'When it's over, you can stay with the department or go back to your life, up to you.'

I was everybody's favourite guy. I still didn't get it.

Over by the window, Danny's face gave me nothing.

McLaren said, 'You're not the only one we've talked to. We've already been to Arkansas and Alabama. This morning, it was Baton Rouge; tomorrow, it'll be Miami. Already there are twenty people on board in Texas.'

He almost smiled.

'It's a big place. If we're lucky, we'll have a dozen just like you in Louisiana by the end of next week.'

'Just like me doing what? Can somebody spell it out what're you asking, exactly?'

McLaren answered. 'Go undercover.'

'Undercover?'

Rutherford leaned his elbows on his knees. 'There are too many shows over too big an area to do anything beyond sticking a pin in the map. And whoever is there for us has to be able to move around. Mingle without being noticed. Twenty, even a dozen, may sound a lot, but in Texas? What we are setting up is the longest of long shots, we get that, but it's a try. The chances of our psycho showing up at a pageant where we have an officer in position are somewhere between slim to non-existent. Probably a giant waste of time. The alternative is to plod on, playing out the usual moves, until we get a break. If we get a break. That could be years. Or never.'

Delaup jumped in. 'We're stretched real tight with this Julian Boutte thing.' He looked at me like it was my fault. 'You were a great detective. If anybody can help, you can.'

The Captain was reaching out to me. Maybe because his officers were being invited to what would otherwise be an FBI party, or maybe he was as fired up as the rest to bring an end to a run of horrific crimes. Pressure from above was getting me the kind of appreciation I'd never had when I worked for him, even though my cases solved percentage was usually the highest in the department. Suddenly, I realised what my "unique position" had to be, and Danny Fitzpatrick's behaviour began to make sense.

'Hold on. You say undercover, you mean, you want me to go to these events?'

'Right. Your niece competes. Molly, isn't it? Great little singer from what I hear. A guy on his own would stand out.'

I fought to keep my voice even. 'Who fed you this crap?'

But I knew, didn't I? Now the truth was on the table, Fitzpatrick didn't avoid looking at me. 'We were kicking round ideas. Then, I bumped into Catherine. She told me Molly won a pageant, and the whole thing came together.'

My sister hadn't told me. I wasn't sure how to react. Rutherford opened his briefcase and took out a handful of ten-by-eight black-and-white photographs. I knew what they would show. I'd seen enough of them to keep me in nightmares for the rest of my life.

'So, everybody involved – the twenty in Texas and the rest – have kids entered in these gigs. Am I understanding it right?'

Rutherford said, 'I can show you what he did to the little boy in Baton Rouge, but I'd rather not.'

'Don't bother. Answer the question. Are you saying officers are putting their own children on the line to catch this guy? Is that how it is?'

He met me full on without evasion. 'No. That isn't how it is.'

'But you want me to run a stake-out with my family as bait?'

The agent rolled his tongue over dry lips. 'We don't see them as bait, and it's the best scenario we can come up with.'

'Forget it. Absolutely no.' I pushed myself out of the chair. 'Good luck with finding somebody. I'm not your man.'

Rutherford held up his hands. 'We appreciate it isn't easy to say yes to what we're asking, though, in reality, you probably won't come within a hundred miles of this monster. Then again, we might get lucky. He might be sitting next to you, third row from the front.'

'Look, I quit for a reason. Deceiving my sister and her husband isn't in the plan.'

'Try it like this: you just being there means their little girl will be safer.'

I shook my head. 'It won't work. I'm against everything about that scene. Hate it. My sister knows how I feel. Molly or no Molly, she wouldn't buy me just tagging along.'

Agent Rutherford shuffled the images in his hand and picked one of them out. 'Sure you don't want to see this?'

He didn't push it. We both knew he was right. McLaren summed up the meeting in one question. 'In or out, Mr Delaney?'

* * *

I gave them my answer and left before I changed my mind. Halfway down the corridor, Fitzpatrick caught up with me. I turned to face him, already sure what he was going to say, and just as sure how I would respond.

'Delaney, listen.' He put a hand on his heart. 'Mea culpa. Sorry for springing that on you.'

'Is that what just happened? I was wondering.'

He stood in front of me. 'Look, I can imagine what's in your head right now.'

'Can you? I doubt it.'

'Nobody planned it. Nobody said, why don't we drag Delaney back in? That wasn't how it was. The Bureau's never keen to let anybody put a foot on their territory; they'd rather fail than give ground. This is different. Rutherford and McLaren are desperate. They haven't got a clue. Literally. They're not even sure how long this thing's been going on. They're drowning. Hell, we're all drowning. You remember how that feels, don't you?'

'Yeah, I remember. But you've known about this since the kid in Baton Rouge. I'm asking myself how you could think it was okay to stick my face in the frame without a word to me.'

Fitzpatrick took a step away.

'And not just me. Catherine. Ray. Molly. You've been to their house, sat round the table with them. You were there when Molly was baptised.'

'Delaney …'

'If they were strangers, maybe I could understand, but they are special. They trust you, for Christ's sake.'

He held up his hands. 'All right. I should have spoken to you about it first. My bad.' Danny spread his arms to convince me I had it wrong. 'Catherine and Ray don't have a problem with this pageant stuff; they're fine about it.'

So fine, my sister hadn't told me.

'Well, good for them. Putting their six-year-old daughter in danger might change their minds.'

'The odds are a thousand to one against.'

I let my anger roll over him. 'Maybe you should show them the photographs Rutherford was so keen for me to look at? Let them decide if a thousand to one sounds worth a bet.'

'Catherine was laughing. It was a hole in the wall, some community centre over in Gert Town. Besides, she had to have read about Timmy Donald or saw it on the news.'

'Danny, she was laughing because she doesn't know what you know. She thinks that kid was an isolated case, and nobody's about to let her into the secret. I've just agreed to use them. It stinks. So, don't tell me about fine. I'm not fine and that's for damn sure.'

'So why say yes?'

I didn't reply.

'Should've warned me. Given me time …'

'Time's overrated. You might have said no.'

'Still might.'

'No, you won't, and I'm pleased.'

'Yeah. Delaup said as much.'

'I mean it. Hangin' with the good guys. Could get to like it again.'

Fitzpatrick had a short memory. Last time I'd looked, the good guys hadn't been so good.

* * *

Seven Years Earlier

The name had been changed from Internal Affairs to Public Integrity Bureau. To protect the innocent? I didn't think so. Otherwise, it was the same deal. A man was on a slab in the morgue, and the question that had to be answered was why.

There were three of them in the room: two PIB officers on the other side of a desk and Anthony Delaup, off to the side with his tie loosened and his shirt sleeves rolled up, gazing at his shoes. When I came in, their expressions didn't alter. I got it. They had a job to do. At the end of the day, they probably kicked-back and sank a few tubes in front of the TV like everybody else and wondered if re-mortgaging the house really was the best way to get out from under the mountain of debt that had been building for half a decade.

An overhead fan moved air around without making a difference to the temperature, which had to be in the seventies even now. The PIB guys kept their jackets on, introduced themselves as Mortimer and Sands, and got to it. Nobody shook hands.

Sands laid out the ground rules. 'Just so you know, Detective Delaney, the tape isn't rolling. You don't need a lawyer, unless you think you do. We've read the statement you made and want to satisfy ourselves that what you signed off on corresponds with what you say now.'

'I understand.'

'Okay. Start at when you got the APB and take us through it.'

I did. When I finished, he changed his approach to asking things he already knew.

'How long have you been with the NOPD?'

'Fifteen years.'

'And as a detective?'

'Eight.'

Mortimer made an unnecessary note; the information was in front of him. For the first time, he made a contribution with sweet talk meant to soften me up. 'Your arrest rate is impressive, the best in the department, what's your secret?'

On the face of it, a straightforward enough question, except with these guys nothing was ever straightforward. Everything had an angle. I shrugged.

Mortimer piled it on with a big spoon. 'Got quite a rep. Practically a hero.'

He read from my file.

'Two letters of commendation for "outstanding work in the line of duty." And a medal of merit. Impressive.'

I let him tell it.

'Obviously you're an exceptional officer, Delaney. Wonder why it is you've never gone for promotion.'

'I like where I am.'

'You like where you are. Maybe that explains the downside to an otherwise stellar career. If you got promoted, you'd have to wade through the politics. Compromise. You're a guy who doesn't believe in compromise.'

'Am I? First I've heard about it.'

'That's what we've been told.'

Suddenly, I saw where this was this going and where it had come from. One look at Anthony Delaup's face confirmed it. Sands said, 'Cedric and Juli Boutte are animals. No argument. Nevertheless, they have rights just like every other citizen. Or do you disagree?'

It didn't deserve a reply, and I didn't give one.

'Cedric Boutte never fired his gun. It was still in the waistband of his pants. Given the situation, adrenaline would be running high. Is it possible you reacted too quickly?'

He knew what I would say. So why ask?

'No, it isn't.'

'It isn't possible?'

'No.'

'In your statement, you claim you warned him you were about to fire.'

'I claim it because it's true.'

'But if his gun wasn't in Cedric's hand, you shot an unarmed man.'

'He was strapped. He went for it.'

'How did you know he had a gun?'

'I saw it.'

'How could you if it was behind his back?'

'He was high. Dancing around. He turned.'

'Where were you when this happened?'

'Outside. Underneath the window.'

'And you were certain it was a weapon?'

I glanced away. One answer per question was all he was getting. Sands started to pace the room, a finger pressed against his lips.

'I'm trying to imagine the scene. Help me out, will you? You're hunkered down at the window, listening to what's going on inside. You take a chance, sneak a look and see the woman and the brothers. At best you get two, maybe three seconds. But God's on your side. You catch Cedric boogying on down in the right direction for you to make the piece stuck in his pants. That about right?'

'Except for the God bit, close enough.'

The PIB officer pulled at his jaw and made a face at his partner. 'Awful lucky, don't you think?'

'Luck had nothing to do with it.'

'Yeah?'

'He tried to outdraw me and ended on the losing side. Sorry if that complicates things for you. I'll bear it in mind the next time some punk does the same. Never realised a dead cop was the preferred option down at Public Integrity.'

Mortimer chimed in. 'Don't get snooty, Delaney. You killed a man who didn't have a gun.'

'He had a gun.'

'Not in his hand.'

'If I'd waited until it was in his mitt, we wouldn't be having this conversation. Can I remind you, they'd abducted somebody and were getting ready to torture her? Already made a start.'

Sands sat on the edge of the desk with his arms folded across his chest. He shook his head. 'Nobody here is unsympathetic to the situation you found yourself in, believe me.'

I didn't believe him.

'But here's the thing: when we catch Julian, he's going to swear you killed his brother in cold blood. He'll be the only witness.'

'Again, can I remind you, in case it's slipped your mind, there was another person in the room; the woman. Boutte slit her throat. That's why it comes out his word against mine. What's new?'

'I'll tell you what's new. The NOPD can't handle more bad publicity. Confidence is low. The public needs to be sure they can depend on their officers to enforce the law fairly, and at the moment, they don't.'

'So, you'll hang me out to dry, that it?'

He pursed his lips as if he was talking to a child who didn't understand how the world worked. 'In the long run, this will blow over. Meantime, you're suspended without pay.'

So much for informal. What had actually gone down with the Boutte brothers was neither here nor there. They intended me to take one for the force; without pay was the clue. Across the room, Delaup was still in a staring contest with his shoes. During the entire fiasco, he hadn't uttered a word.

Sands put it on the table. He said, 'There are bigger issues than a dead scumbag. We have to be seen to be cleaning house. Don't take it personally. It's a matter of trust. I have to ask you for your badge. You'll be notified of the where and when.'

'You can't be serious.'

Mortimer gathered his papers together and stood. 'We don't do jokes, Delaney. I'd lawyer-up, if I were you.'

* * *

Something had ended for me in that room, and seven years on, the sense of betrayal was still with me. Delaup, the department, and the whole goddamned NOPD weren't friends. Danny Fitzpatrick was the exception, and I was mad as hell at him. There was nothing to do but put the bad thoughts behind me and get on with my life.

The week dragged by with not much to show. I hadn't spoken to Stella since the last time we were together. She had to be wondering what was going on. Normally, we'd spend Friday night through to Monday morning together. On Saturday, we'd go to the gig at Mr MaGoo's; on Sunday, if the Saints were at home, I'd go to the game with Cal Moreland and head over to Catherine and Ray's for a while, while she visited some of her girlfriends. We'd hook back up later, at my place or hers – we both preferred our own. It worked, except here I was on Thursday, cancelling those arrangements. When I spoke to her, I heard surprise and disappointment come down the line.

'Why? What's wrong?'

I lied. 'Nothing. Just a shitty week. You'll be better off without me.'

'Shouldn't I get to make that decision for myself?'

'Absolutely. But whatever you decide, I don't want you to come.'

She kept her anger in check. 'Then, I won't. Give me a ring when you can fit me in, why don't you?'

She ended the conversation abruptly. Without knowing it, Harry Love had started a trend.

I waited until Friday to call Catherine. A child had been murdered, yet she'd still taken Molly to one of those damned events. I was angry. And I felt guilty about how I intended to use her. When I'd calmed down, I went into my act. The phone unhooked from its cradle and banged on the wall a couple of times before anybody spoke. Molly. And her technique still needed some polish.

'Hello?' The small breathy voice created a question out of a greeting.

'It's me, Moll.'

'Delaney, I won the pageant!' She pronounced it with a big, exaggerated tee, making her sound very polite. 'I won. I was first.'

'That's great, honey.'

'I sang a song.'

'Fantastic, baby. Put Mommy on, will you?'

The telephone got beaten-up again. Catherine spoke, 'Vince, hi.'

'Hi yourself.'

I was about to blurt out what I knew but caught myself in time. 'Tried to get you earlier, but everyone must have been out.'

'We were.'

'Just wanted to check on Sunday. See what time you want me over.'

One end of the line was quiet, too quiet, as they used to say in old cowboy movies just before the Indians attacked. Her voice was a monotone. 'Whenever will be fine.'

'The mouse seems excited. What's all that about?'

She hesitated. 'Tell you Sunday.'

Unease crept over me. 'Tell me now. I want to sleep tonight. She says she sang a song. Won something. What's she talking about?'

Catherine let out a long slow sigh at the other end. 'We let Molly sing in a competition. She won, that's all.'

'What kind of competition?'

'A pageant. Just a local one. The kids sing a song, and somebody ends up the winner. Molly was the winner.'

'A pageant?'

'Only a local one.'

'Where?'

'Here. In the city. A community centre, no big deal.'

'Fuck's sake, Catherine. You can't be serious? You knew about that Timmy kid, right?'

Oscar-winning stuff.

Catherine cut our conversation short. 'You'll hear all about it Sunday. I've got to go.'

I put the phone down with Delaup's words playing in my head. *We've got a serial.*

Sometimes, I fooled myself into believing I was a pretty cool guy. Then, there were the other times, times like this, when I didn't know what "cool" even looked like.

Seven

The club was cramped, smoky and dark, with tables at the back and a tiny square of dance-floor at the front. I turned up late, so they started without me; it was that kind of gig. Punctuality came well down the list. Nobody asked where I'd been or why I hadn't made it in time. The band didn't have a name, and everybody in it was a cop with the exception of me.

I got my guitar out of its case and joined in on a number, warming up and getting in tune. At the other side of the stage, Danny sat folded over his Fender Jazz. He nodded to me and went back to the music. In the long run, we would be all right, although he was on my shit list and knew it.

During the break, Danny strolled over and knocked his beer bottle against mine. 'No Stella?'

'Washing her hair.'

'First gig she's missed, isn't it?'

'Is it?'

He faced me. 'Look, Delaney. I get it. Delaup sold you down the river, and you haven't forgotten, but this isn't about Anthony Delaup. It's about stopping a child-killer.'

'Let's not go that road again, Danny.'

'And I understand why no Stella.'

'Do you?'

'Yeah. Afraid lightning will strike twice.'

He'd got it in one.

'I offered to put a couple of men on you, and you turned me down. Okay, so what if I put two or three guys on Stella?'

'Delaup won't agree to that. Not with the pressure the department's under right now.'

'Fuck him. I'm talking off-duty. There are plenty of officers who remember Vince Delaney and would be willing to help. All I have to do is ask. What went down before can't be allowed to happen again.'

Finally, he'd said something I didn't disagree with.

'Better than Stella thinking you've cooled on her.'

'It's okay. I've got it covered.'

'As for Molly, she's safer now than she was a few days ago with her uncle on the case.'

It was true. At least, I hoped it was true. 'Except I'm deceiving her parents.'

'But in a good cause. Do you really think Catherine would want you to turn away from doing everything you could to catch this maniac? She wouldn't.'

Fitzy was on a roll; making sense.

'Delaup's a faithless fucker. The FBI isn't asking you to do diddly for him. And for what it's worth, I'd do the same again. Now, let's get back on stage and kick it. Your audience is hungry for you.'

'Yeah, yeah.'

'Think I'm kidding. Take a look around. It's you they're here for, fella.'

Maybe he was right, and maybe he was wrong. It didn't matter; we played, got paid and went home.

On Sunday, over at Catherine's, the only person I talked to about the pageant was Molly. After dinner, she sang the winning song for us. Three times. All day, my sister was quiet around me. I guess I must've been the same, though in my case, it was guilt.

At the door, for the first time, she mentioned what lay between us. 'Look, Vince, we thought a lot about taking Molly to the contests. In the end, we decided to go. There are monsters everywhere; you can't outrun them all. And we're with her every minute.'

Catherine turned the focus on to me. 'She'll be looking for you; you know she will.'

I could hate myself later; right now, I needed to get on the team without causing suspicion. I played the man-at-a-crossroads routine. 'I won't let her down. I'll come.'

'That's great. And thanks.'

'For what?'

'You know.'

I did know, and it made me feel like shit. I kissed her cheek. Back at my place, I showered, went to bed early and watched TV. Now and then, Lowell padded through: just checking on me. 'She ain't here, boy. She ain't here.'

He was unhappy; he blamed me. I defended myself. 'Don't give me that. You know what this is about? It's for her own good.'

His eyes bored into me.

'What choice do I have? Remember what happened the last time with this guy.'

He still wasn't having it, and left.

I shouted after him. 'Okay. Suit yourself. But I'm right. You know I'm right.'

During the post-game analysis, I turned the volume down and thought about what I'd agreed to. In all likelihood, I'd never be called on to do anything harder than cash my new paycheques. It sounded fine. So why didn't it feel better?

Eventually, I switched off the television without knowing what I'd been watching. Darkness engulfed the room. It didn't hide me.

The crimes so far straddle five states; that's an awful big playing field.

It'll only be local.

Any idea how many of these take place every year in this country?

In or out, Mr Delaney?

* * *

I was woken by my phone ringing. It was Agent McLaren. His voice sounded far away. 'Delaney? Sorry to call you so early. There's been another attack.'

'Where?'

'Tulsa, Oklahoma.'

'Pretty far travelled.'

'Yes, indeed. I'm still at the scene with Jim Rutherford.'

'Our guy?'

'Looks like it. A seven-year-old girl, Mimi Valasquez. Familiar details: strangled, body dumped in an alley, yards from the hall where she was competing. Mimi got through to the final. Didn't want to go with her mother to pick up her brother from his swimming session. Mrs Valasquez left her in the audience watching the other kids. She never got to perform again. When her mother returned and couldn't find her, she became hysterical. The police were called and discovered the kid eight hours later. Missed it first time 'round because the body was squeezed into a cardboard box. It's our guy, all right.'

'Don't tell me?'

'That's right, no forensics.'

I breathed out slow. Down the line, I could tell McLaren felt the same. 'What kind of pageant was it? How big?'

'Not big.'

'Should make it harder to go unnoticed. How can a stranger come and go without attracting attention?'

'It's a question, isn't it?' He sounded tired. 'Anyway, we're coming back to New Orleans to feedback and update. We'll do the same thing in every state.'

'Hope you like flying.'

'Hate it. At least it gets me out of being the media guy. Nobody needs that shit.'

'Thanks for the status check. See you soon.'

I thought about Mrs Valasquez, Mimi's mother. How was she supposed to get over it? In that alley, yesterday afternoon, the life had been squeezed from her too.

My mind panhandled what McLaren had said. Two things struck me as unusual. No trace evidence told me our killer was very, very careful: very prepared. And, how could a murderer drift in and out of places without a single person seeing them?

The biggest mystery of all.

Part Two

Sorry Seems to Be the Hardest Word

North Le Moyne, New Orleans

Clyde Hays counted coins into the cupped palm of the fragile hand. 'And thank you,' he said when he was done, ending the transaction with an easy smile. He knew the Creole lady on the other side of the counter; she'd been a customer of his many times in the past. The woman took her change, adding it with painstaking slowness to her purse and began to rearrange her shopping bag, squeezing the latest purchase in beside the others. The whole exercise was a trial, a test of stamina and memory. She was determined to conduct her own business in her own way, so long as the world didn't need her to hurry. Clyde thought of his mother, another lady who'd refused to be rushed and had lived to be ninety-one.

No problem, he had all day.

The woman chastised herself under her breath, checking off some mental list. The bell on the door tinkled. Two clean-cut men came in, their eyes hidden behind sunglasses. Clyde saw them over her shoulder. They stayed by the entrance, happy to wait. When she was satisfied she had everything, she gathered her cardigan round her, lifted her bag and headed for the door. The men stood aside to let her pass and held it open: a nice touch.

When the door closed, they stepped forward. One of them took off his shades and inspected his surroundings, lifting tins, reading labels. His friend picked up an apple and took a bite, locked the door and drew the blind. They grinned at each other.

Clyde Hays had run the general-goods store for forty years, and in that time, it had never been closed on Saturday. Never. His whole adult life had been spent behind the polished mahogany counter. He was proud of the fact his business kept to the opening hours posted on the window. Even during Katrina. Even then.

There had been no customers. That wasn't the point. Hays General stayed open. Until now.

The strangers were enjoying themselves, smirking and wisecracking; powerful guys, six feet tall. Their kindness to the old lady had been a mockery.

'What can I do for you fellas?'

'Been here long, old guy?'

Clyde tilted his chin. 'All my life.'

'Well, time for a change. From today, this store is under new management. You'll still be here, but you'll be working for us. Every week, we'll be round to collect our management fee. One hundred dollars. Make sure you have it ready.'

Clyde couldn't believe it; the guy was serious. 'Go to hell.'

The shakedown artists laughed. 'Look on it as an investment, pops.'

'Why should I pay you anything?'

'Like my friend says, it's an investment against bad things happening. New Orleans can be a dangerous place, don't you know that?'

The leader leaned over the counter, opened the till and removed four twenties and two tens.

'One hundred dollars. Starting today.'

'Get out of my shop before I call the cops.'

'I guess you don't hear so good. This is our shop now.'

Clyde lunged at the man stealing his money. The thief caught his wrist and forced his arm up his back until a bone snapped. The shopkeeper screamed in pain and collapsed on the floor. For the first time in forty years, Clyde Hays was afraid.

Eight

It was after nine when Bob Renaldi picked up Gran Russell and brought her to their house. Katie was in bed asleep. Emily Russell had asked for this meeting, and her daughter feared the worst.

'Tea, Mama?'

She forced a casualness she didn't feel into her question.

'Tea's fine.'

Mrs Russell took a sip from her cup and said what she'd come to say. 'Last Saturday was the saddest day of my life, and the most embarrassing. To see our Katie humiliated like that … the disappointment, the shame …'

Bob Renaldi tried to stop the inquest becoming overwrought. 'We feel the same, Mama, though shame is maybe a bit strong, don't you think?'

'No, I don't, Bob. No sir, I don't. Shame was in my heart then and still is.'

Bob accepted the reprimand. If he told the truth, he felt much the same. They'd let Katie down.

'You're right, Mama,' Eadie said. 'A hundred percent. Every time I think about it, I want to cry. It'll never happen again. Bob and I are agreed. You were right. Katie wanted to take part so much, but it was a mistake.'

She felt better for saying it out loud.

Bob said, 'That isn't the place for our Katie.'

Gran Russell studied their faces. 'So, you're saying she won't be going in for any more competitions, is that what I'm hearing?'

Bob and Eadie nodded. Emily Russell surveyed them some more before she spoke.

'Well, that's a mistake too.'

Bob struggled to keep up. 'What do you mean?'

'I mean it would be just plain wrong to quit on such a low. That girl's liable to be scarred by what happened on Saturday. I know I am. We can't leave her with something to carry around, weighing her down inside for the rest of her life.'

'Are you suggesting we should allow her to go through that hellish experience again? Mama, I can't believe you. Katie was so hurt by it. You saw her.'

'She was, but that other girl, that Molly, she didn't look too hurt to me. She looked well pleased with herself.'

'That kid was good.' Eadie lowered her voice. 'Probably went on to win it.'

Bob Renaldi readied to move into his role as referee.

'So, what're you saying to us, Mama?'

'First up, I'm not suggesting we just send Katie back out there for more of the same. I'm saying we've got some damage to undo, and the best way forward is to go back in there. But prepared this time. Practised to the point where big mistakes won't happen, so small mistakes won't matter. Rehearsed.'

This was out of left field.

'How's all this going to happen? How can we lift Katie up to a standard where she might have a chance of winning something? We'll need a good tune – something up-beat – a routine and a costume. At least one.'

'But it attracts the wrong kind of people. That was what you said, wasn't it? How'd you feel about that?'

Gran Russell didn't hesitate. 'I still think that's the way of it. We'll all be there to make sure our Katie's all right.'

'Ok. Who's going to train her and when?'

'We will. You and me. During the week, we can go to my house after school.' She smiled at her daughter. 'You can learn to play whatever song she's singing.'

'I'm going to play? You want me to play?'

'That's right.' Eadie's mother had waited a long time to be able to say it. 'And I don't want to hear another word about those goddamned piano lessons. Not ever.'

* * *

'Chin up! Eyes on the judges not the ground! Wherever they are, that's where you gotta be looking!' Mia Johnson's voice was stern, cutting across the music from the CD-player. On the stage, her daughter, Jolene, went through her routine. No cowgirl costume, this morning, just jeans and a shirt. The girl's eyes rarely left her mother. Joe Johnson didn't know Jolene wasn't in school; his wife hadn't told him. But how else was the child supposed to get better? A couple of hours in the evening after school just wasn't enough.

It was all about choices, wasn't it? If they wanted Jolene to succeed in competitions, sacrifices had to be made – like giving up your only day off work, like cutting school to practise. For Mia, it was an easy decision. Wednesdays would become rehearsal days. If her feet were killing her and her back ached, so what?

'Too slow! Faster out of that twirl, you're goin' to sleep in there!'

Mia used her thumb to stop the music, pressed another switch to rewind, then started again. The girl watched for her cue, her face stiff with concentration. She mouthed a silent count-in, calling out the beats in her head. Her mommy paced the garage, examining the performance from every angle, polishing the moves until they segued into each other.

'Again.'

When the song ended, Jolene sat on the edge, her slender legs dangling. She rubbed her eyes. 'I'm tired, Mommy. I want to stop.'

Mia stood, hands on her waist, witnessing another kind of performance.

'I need to go to the bathroom.'

There was a whine in the voice that pleaded to be understood. And she was. Her mother had caught this act a thousand times.

'OK, let's take five and you can go.'

Jolene scooted into the house. Mia sat where she'd been. Tired? If anybody wanted, she could show them what tired looked like. It was normal for Joe Johnson's wife to be working three jobs. Now, it was only two; low-paid, mind-fucking positions that took a whole lot more than they gave. Mia couldn't remember when they had last had a holiday – not since Jolene came along – that would make it six years. How could that be healthy for her and Joe? No wonder they didn't spark together like they used to. Work, work, work was all they ever did, and at the end of the day, always a dollar short.

Joe was a good man who struggled with the responsibilities of marriage and fretted about money. Sometimes, she'd catch him with his worry-head on. His eyes would tell her he was someplace else, counting and figuring, never at ease. They were going through a bad patch. That was how she saw it: a bad patch, not the end of the marriage, the way Joe had called it. After nine years, she wasn't too concerned about their long-term future together. They loved each other. Deep down, she was sure of it.

Yes, of course they did. Mia could be a bit wild with cash but, hey! Why were they both grafting their tails off if the best they could do was stand still? The pageant stuff wasn't cheap when you added it up – entry fees, travelling, costumes – even when some lying brought the costs down, it was still an expensive interest. But Jolene loved it, Mia did too; it was just Joe who needed convincing it was money well spent. But it was. It gave them something they could all do together one or two weekends every month as a family, and created a focus for spending time with their child. The money would go anyway; that's what money did. This way, they had a trip away, plus the bonus of seeing Jolene do her stuff.

Her father thought she had no talent. That wasn't so, coming third in Baton Rouge ahead of some good kids proved it, to Mia

Johnson at any rate. Though after what happened to the little boy, thank God Joe wasn't there. That would be the end of the dream. He was working every hour he could, because they were broke. When he got home, all he wanted to do was fall into bed and sleep; too tired to watch the television news. Besides, where was the mother? If she'd been paying attention, it wouldn't have been possible for someone to harm the child. Really, when you thought about it, with so many people around, being in a pageant was just about as safe as playing in your own backyard.

Jolene reappeared and sat next to her mom. Mia put her arm round her. For precious seconds, they were pals.

'Remember, your daddy doesn't get to know our new arrangement. He thinks school's important, and it is, but so's this. We're just dividin' up time to cover everythin'. Don't go lettin' him know, y'hear?'

Jolene shook her head.

'Good girl,' her mom said. 'Now, let's get to it, 'else we're wastin' our time.'

They got up.

'Ok, sugar, I want us to practise our vocals so we'll go through the routine. This time, concentrate on your voice. Think about singin' the words.'

The music began. Jolene Johnson started to sing. Thirty seconds in, her mother stopped the backing-track.

'Again.'

An hour and twenty-odd attempts later, Mia gave up. They had a problem, a big problem. Not something she could fix.

'We're finished, honey. That's it for today.'

'Do I have to go to school now, Mom?'

'No,' Mia Johnson replied. 'You don't have to go to school.'

'Great!'

Jolene rushed off, unaware. She could dance a bit and deliver the routine with plenty of energy, but she couldn't stay in tune. She was flat, sometimes sharp. Other times, she lost it altogether. She needed professional help. Jolene needed a voice coach, someone who could teach her to sing. Mia resigned herself to the truth. It was disappointing, of course. Still, lots of the children got tutored. Jolene had to have lessons. No point beating around the bush, she'd tell Joe tonight. That would be fun.

* * *

Mia had found a voice coach over in Kenner, Jefferson County, which was good news. The first problem was that the only available slot was a Saturday morning. The second was the fifty-dollar fee. Breaking the bad news to Joe was easy. His face gave her nothing. He shrugged his shoulders and kept on eating.

Mia grinned at her daughter. 'We've got the green light, honey.'

Joe drove, even though Saturday morning was the only day he didn't have to get up at the crack of dawn and drag himself to work one more time. The singing teacher's name was Miss Wilson, a florid-faced woman who liked things just so. Inside her house, nothing was ever allowed to be out of place.

Miss Wilson was in big demand, had been for twenty-five years. Her "students," as she called them, came to her from all over the state. One or two actually had a voice, so their technique benefited from working with the teacher. Mostly, her job was to help people get the best out of not very much. The rise in competitions, contests and pageants meant a bonanza for Miss Wilson, allowing her to travel for two months of the year.

She preferred cruise ships, searching for Mr Right and finding him on the odd occasion. In those surroundings, she could be the woman she believed herself to be. Everyone was a stranger to her, and she was a stranger to everyone. It was exciting. Whatever Miss Wilson missed out on in her life, it wasn't the capacity to fantasise. Prim and exacting at home, she permitted herself to be frivolous, even coquettish, on "her travels," as she liked to call them.

Miss Wilson was a dreamer, and the fifty bucks an hour she charged paid for those dreams.

'Doh, ray, me, fah, soh, lah, te, doh! Doh, te, lah, soh, fah, me, ray, doh!'

Jolene Johnson did her scales, missing most of the notes on her way up. Any that escaped got missed on the way down again.

'Weeell.' The teacher hesitated. It was important to establish what could be achieved with a student from the very start, otherwise, trouble lay in store. 'I can help with her breathing and timing. I can't make her Celine Dion.'

'But you can help her?'

Mia picked the words she wanted to hear. Miss Wilson repeated herself, weighing the many hours of Saturday morning purgatory ahead against an extended wardrobe for her next trip.

'I can get her breathing better. Better breathing brings confidence to a performer.'

'Doh, ray, me, fah, soh, lah, te, doh! Doh, te, lah, soh, fah, me, ray, doh!'

'Great. That's great, Miss Wilson. And can you get her to stay on the tune?'

'As I say, Mrs Johnson, I can help Jolene with her breathing.'

'Doh, ray, me, fah, soh, lah, te, doh! Doh, te, lah, soh, fah, me, ray, doh!'

Nine

Rutherford and McLaren were flying in for a noon meet. I didn't feel like biking. Lowell was having none of it. When I lifted the car keys, he went to the table and picked the harp up in his teeth.

'Sorry, fella. Not today. I'll only be a couple of hours. So, what's it to be, rock or blues?'

The look in his eyes told me he was too blue for blues, so I put on Bayou 95.7, the classic rock station, and left with Bon Jovi ringing in my ears. I knocked on Mrs Santini's door. She was ahead of me and gave a thumbs-up from her window.

Although I was fifteen minutes early, people were there, ready to begin. The room was more crowded than before. Besides Danny and me, another dozen I didn't recognise sat or stood around.

Danny came over with two cups of coffee and passed one to me. 'Boutte hasn't surfaced. That doesn't mean he's gone. Stay careful.'

I let it slide, reluctant to get into it with him.

He took a sip of his drink. 'You know about Tulsa?'

'Yeah, McLaren called from Oklahoma this morning.'

'That makes six. I want to stop this guy.'

His voice was quiet; serious. The coffee was strong, lukewarm and unpleasant.

'We all do, buddy.'

The room hummed with conversation. We didn't contribute; we'd said enough.

Right on the button at twelve, Delaup came through the door flanked by Rutherford and McLaren. The agents looked tired. Another man, tall and thin, with a small moustache, followed at their back. No one I'd met before.

The four of them sat down. Delaup thanked us for coming then Rutherford stood up – unnecessary at such a small gathering.

'On Saturday night, the body of Mimi Valasquez was found in an alley in Tulsa, Oklahoma. She'd been strangled after competing in a kiddies' event and left in a cardboard box yards from the venue. Whoever killed her took a hell of a chance. Her mother was only gone a short while – had to collect Mimi's brother from the swimming pool – and the kid was dumped in daylight. It's possible he put the body in the box first. That way all anybody would see is a guy getting rid of trash. The MO matches the others. This is the same guy. That makes six.'

His voice was flat.

'There are no eye-witnesses. Once again, forensics found nothing, most probably because there's nothing to find.'

Agent McLaren said, 'Any observations at this point?'

I raised my hand.

'Mr Delaney?'

It was a strange feeling to be the only one in the room without a job title. Intimidating in an egocentric kind of a way. I'd been Detective Delaney for years and never missed it, until now.

'You said whoever killed her took a chance. Seems to me that's how this guy works. In every case, the chance of discovery is high. All the homicides are in public places, all in daylight, and of course the victims are children. Vulnerable, yes, but liable to scream the place down, too.'

'Point well made.'

He turned to the stranger sitting along from him.

'Mr Diskins. Would you like to introduce yourself and respond?'

Unlike Rutherford, he didn't stand. He didn't need to; his voice cut across the room, loud and clear. 'Charlie Diskins. I'm a profiler with the FBI. So far, this guy has killed six children, and going to what Mr Delaney said, in every case, he took an almighty risk, suggesting the threat of being caught is part of the thrill; as big a part of the motivation as the violence. Our perp never leaves any trace, which means he's thoughtful about his business. Shows he's under control, in some ways at least. No sign he used drugs to subdue the victims, yet the acts are committed in crowded places. Our killer thinks he's cleverer than we are to the extent that detection is only a theoretical possibility to him. Exciting, yes, though unlikely to end in his capture.' He paused for effect. 'That belief is a big plus for us; it means he'll make a mistake. In his arrogance, he'll drop his guard. We'll get our chance. We need to be prepared to take it.'

He eyed the solemn faces in front of him. 'Six attacks in six states; victims from both sexes. You know from your own experience, but I'll say it again: these crimes are about power. We're up against a super-ego. Lucy Gilmour is the only one spotted with a stranger. So, the question to ponder is: who can walk around at these events without causing suspicion?

'Most of the crowd are women – some men; fathers, grandfathers, brothers, though the brothers will be kids, too. There'll definitely be workmen, like venue staff, an electrician or a plumber grafting on the weekend. Janitors. Judges. Caretakers. Maybe catering people. Everywhere had these types at the time of the crimes. No doubt this stuff has already been covered, but something must've been missed. Track them all down again so we can cross them off the list a second time. Believe it or not, some of these children have their own hairdresser, performance coach, even make-up artist. It's incredible, though those aren't so likely at a local event. There's a whole other world happening out there, people, most weekends of the year. Normally, it would pass us by, except nothing about this is normal.'

A hand went up. 'Detective Eddie Clementon. Who're we looking for? What's your best guess?'

Diskins answered with unashamed candour. 'Don't have one. All I can do is speculate. On the basis of the not-very-much we have so far, I'd say our perp is male, twenty-five to forty-five, perhaps a well-known face on the pageant scene. It could even be a parent using a child as a cover.'

'How sick is that?' someone said.

'Sick. But sick is the keyword here. In all probability, he's a family man Monday to Friday and a monster on the weekends.'

Diskins had told us pretty much what we already knew. No evidence existed to support anything more specific. His final comment was about the media. 'The decision's been made to keep the serial connection out of the news. That would give an advantage to the killer. He would know we're on to him and probably go to ground, for a while at least.'

The woman in Detective Nancy Corrigan slipped out. 'Shouldn't we be warning people?'

'We have. It doesn't stop them. They believe – if it happens at all – it'll happen to somebody else. They're sure they can protect their own children. Notices were sent out, after Timmy Donald was killed, to every known pageant venue. We also placed a public information notice in *Pageantry* magazine that ran for three issues. It's public knowledge, Detective. Draw any more attention to ourselves, and we'll be telling this animal we're waiting for him.'

Corrigan flushed under the rebuke. It was a fine line, and everybody knew it.

Captain Anthony Delaup got to his feet. 'The FBI has a plane to catch. Everybody else stay in your seats, please.'

Rutherford, McLaren and Diskins left. Off to do the same show in another state. I didn't envy them their job, nobody did. Running around, coming up dry, trying to believe they could crack this thing. Trying to make us believe it, too.

We settled down to listen.

Danny took the floor. 'Our job is to keep on looking. Revisiting the familiar until it gives up its secret. Hard going. We don't have a choice.'

He pointed to two detectives and gave them names.

'Morrison and Santana, compare the list of competitors in all six pageants where our guy took a child. Corrigan and Lawson – tough one, sorry, guys – I want you to interview our victims' parents one more time. Go over their statements.

See if they can remember something. Anything. Millar and O'Rourke, talk to every ancillary person connected with the Baton Rouge event, and cross-check with Corrigan and Lawson anyone who used or uses professional assistance – hairdresser, dance teacher. All of it. First thing Friday morning, be prepared to feed back to the group. And copies of everything for everyone. Agent McLaren will be the task-force co-ordinator. He knows the teams working the other states. The paper will come through him. I'll pass it on. Right now, we have one attack to investigate. Baton Rouge. By the end of the week, I expect us to have something to contribute. Thanks, folks.'

He clapped his hands the way they do on TV cop shows to get the team moving.

I watched them file out. One or two said goodbye – to me, to their weekend, to any family plans they might have had. That had once been my life. I didn't miss it a bit.

When everyone else had gone, Delaup, Fitzy and myself were left.

'No assignment for you, Delaney. Least not out front.'

Danny spoke to me. 'What's your plan?'

'I'm going with the family on Saturday. Molly wants to see if she can make it two in a row. Report on Monday.'

Both of them shook my hand.

'Glad to have you back.' Delaup sounded as if he meant it.

'Good luck,' Fitzpatrick said. 'Sorry I got you into this.'

'A man's gotta do … right?' At the door, I turned. 'Let the games begin.'

* * *

If the games did begin, nobody noticed. Saturday came and went, and nothing happened. Molly was second, which didn't please her. All the way home, she sulked, behaving nothing close to the angel her fans imagined and more like a five-year-old girl who hadn't gotten her way.

At the event, I sat through hours of precocious no-talents, and the nearest I came to a violent confrontation was when some kid sitting behind me insisted on pressing his knees against the back of my chair.

Seeing Molly do her stuff was a thrill. I could tolerate the event more easily than I thought, and though the pageant was ham, it was a family day; harmless fun, and the youngsters seemed to love it. I divided my time roaming around, watching the adults a lot more than the kids.

If the killer was there, I didn't see him.

Ten

When the Governor of Louisiana, John J McKeithen, toured the Houston Astrodome in 1966, he was quoted as saying, 'I want one of these, only bigger.'

Looking around as the Superdome filled up, I guessed he'd got his wish. In the seat next to me, Cal Moreland struggled through a giant packet of potato chips. How he could be hungry already was a mystery, we'd only finished eating an hour ago.

Cal is my oldest friend. In the season, we meet up for home games. Football is the excuse to get together.

He said, 'What do you think?'

'First game, too soon to tell.'

'Yeah, we know that, but what do you think?'

'I think I'll wait and see.'

'Know something, Delaney, you're too cautious, always have been. Even when we were kids. You need to take a chance, cut loose.'

I'd heard all this from him before and couldn't agree with any of it. 'Ok, I'll go with Florida.'

I knew that would get him, and it did.

He exploded. 'The Buccaneers, are you shittin' me?'

'Why not?'

'Why not? Because we're here to see our team win. We're here for the Saints.'

'And I'm rooting for them. You asked me what I thought.'

Frustration bloomed on his face. Cal was always better-looking than I was: taller, blond, blue-eyed and much more reckless. Impetuous. I was darker, brown-eyed and steady by comparison. For years in our youth, I got the girls he didn't want.

Cal Moreland had always represented something special to me. Larger than life, full of fun, full of shit. There was a time when I wanted to be him. But we were different. He was built wild: didn't play music, didn't like dogs and had no brothers, sisters or children – so no nephews or nieces. Cal joined the NOPD three years after I did, always working out of different districts from me and finally making detective, third class. Soon after, I was gone. In truth, most of what we had was in the past. Those season tickets we'd scrummed-up to buy a long time ago represented what was left of common ground. We'd come a long way, not always together, but here we still were.

'Fifty on our boys, by four,' he said. 'It's called faith. You want to try it.'

* * *

The following day I was at my desk, checking bills, when the phone rang. It was Harry Love. He wanted a background check on a prosecution witness, a Johnnie G Miller. He needed it as soon as. Two, maybe three days of my time in billable hours. Not a lot, still, it was money. I fingered the harp in my pocket without any intention of playing it. The guitar and Lowell rested in the corner. It was one of those days where everybody seemed low for no reason.

A memory came to me: the delight on Cal's face when the Saints finished off a forty-two-yard catch and run to lift them to an opening-game win over the defending champions, Tampa Bay Buccaneers.

He crowed. 'I told you, I told you: no quarter.'

'Yeah, you did. A good start.'

'A great start.'

I waited and wasn't disappointed.

'We could go all the way. We've got the right stuff this year.'

'Maybe.' The immediate aftermath of an opening-day win was no place for moderate talk. 'A lot can change during a sixteen-game season, Cal.'

He shook his head. 'I don't get you. We can win this thing.'

'You think?'

'Who knows where the road goes, Delaney?'

'Anyway, you won fifty dollars.'

'Oh yeah, so I did. So I did.'

Voices from outside brought me back. I grabbed the bills off the desk and stuck them in a drawer. The door opened, and a cinema line came through it. There must have been fifteen or twenty people, mostly African Americans with a handful of Asians, Koreans or Vietnamese, and one or two who looked to be Hispanic or Latino; there were no white faces in the group. I brought my chair out from behind the desk and placed it beside a woman standing at the front. She thanked me. Then, I perched on the edge of my desk and looked at them.

These were not young people, most were at least in middle-age and some a lot older than that. They looked at me. I looked at them. Each waiting for the other to begin. The silence was broken by a voice from the back, a man's voice, deep and gravelly. 'Nice dog.'

'So, how can I help you folks?'

Feet shuffled and heads went down. The woman at the front surprised me by standing up.

'My name is Pricilla Bartholomew, Mrs, and this is my husband, Willard. Thank you for seeing us without an appointment, Mr Delaney.'

Mrs Pricilla Bartholomew was a tall lady; slim, edging sixty I guessed, with ramrod posture and clear eyes. Easy to imagine she'd been a looker. And there was an intelligence it was impossible not to notice. 'We need your help. Plain as that.'

'Tell me about it.' I repositioned myself on the desk to listen.

'We're here representing the traders and business people of North Le Moyne and the surrounding area. There's more of us, a lot more. I can introduce everybody, if you like. That would eat up your time, so I guess I'll just stick with telling you the facts. It was me who proposed coming here. Saw your box in Yellow Pages and persuaded the rest we jump right in and come down today. You looked like somebody we could afford.'

She spoke without offense. 'And now, we're here.'

So, it was true: it did pay to advertise.

'We own a deli, Willard and me, have done for almost thirty years. Used to be my father's. When he passed, it came to me. Originally, my family was from Asia. We specialise in spices and sauces from the region. Everybody here is a small trader. Nobody's making a fortune down our way.'

I believed her.

'We were doing all right until two months ago. That's when it started.'

'What started?'

'The threats, the violence – Clyde had his arm broken. They went to every store and laid out how it was going to be. From now on, they said, they would make sure nobody bothered us. If anybody did, they'd sort it out.' She took a breath. 'They wanted money, of course, for this service, as they called it. One hundred at first. It's gone up to two.'

She tilted her chin proudly. 'It's killing us, Mr Delaney. Not just the money we can't afford, but the worry, the constant fear and the disgrace of knowing we stood for this, even for a minute. We're all hard-working people, who just want to be left alone to run our businesses, raise our children and live our lives. It can't go on.'

'Mrs Bartholomew, all of you, what I'm hearing is extortion. Organised crime. Really, this is a matter for the police. I can make a call. Put you in touch with a guy I know. This isn't what I do, I'm sorry.'

Pricilla Bartholomew held me with her eyes. She was the one I had to convince.

'I'm not unwilling. It *is* a police matter. Extortion is a serious crime. You need the police.'

She let me dig a hole for myself.

'That's why we've come to you. These people *are* the police.'

Eleven

'They told us.'

The voice hadn't come from Mrs Bartholomew; she was busy watching me. I spoke to all of them, although really only to the tall, proud woman at the front.

'They told you they were the police?'

Her face remained impassive. The gritty voice that had commented on Lowell said, 'Yeah, that's right.'

'You say it began two months ago?'

'Yes. About that.'

'How did it actually start? What was the first thing that happened?'

Cilla looked back over her group and nodded to a small black man over to the side. 'Tell him, Clyde.'

He fidgeted with his hat, and when he spoke his voice was quiet. 'One day, two young fellas showed up. Walked in as if they owned the place, started lookin' around. I remember I was servin' a customer at the time, but I saw 'em. There was an arrogance, a cock-of-the-walk kind of thing, the way teenagers act around each other in public, know what I mean?'

I knew what he meant.

'When the customer left, I asked, "What can I get you fellas?" They just smirked across the counter at me. One of them palmed an apple 'n took a bite out of it. The other strolled over, drew the blind and locked the door. My place, closed in the middle of the day. Never been known.'

Clyde pulled himself up to his full height.

'I wasn't afraid, but I wasn't happy either.'

It was important to him to get that out. Get it said in front of his peers.

'Anyway, they told me my store was under new management. That was their expression. The new bosses wanted one hundred dollars from me every week from now on.'

The hat in his hand was taking a beating.

'"Why would I pay you anything?" I asked them. "Look on it as an investment," the one by the door threw in. The first guy leaned over, opened the till and counted out one hundred in twenties and tens. "Startin' today," he said, and he laughed. They both did. I told them to get out of my shop before I called the cops. "Save your dime, grandpa." One of them grinned. "We are the cops." Then, he broke my arm.'

Clyde cast his gaze around the group.

'Heard everybody got a visit, same speech too. Now they come in every week for the money, except three weeks ago, it went up to two. Two hundred a week, eight hundred a month. Money like that isn't hangin' spare in my business. I'm payin' them out of my wages. No other place to find it.'

He wasn't nervous anymore; he was angry. The hat got it just the same. He was done and disappeared behind a bigger guy, which could've been anybody in the room.

Cilla said, 'Everybody has a similar story.'

Heads bobbed and lips moved in agreement.

'Okay. Is it always the same two guys? What do they look like?'

Willard Bartholomew chimed in, without waiting for his wife to invite him. 'Late twenties, clean-cut, real short hair, tallish – well, taller than me anyway. Look the way cops look out of uniform. Tell them a mile off. Same two all the time. Always doing that good cop, bad cop routine. One of them does the smiling, while his friend does the threatening. In the beginning, we put up some resistance, refusing to give them the money, closing up on collection day: making noises about what we'd do. They just laughed. Then, they came 'round to a couple of stores and trashed them. That brought us into line. We realised we had trouble that wasn't just gonna go away.'

'And you could identify these guys, no problem?'

'In our sleep.'

'You said there's more of you involved. How many more?'

'Around a hundred.'

I did the math: over a million dollars a year in this neighbourhood alone. Nice. If they operated in other places, very nice indeed.

'So far, you've paid these guys and done nothing about it, all because of something they told you about themselves that might not be true. What if it's a con? What if the whole scam depends on you believing them?'

Silence.

The coarse voice at the back spoke for all of them. 'They're cops. Dirty, with our money.'

I didn't dispute it.

'I'm working for you now. But there's a condition. I call my own shots.'

Willard said, 'What does that mean?'

'It means I decide how to play it.'

He spoke to himself. 'You're gonna involve the police, aren't you? We're telling you who these bastards are and you don't believe us.'

'I'm keeping our options open, that's all.'

He didn't believe me, and neither did I.

'Look, I worked for fifteen years with the NOPD. I know people in there. I'll think on it before I do anything, but right now, my gut tells me to talk to a friend or two.'

A murmur of discontent ran around the room. I guessed I was already challenging the most important condition of my employment.

'This is our lives you're gambling with, Mister.' Willard again, he'd taken over from his wife. 'We're the ones in the firing-line.'

It was a popular view. The noise of dissension swelled in the room. I sensed rebellion. Except my position wasn't negotiable. How could I help without enlisting help myself?

'Listen! Just listen! You want me to gather evidence against these guys, and I'll do that. My way. So, in or out?'

In or out, Mr Delaney?

The brusque ultimatum restored silence and the balance of power. When they'd quietened down, I approached their objections more gently. Good cop, bad cop, all in one. I wondered if Willard Bartholomew had picked up on it.

'Folks, I know how serious your situation is. The last thing I want to do is endanger anyone, trust me on that, but if what you believe is true – that no one on the NOPD is clean – then that begs the question: assuming I get evidence of this felony, where do you want me to take it? Not to the police. To a judge, maybe? What makes us think we can depend on that guy?'

'Internal Affairs.'

Someone watched too much television.

'They don't call them that these days, and they're police officers, too. Different remit, that's all. Still cops. So, who?'

Cilla Bartholomew called time on my little circus. 'We take your point, Mr Delaney.'

She spoke with an austerity I guessed she reserved for bullies and assholes.

'Then, tell me what to do?'

She stroked her sculpted nose. 'Can we have a few minutes? We need to talk.'

'Of course. Take as long as you want.'

'It's a big decision.'

'I understand. It's a big decision for me, too.'

* * *

'Can you come back in please, Mr Delaney?'

Inside, things had changed. Cilla got straight to it.

'We've talked, and I'll be honest with you, it was a close-run thing. Maybe if we'd banished this thing at the start, showed them we couldn't be scared so easily, we might have got the monkey off our backs. But maybes don't matter. We are where we are. So, we're going with you. Do as you see fit.'

I thanked her with a nod.

'I've got a couple more questions before I can get started. First, do these jokers always show up on the same day?'

Gravel Voice answered. 'Tuesdays or Wednesdays.'

'Always on a Tuesday and Wednesday?'

'Yeah.'

'Second, anybody see the car they drive?'

Nobody had.

'All right, starting from tomorrow, I'm working for you. As for tactics, I haven't decided yet. It's more important to get a look at these guys, find out who they are, and what their connection might be. For the next while, when they come around, just pay them. Don't cause any trouble. It won't be for too much longer.'

They filed out. Willard Bartholomew was one of the first to leave. That told me something. His wife stood at the back, shepherding the stragglers homeward. I fell into step with her. Out on the landing, a bottleneck had built up that was gradually sorting itself out. We stood for a moment, allowing the delegation to negotiate the steep incline down the wooden stairs. The street below was wet. New Orleans was in the middle of a week of thunderstorms. From somewhere, the smell of jasmine drifted on the clean air.

'Thank you for your time, Mr Delaney.'

'Thank you for your faith in me. I got the impression Willard doesn't share it.'

She had nothing to say to that.

We waited in silence, then she asked her question. 'How high do you think it goes? You said they sounded organised, that extortion's a serious crime. Surely somebody must be protecting these bullies, don't you think?'

I did think. That's what I had to find out.

'Who knows?'

She offered her hand, bowed a little and half-smiled. 'I'm leaving with something I didn't have when I arrived.'

'Really, what's that?'

'Hope. You've given me hope, and I thank you for that. Though we never did discuss money, did we?'

'Don't worry. I'll charge you something.'

She turned away, satisfied, stepping carefully down the rickety stairs towards the others already walking up Dauphine. I looked at my watch – 5.30 p.m. On one hand, I was back working for my old boss, helping the police chase a psycho who'd left a trail of dead children across six states. On the other, I'd taken on a case where they were the probable perps.

Lowell watched them go and looked at me.

'I know, I know. I'm supposed to be out of this. Don't nag.'

Twelve

I spotted them at once, and Willard was right; even in suits, they looked like cops. They came strolling down the street, laughing and kidding around, stopping in at one store after another to make their Wednesday collection. A few minutes later, they'd be out again, hands in pockets, following passing girls with their eyes. Whatever they were saying to each other must've been awful funny, because they kept smiling all the way down the street: just a couple of extortionists, happy in their work. My camera whirred and clicked, recording their good mood. It wasn't going to last much longer.

Both were fair-haired, one more blond than the other. He was always a half-step ahead of his partner, which told me who was the boss. But the organiser of a big-money racket? I put them down as late-twenties, probably patrol cops with no rank. Could be they'd happened on a way to earn real money and were taking it. No operation. No Mr Big – nothing like that – just rogues on the make.

They passed me, and I let them go, still clowning and joking. They were tall, and I had the impression of hours spent working out. One of them carried a training-bag with *Nike* on the side. Easy to appreciate how intimidating they would seem if they showed up in your store demanding money, grinning as they emptied the register.

I moved the car in the direction they'd come. Sixty minutes later, they were back, still laughing. They say crime doesn't pay. Going by these guys, not only did it pay, it was a hell of a lot of fun. At one point, the junior partner looked over to where I was. For a moment, I thought he'd made me, but no, laughing-boy joined with his pal in a new hoot. These guys believed they were invincible, systematically hitting on one trader after another and having a ball.

And that was the thing.

They were a couple of punks having a good time. I wondered where that level of confidence came from. Not bothered about drawing attention to themselves, yet I was watching a felony in progress. How come? Could they really be that dumb?

Of course they could. They'd probably smoked a joint or two before starting out and were still getting the benefits.

Their last stop was a hardware shop. They were inside about three minutes. When they left, a man in overalls followed them to the door and watched them go. I didn't recognise him; he was one of the faceless people I was representing. His hair was pulled back, his expression was grim. He stood, hands on hips, spat on the sidewalk and went back in. He didn't know I was there. Even if he had, what difference would it have made? Another two hundred bucks had just said goodbye.

When they made a left, I got out and followed them. Further on, they stopped at a muddy-brown '04 Ford. They weren't spending the money on wheels. I ducked into a doorway as they rolled by and got the licence plate.

Before the day was out, I'd know who they were.

* * *

'So, what do you need?' Fitzpatrick's mouth might have been programmed.

'Just the ID.'

'All right. Two hours.'

I went back to the office to wait. My dog was there, and he needed a walk. After a promenade around Jackson Square, we settled down. I took a look at the Word Jumble, though to tell the truth, my heart wasn't in it, so I stared at the walls instead. I may even have dozed off. Suddenly, there was a noise outside. Lowell's ears went back. He growled; never a good sign. My first thought was Boutte. I opened the drawer as quietly as I could, took out the gun and crept towards my door. Surely those two apes hadn't followed me here? I must be slipping. The click of the hammer cocking was loud as thunder. In one continuous movement, I turned the handle and pulled back the door.

Nobody. But Lowell had growled.

'You're losing it, buddy. He's probably a thousand miles away by now.'

The gun went back in the drawer, Lowell went back to his basket, and I went back to waiting, the excitement over for now.

Danny called. 'Name's Ryan Hill. Two-seventy-two Madeleine.'

'Thanks, Fitz. Ever heard of this guy?'

'I haven't, no, but it's funny you should ask.'

I beat him to it. 'Because he's a cop.'

'Right.'

'Which district?'

'Fifth.'

'Thanks, buddy.'

Because of Fitz, I now knew who the guy was, where he lived and what district he worked out of. Cal's district. He'd know these guys.

They were already on their way to jail.

Thirteen

'I don't believe it. I don't want to believe it.'

'It's true. Wish it wasn't, but it is.'

'Tell me again from the start.'

It was three o'clock in the morning, and the air was warm. We were sitting beneath the green and white awning of Cafe Du Monde on Decatur, just us and a handful of people with nowhere to go killing time until the sun came up. Not far away, the Mississippi rolled in darkness to the Gulf, and in the black sky a lonesome night heron called to his mate. I took a sip from my café-au-lait; the chicory softened the harshness of the bean, adding an almost chocolate flavour: comforting. And tonight, I needed comfort. What I had to tell Cal Moreland wasn't easy.

He listened without interrupting as I explained how the traders' delegation had come to me and their feelings about talking to the police. While I spoke, I watched him clench and unclench his fists, the colour draining from his face leaving it pale under the lights. When I finished, he said, 'And this has been going on how long?'

'A couple of months.'

Cal exhaled so hard it was more like a snort. His hands gripped the edge of the table. 'We're talking real money here, Delaney. Real money.'

He absently shredded a paper napkin, reacting exactly as I'd thought he would: disbelief, anger and shame in a predictable procession. His face was ravaged by lack of sleep: the corners of his eyes were marked, and the skin on his forehead was dry, flaking. He looked like a guy working too hard, worrying too much. I needed his help even more than Danny's, because he was an insider. He could get closer than I ever could. I wasn't using him: he wanted in.

In or out?

'Fuck!' He swore quietly and viciously to himself; the coffee cup trembled in his hands when he lifted it to his mouth. I'd never seen him so angry.

'Scum-sucking bastards. What do you need?'

'Complete discretion. Anything else puts my clients in danger. They don't want the police. "No police, we don't trust them." Their exact words.'

'Who can blame them?'

'The only ones who know what's going on are the clients, me, and now you.'

'And the perps.'

'To answer your question about what I want. Two things: the name of the other guy and a quick end to the extortion.'

'First one's easy. You'll know who he is later today.'

'Good. After that, we need a plan. They do their rounds Tuesdays and Wednesdays. I want to be ready to strike.'

I could tell what Cal was thinking. 'You'll be there?'

'Wild horses,' he said. 'It's gotta be.'

We toyed with our coffee in silence for a while until Cal broke it.

'This is bad, Delaney, really bad. We don't need this shit.'

'I know.'

'No, you don't.'

The frustration and disappointment bubbling inside him surfaced. 'You're out of it. Fuckers like these do more damage to their fellow-officers than anybody else. Yeah, even the victims. We have to work on after it all dies down, except it never does, not for us. No one wants to talk to us, help us. We become the enemy. People think it's legitimate to feel that way because of rotten cops like these two.'

He was wrong. I knew what it was like to be distrusted because you had a badge.

Cal wasn't finished.

'Let me tell you what you don't know. We'd been called to assist at a scene where some Caucasian crackhead had gone crazy, taking his wife and child hostage in his flat. Nobody could get near the guy. He warned us he was going to waste both of them. We waited for hours trying to talk him down.

'There was something about that night. It had been a beautiful autumn day, crisp and clear with blue skies. A good-to-be-alive day. Winter was coming and that was okay. It meant Thanksgiving, Christmas, New Year and on to Mardi Gras. It was easy to be optimistic.'

He told his tale, and I watched him, noticing for the first time how old he looked. Everybody gets older; with my friend, it seemed to have happened right before my eyes at three-twenty-five a.m. in an all-night diner, the only witnesses me and two cups of cold coffee.

'Anyway, the situation was critical, heading for only one outcome. By this time, a big crowd had gathered out in the street. We heard a single gunshot. Me and two other officers crept along the balcony, shot the door out and dived into the house. I'd never been so scared in all my life. It looked like Beirut in there: clothes, food, toys everywhere – and the smell.'

Cal screwed up his face.

'The body of the mother lay in the hall. She'd caught a bullet in the back trying to get to the door. The guy was screaming at us to get out, get away, waving his piece around, showering us with crazy talk about what we were making him do, all the time hugging a baby close to him. I didn't stop to think it out. I shot him and raced forward. The gun fell from his hand, and he went down in slow-motion. I scooped the kid out of his arms before he hit the floor, dead. Then other officers appeared. The whole thing was a dream. I left the flat carrying the child in one arm. Didn't even know I was still holding my gun in the other. In the street, a woman officer took the baby. I realised I still hadn't holstered the gun. The beautiful day had turned into a night of flashing blue lights, loud noise and the sound of my heart exploding out of my chest.

'The crowd knew what had gone down and parted to let me get to my car. A black guy stepped in front of me. To tell the truth, my head was someplace else. I never even saw him coming. He looked at me for a couple of seconds, gathered spit in his mouth and fired it at me. It fell short. Some of it landed on my shoe. Nobody said or did anything. He walked away, and they let him go. The adrenaline pumping through me stopped. I was cold. I wanted to cry.'

Recounting the incident added more years. His eyes glazed over. For a moment, I thought he was going to break down. Instead, he got a hold on himself and locked his eyes on mine, asking me to understand. I did. He'd just risked his life to save a child, yet was still despised. Still the one on the other side.

'I lost something of myself that night. And I never found it again. Don't expect I ever will. You learn to live without it, make some adjustments.'

'Pick yourself up, brush yourself down?'

'Something like that.'

I knew guys who'd lost their soul trying to shore up the breaking dam. My surprise was that the confident, exuberant friend of my imagining had become a casualty, as much as the woman on the floor of the grubby flat with a bloody hole in her back.

'These punks can't be allowed to exist. The job's already too hard. Whatever you're planning, include me in.'

'I knew you'd say that, but it's good to hear.'

I smiled. He smiled too.

'Okay. When do we move? I aim to put an end to this thing.'

'Wednesday. Let them get comfortable, get in their groove, then we hit. Catch them in the act. Eye-witnesses, evidence, the whole nine yards.'

'Expect my call as soon as I've identified the other guy.'

'Fine. Only a slip on our part can let these guys get away. Talk to nobody. Nobody.'

I sounded like a paranoid asshole.

'"No police, we don't trust them,"' he said, quoting what I'd told him, grinning without humour.

I followed him with my eyes as he left. He wanted this mess cleared up as much as I did – given what he'd told me – maybe more. The next eight hours were lost to me. I didn't toss or turn or dream. Who knows how long I would've slept, if my phone hadn't wakened me. It was Cal. He sounded better.

'Raymond Clark. Twenty-seven. Partner of Ryan Hill. Both been with the NOPD for two years. Unexceptional people who aren't going far.'

'Hard to believe these two possess the entrepreneurial talent to take this on by themselves, don't you think?'

'Yeah, I do think.'

'Wednesday, just as we agreed. The only people who know are me and you. No leaks. No opportunity for these goons to head for the hills. Call me if anything changes.'

'We've got them, Delaney. Absolutely.' He was back to his confident best. It was good to hear. 'A week from Sunday, we'll be sitting in the Dome watching the Saints whip the 49ers and these punks'll be behind bars.'

* * *

The call to Stella wasn't easy to make, but there was no other choice. Until Julian Boutte had been recaptured, the less I had to do with her the better. I could guess what her reaction would be when I broke it to her, and I wasn't wrong.

'Listen, Stel. I'm snowed under. This pageant thing is picking up speed.'

Her response was guarded. 'You're saying what, exactly?'

I hesitated. 'Think I'm gonna need a couple of weeks' space to get out in front of it.'

Silence.

'You mean time away from me?'

'No. I mean time to deal with what I'm into.'

Stella was nobody's fool.

'Take as long as you like, Delaney. And when you're ready, maybe you'll tell me what the hell is going on?'

Fourteen

The child stood apart from the crowd, clutching her meaningless inkjet certificate in both hands. Her mother talked nonsense to the other moms, in a circle, comparing stories that flattered them and defamed their husbands.

Andrea Hassel was bored. The competition was still going on, people coming and going, hurrying their kids along. It didn't concern her anymore today; her section had already performed and been judged. The girl wanted three things; her mommy's attention, the bathroom, and to go home.

She tugged the hem of her mother's jacket, trying to get her to detach from the conversation and attend to her. 'Mommy.' Her voice was a thin whine. Though she was only five-years-old, Andrea had long identified it as the sound that got results. She was too young to understand chatting with the other moms was part of the fun for her mother.

Like all children, she was the centre of the world.

But her mommy was busy right now impressing two women she'd met at the pageants. They boasted to each other about costs and sacrifices and the difficulties brought by loving their children as much as they did, agreeing the benefits to Justin or Tammy or Samantha far outweighed any considerations of self. It was for the children, wasn't it? All for them.

'Well, well,' the stranger said. 'Aren't you the pretty one?'

Andrea's tiny face looked into the smile, her hands balled in small fists rubbing at her eyes, a preamble to tears that hadn't arrived yet but were on their way.

'I heard you sing. You were very good. Is this your certificate? Let me see.'

The child handed over the paper.

'My, my, look at this. "This is to certify that Andrea Hassel won first prize in the three-to-five-year-old section of the Modern Miss Johns Creek Pageant."'

The paper was rolled and handed back. Andrea accepted both it and the stranger. Less than a yard away, she could hear the mommies talk. That's what it sounded like; talk, talk, talking and no listening.

'I want to go to the bathroom.'

Christ, did these kids ever say anything else?

Fool. Don't be a fool.

She's nice though.

Unwise! Unsafe! Unnecessary!

Fuck off! I know what I'm doing. Besides, she's perfect. Look at the light in those eyes. Don't you want to be there when it goes out? I know I do.

Agreed. And the mother's wrapped up in herself. Perfect.

'Do you, honey? Well we can fix that, can't we? Let's see now. I think the restroom is through here.'

The Watcher couldn't help admire the skill, the balls. The risks were running higher and higher, it was true.

But the rush. Wow!

Fifteen

The Monday meeting was becoming something to dread. As soon as I arrived, I knew I'd be hearing more bad news. At the previous one, we'd gone through the lists of competitors and their families, workmen, catering people, etc, and listened to who was where and when; who employed extra help to assist the young performers. It produced zip and was depressing as hell. If anything, it magnified the size of the problem facing the agencies. I understood why the FBI had included us. Even with the locals involved in every state, it needed a miracle.

All the usual suspects were there. I got myself set up with coffee, took a seat at the back and switched off my cell. Further down, Fitzpatrick and Delaup had their heads together. Everybody looked tired and serious.

Agent McLaren opened it up. 'Good morning. Most of you have probably already seen the news on TV.'

I hadn't. It was only six-thirty a.m. Yesterday, the television had stayed off.

McLaren brought me up to speed. 'On Saturday, he hit again. Johns Creek, Georgia, this time, making it seven attacks in total. There is no centre to this thing, and to be honest, it's a much bigger playing field than we can cope with.'

He cleared his throat.

'Andrea Hassel was lifted from under her mother's nose. Her body was found in an unused room – strangled, same as the others.'

Beside him, Agent Rutherford looked beat. He kept his head down. The murders were taking their toll on him.

'It's difficult to find anything new to say. Fortunately for me, that's Charlie Diskins' job – Charlie?'

Diskins gave McLaren the briefest of nods and addressed the group. 'Seven attacks. Seven dead children. Is there anything positive to take from the latest atrocity? Well, as a matter of fact, there is.'

I was glad to hear it, because from where I was, we stood every chance of coming a very poor second to this fruit. He'd got to call all the shots. Unless he made a mistake, how were we ever going to catch him?

'The attacks themselves are happening closer together. After Lucy Gilmour, who we now believe was the first one, five months passed before the Dulles kid was killed. Four until Billy Cunningham. The interval between the killings was measured in months.'

He let everybody catch up. We knew where he was going. 'Pamela White was three months ago, Timmy Donald seven weeks, Mimi Valasquez a couple of weeks, and now Andrea Hassel: two days. Whatever crazy urges make him do this are racing away. Based on the time progression, we can expect more deaths, and soon.'

I felt sick listening to the roll call of murdered children and the dismal prognosis.

'The latest attack on Saturday was particularly audacious. Bold beyond belief. Agent Rutherford interviewed the mother.'

Diskins signalled for Rutherford to tell it his way.

'The mother says the child was standing beside her in a room full of people. One moment she was there, the next … and nobody saw or heard anything.'

Rutherford was low on energy. He left it there.

'That's where we can take a little heart.' Diskins was back in the driving-seat. 'Sometimes, you hear serials want to get caught. I've never been sold on that idea. With this one, a child is abducted from her mother's side and killed, and nobody notices. Here's what it tells me; our perp has – not a wish to be stopped – but an enormous ego. A super-ego. He thrives on the danger. Loves it. He'll make a mistake. No ifs or buts, he'll go too far, trust me on that. Questions?'

I hated to pour cold water on our efforts, but it had to be said. 'Surely if this guy keeps moving states, we're wasting our time? Shouldn't the neighbouring states to Georgia be on alert?'

'Good point. Already done. But he might double back and catch us with our pants down.'

Everyone desperately wanted to believe Charlie Diskins; it was all there was. The next hour was spent with updated reports on the results of all the cross-checking that was going on. The same work was being done by teams in the other states. I hoped somebody, somewhere, would make a connection, spot something everyone else had missed. What had been discovered took no time to tell.

The meeting broke up. I overheard two detectives talking, and my ears picked up.

'Of course, they'll investigate, but …' a neat, late twenties brunette was saying to her colleague, busy repacking his briefcase. He didn't commit himself.

I interrupted. 'Excuse me. What did you just say?'

'We're talking about last night. I was telling Dale what I'd heard on the 'vine. Bound to be an investigation with a thing like that.'

'What do you mean?'

'Around ten o'clock, there was a raid on a house near Canal. Drug bust, I think.'

'And?'

'Two of our guys went down. That's all I know.'

My mind had already moved on, directing my hands to retrieve the cell from whatever pocket I'd hidden it in.

'Fuck,' I said, irritated with myself.

I found it and switched it on. The usual palaver of entering pin numbers and welcome messages frustrated me. Finally, I had service. I'd missed a call. No message. It could be a call from anybody about anything except some sixth sense said it wasn't.

I pressed caller ID and Cal's number showed; he'd tried to reach me at nine minutes past seven. Of course, he couldn't because I was in the meeting. I pressed redial on my way out and headed down the back stairs. From experience, I knew no one used them.

He answered at once. 'Delaney. Tried to get you earlier.' He sounded agitated.

'Had my phone off. What gives?'

'You've heard about last night? The bust?'

'Only just heard.'

'Two officers down.'

'How bad?'

'Both dead?'

I could guess the rest. 'Who were they?'

The line went quiet.

'Hill and Clark. Convenient, or what?'

'I'll call you later, Cal,' was all I could get out. As quickly as it had begun, it was over. The thugs who'd terrorised a community were gone. After I talked to Cal, I'd tell Cilla Bartholomew. She could give the others the good news. For me, there were still too many unanswered questions: who was behind it? How high up did it go?

Now, we'd never know.

It was a result, of sorts. But in the words of Cal Moreland, "Convenient, or what?"

* * *

I spent the rest of the morning working on the Harry Love case I'd neglected. Not a good idea. I needed the work. Johnnie G Miller turned out to be a witness whose testimony might well put Harry's client away. Harry expected me to uncover something to discredit Miller in court. Unfortunately, there was nothing. Johnnie G turned out to be a stand-up guy. Harry wasn't going to be pleased.

The dog deserved a change of scene, and my work ethic was shot. Though it was only eleven o'clock in the morning, we headed for the Chartres House Cafe and got a table out on the patio. Chartres was dog-friendly and no wonder; Lowell drank beer twice the price of his usual tipple as if money grew on trees. To keep him company, I had a couple as well. Later, I had two calls to make: one to Cal Moreland, the other to give Harry Love the bad news about the witness.

The day was a bust.

* * *

When we'd had our beers, we walked around, taking in the sights and smells of old New Orleans: the French Quarter which, as it turns out, is arguably Spanish, sparkled in the sun after a downpour lasting less than a minute. I felt like a tourist watching the people on Jackson Square. The attraction of the Big Easy wasn't hard to understand.

I was ducking out of Monday and didn't care. I was only on the periphery of the serial killer investigation. The deaths of the dirty cops had brought some kind of result, but it was too early to tell exactly what. So why was I having such a shit time?

Since Danny had given me the news about Julian Boutte, I'd been on edge, looking over my shoulder and double-checking the street outside from whichever window I was closest to. And the old water-and-well thing was true: I really missed Stella. When this was over, if I wanted her in my life, something would have to change.

Then again, how could it? I wasn't a cop anymore – hadn't been for seven years – yet people I loved were still in danger. The past, it seemed, was determined to hold on to me.

* * *

Seven Years Earlier

On a balmy evening, I was driving back from a stake-out at the end of a long, hot and fruitless day when a phone call changed my life. Minutes earlier, I'd dropped Danny Fitzpatrick at his place and watched him walk up his drive. He was tired and so was I. Fitz waved over his shoulder without looking back, and I pulled away, happy to be going home.

On Lake Pontchartrain, two pairs of frigate birds flew together, low above the water, with an orange sun dissolving in the distance behind them. After twelve hours in a stifling car, I was running on empty, thinking about a shower and sleep. Or maybe just sleep. I reached across to the passenger seat and opened my cell.

Julian Boutte laughing evil down the line snapped me awake.

Boutte hadn't crossed my mind much in the week since he'd thrown himself through the window in the shotgun. The hunt for him was still going on, and though the police had tossed the parish from top to bottom, they'd found nothing. No surprise. Algiers was home turf for Boutte; he had friends there who would hide him. An army could search for a couple of decades and still come up dry.

His voice was a rasp; teasing. 'Guess where I'm at, Delaney.'

'Don't know. Don't care.'

Julian sounded disappointed. 'Oh, man. Humour me.'

He'd done his homework; he'd called my cell. In truth, I hadn't expected him to come for me but I'd reckoned without his state of mind: Julian Boutte was insane. That madness would be his undoing. For the moment at least, he was king of the hill. Boutte breathed hard into the phone and I could imagine him grinning.

'I'm not in the mood for games, Juli. More to do with my time. Thought you understood that.'

'You're a busy guy, I get it. Question is: how busy?'

'Too busy to be fucking around with you.'

'Yeah? Got something that'll get your attention. Somebody here wants to talk to you.'

There was a scuffle. Boutte cursed. I heard the slap of skin on skin and a woman cry out. Putting the hurt on females was Boutte's special talent – I'd seen it up close – and he was doing it again. Then, she spoke, her voice frantic with fear, and my heart jumped a beat.

'Delaney! Delaney! Help me!'

It was Ellen.

Suddenly, I wasn't tired anymore. Boutte came back on, giggling the way he had before he'd cut the woman tied to the chair. He whispered into the phone like we were a couple of buds, talking trash.

'Done all right for yourself, gotta say. But if you want a last look, better hurry. Now, Detective, where am I at?'

And I knew.

'If you touch her I'll kill you.'

'Yeah, but where am I?'

'My place.'

'Correct! Make it fast, or don't bother coming.'

I punched Danny on speed dial and got no answer. All I could do was leave a message and hope he got it in time. 'Fitz, it's me. Boutte's at Ellen's. He's got her. Need you to back me up.'

The next fifteen minutes were the longest of my life. Ellen Ames was my fiancée: she was twenty-eight, and in six weeks, we were getting married. It would've happened before – I'd asked her often enough – but what I did for a living had held her back. She didn't want to worry every time I walked out the door about whether she would see me again. I was prepared to give up being a cop. Thing was: I was good at it and couldn't imagine doing anything else.

At the house, Boutte heard my steps on the porch and called to me. 'Come on in, Detective. Fun's about to be begin.'

I pulled my gun out of its holster, opened the door and stopped in my tracks. Julian Boutte stood in the middle of the room, grinning his crazy grin, slowly turning a knife in his hand; the same one he'd used to slit the black woman's throat. Ellen was tied to a chair in front of him. Her head had been shaved, and her hair lay in clumps on the carpet. She was naked. Above the gag, there was terror in her eyes. I'd seen it before in the shotgun in Algiers.

Boutte was re-staging the scene for my benefit, except this time, he was expecting it to come out different. He held the blade against Ellen's windpipe and caressed the pale skin; she shuddered. Cedric's brother was relaxed enough to crack an old joke and enjoy it. 'Déjà vu, all over again, right?'

He giggled.

I repeated the promise I'd made to him on the phone. 'Touch her, and I'll kill you.'

Juli wasn't impressed. The giggle died, and the grin that went with it disappeared. 'Yeah, you said.'

I edged into the space between us. Closer, though not close enough. He guessed what I was thinking and warned me off.

'Less you're faster than last time, forget about it.'

'This is between me and you. Nobody else is involved. Let her go, Juli.'

Dialogue from a B movie. All I had.

'Wrong, Detective. My brother's involved.'

'I gave Cedric fair warning. The decision to move for his piece was his.'

Boutte didn't see it that way. 'Ced and me, we had business with that bitch. It was ours to take care of. You stuck your nose in when you should've kept it out.'

He waved the knife to include the three of us.

'Whatever happens here is on you, Delaney.'

I took a step forward and spoke to Ellen. 'Take it easy, baby. It's gonna be all right.'

She didn't believe me, and she wasn't alone.

Boutte was wired to the moon, rocking on the balls of his feet like a boxer, pumped and ready. He leaned forward with his eyes still on me, took one of Ellen's bare breasts in his free hand and rolled the nipple in his calloused paw: the grin came back. She turned her face away, and I heard her sob. All the while, the knife stayed at her throat, poised to end her life for something she'd had no part of.

Julian switched his attention to the other breast and whistled his appreciation. 'Oh, man. Sweet. You're a lucky guy, Detective.'

Juli Boutte wasn't the first madman I'd faced down, though I'd never had such a personal stake in it. He was about to mutilate the woman I loved.

I kept my voice even.

'I've changed my mind, Julian. I'm gonna kill you, however this shakes out.'

That show of bravado amused him. The manic dance routine got dropped. He put one finger under Ellen's chin and raised her head in a delicate exhibition of power; getting set. But he was having fun and didn't want it to end. Ellen trembled. Fear made her seem smaller. Her eyes pleaded with me to save her; I felt helpless. Watching Boutte doing what he was doing to her made me want to be sick.

Boutte said, 'Gonna give you the same chance you gave Ced. Her blood'll be on your shoes before you get a shot off.'

'Only thing is, you won't be alive to enjoy it. Give yourself up or get wasted right here right now because – hard or easy – I'm taking you down. Depend on it. Your brother made the wrong call. Wondering if it runs in the family. You know, like an idiot gene or something.'

Julian went into his dance, winding himself up, but the performance lacked conviction. Maybe the drugs were wearing off or maybe he was realising that, as it stood, he'd brought a knife to a gunfight: either way, he was faking it. He licked his lips. Like his brother, he probably had a piece in the waistband of his pants and was remembering how much good that had done Cedric.

We stared at each other in a silence broken by Ellen moaning quietly from behind the gag. Boutte wiped a hand on his jeans and changed his grip on the knife, as a thin film of sweat appeared on his brow. I guessed he had mortality on his mind. Bad thoughts for a moment like this. The odds were with him, but he was cracking.

In my years on the force, I'd seen plenty push it as far as it would go, and there was one thing I was absolutely sure of: nobody wants to die.

From somewhere, his faith returned with a recklessness that defied reason. He'd killed his last victim and got away; he could do it again. Boutte's free hand moved behind the chair, in position to tip it forward, just as he'd done in Algiers.

Déjà vu, all over again.

I ignored Ellen and concentrated on the black man behind her. 'Don't, Juli. Don't make me do this.'

Julian's eyes glazed over, and I knew I was talking to myself. He wasn't there anymore. And the nightmare played out: the hammer cocked, as loud as a tree falling in the rainforest. The chair tilted forward and balanced on the front legs. Ellen had somehow struggled free of the gag and was screaming. All I saw was the thin line dripping red on her white skin. Behind her, Juli Boutte's face seemed as big as a Mardi Gras float: a huge target I couldn't try to hit, because Ellen was too close.

The spell was broken by Fitzpatrick bursting through the door. For a vital second, Boutte was off guard. He broke cover and gave me something to aim at. I hit him high on the shoulder and dived to catch Ellen pitching towards the floor. Boutte dropped the blade and staggered away.

Fitz shouted, and this time, there were witnesses. 'Stay where you are, Julian, or join Cedric in the morgue!'

No surprise. I was right: Julian didn't want to die after all.

When the ambulance came to take her to hospital, Ellen wouldn't let me go with her. I put it down to shock, and I guess some of it was.

But deep inside, I knew better.

Sixteen

At eight o'clock in the evening, I was putting new strings on my guitar, and Lowell was asleep in an armchair with Ry Cooder playing low in the background, when a knock at the front door took me by surprise. We didn't get many visitors. Lowell raised his head, and my first thought was Julian Boutte. It would tickle a psycho like him to arrive like a normal person while anyone sane would expect him to come in the middle of the night. I slipped my gun out of its holster, moved towards the window and looked out.

A figure stood in the shadow underneath the porch, and it wasn't Boutte; it was Stella. I opened the door, and she turned her eyes wide and wild in the fading light.

Before I could speak, she let me have it.

'Thought you'd be man enough to tell me to my face, Delaney.'

I checked the road over her shoulder. Apart from a few parked cars, it was empty. 'Tell you what, Stel?'

Her features twisted, and the words rushed out, hot and harsh. 'Don't give me your BS. You know what I mean.'

'You're wrong, I don't.'

I stepped into the hall, and she followed. Lowell rushed to meet her, licking her hand and wagging his tail. Stella took a break from calling me names to pat him, and for a moment, it looked as if the attack was over. Wrong.

'Look. It's been fun. We might even have been in love.'

'We are.'

She ignored me.

'Too bad there are things between us.'

'Things like what?'

Stella waved her arms at the room. 'Different stuff we both bring to the party. Can't be helped. And anyway, it doesn't matter now.'

This was running out of control. Her cheeks flushed, and her voice cracked. 'I'm thinking about going back to New York.'

'Thinking about going or going?'

'Going.'

I stared at her. 'When?'

'A month, six weeks. Soon as I can wrap up the business and sell the house.'

'So, the jury's back and the verdict's in?'

'It isn't like that.' She sighed. 'Let's be honest, shall we? Things have cooled. Okay. It happens. But I never imagined you of all people would be such a coward.'

I got the impression the speech had been rehearsed.

'Stella. Where's this coming from?'

She sailed on. 'Right people, wrong time. Too bad.'

'And in the meantime?'

'That's why I'm here. What do you think?'

I loved her and didn't want to lose her, that's what I thought.

'Would've preferred to be in on the New York decision.'

'Except you would've found reasons for me to stay, even though it's over.'

'It isn't over!'

Stella smiled a sad half-smile. 'Isn't it? From the beginning, I knew there was something. Couldn't put my finger on it, so I didn't ask. You didn't tell me.'

'Stella ...'

'You've kept me on the outside. I haven't even met your family, for Christ's sake. Now, you need space, and I'm supposed to put my life on hold.'

Lowell was standing beside her; his head tilted, waiting to hear what I had to say for myself. Suddenly, it was two against one.

'Stella. Something's going on right now. I can't explain, but I will soon. I promise.'

She shook her head.

'Sorry, Delaney. A girl can only take so much. Enough is enough. For a while there, I really believed we had something. I was wrong. I'm going back home. It's where I belong.'

Lowell whined and brushed against her.

'Do you want to go home?'

'Truthfully? Yes, I do. Being here doesn't feel right now.'

'And New York will?'

Chilly little questions like that wouldn't help.

'I've no idea. It'll be close. Closer than New Orleans.'

We watched her walk into the night. When she was gone, Lowell went into the other room and stayed there. He'd just lost a friend and wasn't speaking to me.

I'd been here before, and I couldn't believe it was happening a second time.

* * *

Seven Years Earlier

The wedding had been big news, somehow managing to find its way into most conversations Ellen and I had. My job was to listen and look interested. Input wasn't required, except to pretend to be cool about being overcharged on everything from the bride's bouquet to the meal. The only thing not costing a fortune was the band: Danny and the rest of the guys had offered to do the gig as a present to us. Fitzpatrick agreed to be my best man with the nonchalance of a friend who assumed the honour was always going to be his. Of course, he was right.

Until Ellen Ames, marriage wasn't something I'd ever considered. But with Ellen, to tell the truth, the more I thought about it, the better I liked the idea.

The scene at the shotgun in Algiers went down six weeks before we were set to make it legal. Forty-three days to be exact, in case anybody was counting.

And anybody was. I was.

Thanks to Julian Boutte, it never happened.

I'd lost count of the nights spent lying in the dark going over it, knowing that if Cedric hadn't grabbed for his gun, my whole life would've taken a different route.

But after …

After, there was only a noise in my head and a feeling in my gut I carried round like a dirty secret.

Ellen's hair grew back, and on the surface, she seemed to have recovered. But talking about it was beyond her, and when she finally did, I heard resentment in every line she spoke. In the circumstances, the wedding couldn't go ahead. The official line we told our friends was that it had been postponed; we both knew different. Pretty soon, the big day didn't get a mention anymore. Ellen wasn't the same woman; her nerves were shot; she jumped at the slightest sound. We stopped sleeping together and spent more and more time apart. On Sundays, browsing the antique shops on Royale, I often caught her nervously glancing over her shoulder, looking for Julian Boutte.

My solution was a dog. Well-meant but not very original in the aftermath of such trauma. I found what I was looking for in a pet shop off Decatur: a tan-and-white mongrel with deep brown eyes and an attitude the other pups around him lacked. To please me, Ellen made a good stab at welcoming him. But really, I realised it would take more than a cute little mutt to return her to me. She named him Lowell, and the two of them rubbed along well enough for a while without forming much of a bond.

Ellen couldn't. Not with the dog, not with me, not with anyone.

She'd lost the ability to trust and with it, to love.

Four months after the Boutte brothers destroyed our lives, I came home one evening to find a taxi purring outside the house and Ellen waiting for me. The look on her face told me what she was going to say as her fingers pulled, almost angrily, at the handkerchief in her hand. And she had a right to be angry.

'Before you speak, I have to get this out. I can't marry you. I can't marry anybody.'

'Ellen ...'

She held out her hands to shield herself from me. 'All I want is to get away from here. I won't ever be able to come to terms with what you do.'

'But I've quit the department. I'm not a cop anymore.'

She shook her head, slowly, as if she was hearing a lie. 'You don't have a badge, but we both know there's no difference. You're still involved, Delaney. And you always will be.'

I took a step towards her, and she moved away. Ellen was afraid of me and everything she thought I represented. Pleading didn't help, though I tried.

'I'll get another job. Whatever's right. Just don't go.'

She let her arms fall to her sides. For a moment, I believed I'd reached her. I hadn't. What Julian Boutte put her through couldn't be forgotten; it would always be there. Always be between us.

She said, 'I don't blame you. But please, don't ask me to live in your world. Please don't ask me to do that, Delaney.'

I babbled like an idiot. Clutching at straws. 'What about the dog? What about Lowell?'

Ellen almost smiled. 'He'll be all right. You can look after each other. Besides, I don't like animals.'

'You never told me.'

'You never asked.'

'Will you write, so I know you're okay?'

She hesitated, unwilling to offer false hope. '... Yes.'

I watched the taxi pull away from the sidewalk. There had been no tears. Ellen was glad to be leaving. She didn't turn her head. Didn't look back.

And I never saw her again.

* * *

Cal and I met in the Cafe Du Monde around nine-thirty. Before that, we'd spoken on the telephone. Both of us were cautious and the conversation lasted less than a minute.

I arrived first. Earlier, I'd mooched around the Quarter on my own, stopping off at a few bars where I was a stranger. In one, I had a Diet Coke, in another a coffee, sitting on a barstool watching a hockey game from Canada. The time passed. Twice I took out my phone on the point of calling Stella. Both times something stopped me.

Cal was wearing a dark-blue windcheater and jeans, looking more relaxed. He slid into the booth beside me and ordered black coffee and beignets.

'Anything?'

'Nothing helpful. An anonymous caller tipped them off something big was going down. Hill used his cell to inform the station-house what they were about. Around ten, they entered the building. Hill was killed with a single shot to the head. Clark got it in the chest. When a patrol car arrived, both officers were dead.'

'Any sign of drugs in the flat?'

'Nope. Cops: zero. Bad guys: two. Or it would be, if we didn't know better.'

'I've been thinking about what you said about it being convenient.'

'Well, isn't it? Just when we're about to interrupt their little number, they get killed? How's that for timing?'

His eyes were bright. His skin was clear; a different Cal from last time

'The options are limited to two. If Hill and Clark were freelancing, working alone, then it's over. Your traders get their quiet lives back. If not, if they were only soldiers, just the bag-men, that means the people behind the whole thing are still out there. We're talking about an awful lot of cash here. A big prize. Somebody's behind it.'

I said, 'Somebody in the department?'

'Don't know about that. The traders got the police connection from Hill and Clark, maybe whoever's running the scam is using NOPD officers, perhaps they were the only ones involved. Could be nothing to do with cops, apart from two bad apples, which would mean the operation is organised and run by people we haven't even thought about yet.'

'Either way, the evidence trail's gone cold.'

'Literally. Everybody's hot to put down the animal that killed two cops. To be expected. My guess is nobody's gonna find anything.'

'So, what now?'

'Wait and see. If it's over, it's over. If two new punks are drafted in, and it's business as usual, then we go back and deal with them same as we would have with Hill and his pal.'

'And if they're cops too?'

'Then, it's goodnight for them. It's got to be, Delaney. There's more at stake than just the crime. I want these guys stopped. Whatever it takes.'

* * *

I called Cilla Bartholomew the next day and told her the news, leaving out the details along with my suspicion. Two bad apples – as Cal called them – got theirs. Was that the same as the scam closing down? Maybe another pair of perps were already on their way to begin the first day in the new job.

'So soon? Thank you, Mr Delaney, thank you.'

I was about to hang up when she added a question.

'Is it over? Really over?'

I replied as honestly as I could. 'I hope so.'

But what did I know?

Seventeen

Another Saturday and another tinsel-covered hall swarming with moms and dads and their noisy kids. Either these people didn't watch the news, or they lived in a La-La land where nothing could touch them. Or maybe I'd been a cop too long.

This morning, we were in Chalmette, where the Battle of New Orleans was actually fought. Until now, Catherine had been as good as her word about keeping it simple. I wondered how long that would last, given Molly's enthusiasm for the whole thing. Winning helped, of course. Last time, we'd lost – something that didn't sit well in the Lothian household – and it explained why I was hearing talk about a new song.

Lowell stayed home with his radio: selections from *Annie* weren't his groove. Or mine, but I didn't have a choice. And I never did call Stella, which was a mistake. She didn't call me either, although I hoped she would. I did hear from Cilla Bartholomew. She sounded upbeat.

'All clear.'

'Great. Let me know if anything changes.'

'I will, and send us your bill, Mr Delaney.'

'Plenty of time for that.'

I left Ray and Catherine with Molly and did some scouting, trying to figure how the killer avoided being seen. Somebody must notice something, even if they didn't recognise it.

I had an idea so obvious, it made me want to shout it out: a disguise. If the attacker covered his own identity by pretending to be someone else, that would allow him to move around without being discovered. What could it be? A workman? A father, perhaps? No, a woman; had to be. There were women everywhere you turned at these gigs. He could go undetected if he dressed as a woman. Who would notice?

I examined every female of any age searching for something that didn't ring true: a voice, a walk, a look; something. After an hour, I was a whole lot cooler on my idea. Plenty of women, none of them remotely unnatural.

I wandered back to the main hall, probably more suspicious-looking than anybody there. Molly came on and blew the house down. Back on top and happy to be there.

I didn't fool myself into believing a killer who committed crimes across five states was likely to turn up at an event when I was there. The odds were against it.

Behind me, the accusing tone could only come from one person.

'I know what you're doing.'

'What? What are you talking about?'

'Can't you ever not be a cop?'

'I don't understand what you mean.'

Catherine spoke, low and serious. 'You're patrolling or snooping or something. You stick out. If I can spot it, so can everybody else.'

'I'm not snooping, as you call it.'

'If you don't want to be here, don't come. If you don't like it ... You look like a creep. I mean it.'

'I can't sit in there all day, Cee. And you're wrong. I do want to be here. I want to hear Molly. But when my instincts as a cop tell me to check things out, I'm going to follow them. It isn't a choice. If anything happened while I sat around doing nothing, I'd never recover. So you understand one thing. I'm gonna follow them. End of discussion.'

My tirade knocked her back on her heels.

'I came to tell you we're going for something to eat. Coming?'

'Yeah, I'd like that.'

Something to eat was melon and sandwiches in the car. Ray must have noticed we had gone quiet. Back inside, the show went on. I did my best not to upset my sister. About two o'clock, the final of Molly's section began. Thirty minutes later, it was over. Another victory for talent – at least that was our opinion. Molly beamed as she collected her scroll, and we moved into the corridor.

The next minutes were spent congratulating the winner, who basked in the praise: a family circle with Molly at the centre, just the way she liked it.

'Hello again, and hi to you, Molly.'

We stopped talking. Catherine searched her memory for a name to go with the face.

'Roy. Reba Roy. Perhaps you don't recall. We met a few weeks ago when Molly won.'

'Oh, of course. How are you?'

'Fine, thank you. Catherine, isn't it? I remember because your little girl was so sweet.'

'Don't make her head any bigger than it already is or she won't fit into the car. Let me introduce you. This is my husband, Ray, Vincent Delaney my brother, and of course, Molly.'

'Reba Roy.'

She shook hands with us in turn and hunkered down to speak to Molly. I made a who's-this face at Catherine. She gave a how-should-I-know shrug back.

'I wouldn't forget you, not with that lovely voice.'

Molly blushed. All of a sudden, a shy little girl rather than a runaway winner.

'You just keep beatin' everybody, don't you?'.

'I lost once.'

'Really? Someone was better than you, honey? I don't believe it. Must've been a swizzle.'

Molly agreed. 'It was. I was the best.'

The woman said, 'She's special. You must be very proud.'

Ray answered, 'We are.'

Reba Roy was in her early forties: slim and good-looking with auburn hair pushed back behind her ears. When she spoke, in an accent most definitely from south of the Mason-Dixon Line, her green eyes sparkled. I liked her.

Catherine captured Molly's hand. 'Excuse us. We need to go get our stuff.'

Ray said, 'I'll bring the car round to the front.'

They moved off, leaving us alone.

Reba smiled and pointed a finger at me. 'Heard about you. You're against this, aren't you?'

Before I could answer, she made her own position clear.

'Can't say as I blame you. It gets a little gratin' at times. The kids are cute, but the adults …'

She pulled the edges of her mouth down into a miserable expression. I laughed.

'All that hootin' 'n hollerin'. And some of the attitudes. Why do they assume everybody'll just love their free-range kids? I'm a mom, I understand it, but if I wasn't …'

Her brown eyes changed with a new thought. She nodded at Molly walking with her mother down the hall. 'Must love that kid a lot,' she said more to herself than to me.

'I do.'

'Easy to see why.'

Our side had had a good run; it was time to ask about her.

'Got skin in the game?'

'Only got one, and yes, my daughter, Labelle. She's older than Molly. She'll be on later. You'll hear her if you're still around. She's good but not real good. Right now, she's with my husband, Peter. We spell each other so nobody has to sit through the whole damn thing.'

I loved the way she spoke. Not just the accent – the easy way she explained herself.

'Unfortunately, we're going home now.'

'Well, next time.'

I shook her hand.

'Tell me something, Mr Delaney.'

'Just Delaney'

'Tell me, Delaney. Do you worry about your niece? Because I know I do with Labelle. Your sister told me you took a view on the pageant thing. Is Molly's safety the reason?'

'One of them, perhaps.'

'Is that why you're here sufferin' like the rest of us?'

I laughed again. This woman was something.

'Maybe it is.'

She put her arm in mine. 'Let me walk you to the door. Got a question I need to ask. Do you still keep up with any of the people you used to work with?'

She held up a hand.

'When Catherine and I met the first time, she told me about her brother; ex-cop, now a PI in the city. Hard-headed; prejudiced on some issues.'

She hurried to reassure me.

'Not exactly how you see yourself? Don't sweat it.'

Reba Roy apologised for my sister. 'She didn't mean to say anythin'. She was uptight about tellin' you they'd been to a show. It sort of came tumblin' out. Wasn't supposed to happen, it just did. Nerves.'

She took my arm again.

'The reason I ask is this. I enjoy comin' to watch Labelle, but I sure do have some sleepless nights. It wasn't ever my idea; it was Peter's. He thought it would be good for her.'

'And is it?'

'I think I'd have to admit, we've all taken something from it. I'm still not convinced. Peter's keener than I am, keener even than Labelle. She'll outgrow this stuff in a year or two. Wouldn't be right if she didn't.'

We were at the door. Through the glass, I saw Ray waiting in the car. Catherine and Molly were taking their time. Reba Roy was working up to her point. I thought I knew what it was. We stopped and uncoupled our arms.

'I'm taking an awful long time to say this, aren't I?'

She fidgeted with her fingers.

'Just ask. Whatever it is, just ask me.'

'Okay. You know kids on the pageant circuit are bein' attacked. Your cop friends must talk about it.'

I hesitated. This was a surprise. Somebody taking the danger seriously.

'Doesn't that worry you? Some maniac runnin' wild? It sure as hell worries me. I'm sorry,' Reba Roy said. 'I get carried away sometimes.'

'No, that's all right. I'm the same. I feel better being here.'

'I understand. Must be difficult to just stand by, with your background and all.'

'Standing by isn't an option.'

Her attention was drawn away. 'There's Peter!' She waved at a man across the corridor. 'Peter! Peter!'

He stopped, uncertain where the cry was coming from then saw her and came over.

'This is my husband, Peter.'

Peter Roy's handshake was strong and definite. He was older than me and a shade taller. His hair was longer and brushed his collar every time he moved his head. He wore a blue button-down shirt under a V-neck sweater, slacks and suede shoes. His wife gazed up at him; he placed a protective hand on her back. They seemed to fit each other.

'Peter, this is Vincent Delaney. You remember I told you about the little girl with the beautiful voice? Well, this is her uncle.'

He looked like a college lecturer, right down to the leather patches on the elbows of his tweed jacket.

'Lucky man. Reba told me she was the cutest thing.'

The timbre of his voice surprised me; higher and much less commanding than I expected. It didn't go with the laid-back rest of him.

'Where's Labelle?'

The urgency in his wife's question was unmistakeable.

'Watching the others do their thing.'

'Peter, we agreed. Labelle is never to be left alone. Not even for a minute.'

'She's happy enough, Reba.'

He looked at me. Women, his expression said. Always on edge about something. Knowing what I did put me firmly with his wife.

'We gotta go. Nice to meet you, Delaney.'

They hurried away, her charging ahead, him trailing behind. I scanned the face of everybody who passed, wondering if the killer was right in front of me.

Can't you ever not be a cop?

No, I can't. And believe me, Catherine, you don't want me to.

Eighteen

The Monday meeting was short: under an hour. Only the local guys were there because the weekend had produced no new activity from the killer which meant the FBI could put their travelling show on hold. Nobody had anything new to report. Delaup gave out the same directive as before: keep looking. Then, he headed off to get an update from the officers handling the hunt for Julian Boutte.

Danny caught up with me in the corridor. 'How goes it, Delaney?'

'All right. What about you?'

'Same old, same old.'

'So I hear. Delaup isn't exactly an ideas man, is he?'

He shrugged the criticism away. 'He's solid enough. It isn't easy to find a way into this one.'

'Guess not. Anything else?'

'Well, we lost a couple of guys last week. Drugs bust that went wrong.'

'Heard about that. Any sign of the perps?'

'None. No sign of drugs either.'

'Suspicious?'

'Not really, just a disappointing lack of evidence.'

'Who were they?'

'One of them was the guy you asked about.'

He glanced at me but didn't push it and changed the subject. 'Not getting very, far are we?'

'Still early days.'

'For us, maybe. Not for the next victim out there it isn't.' Fitzy shook his head. 'This is one smart mother. Wherever he is he must be laughing at us.'

I slapped him on the shoulder. 'We'll get him.'

He needed convincing. 'And so far, no sign of Boutte. Thinking is he's left the state by now. I don't buy it, though it takes the heat off.'

'Doesn't surprise me. Juli has friends in Algiers. Plenty of people willing to hide him for as long as it takes. He'll show himself when he's ready.'

Danny was uneasy. 'Yeah. When *he's* ready. What about you?'

'I'll be ready for him. I'm ready now.'

* * *

The journey to work wasn't as much fun as it used to be. The problem was me. The murders were bad without having Molly at potential crime scenes. My reaction was no different from anyone else's: Reba Roy had shown me that. But it gnawed away at me just the same. No contact from Stella. I wanted to call but didn't. Maybe it was the same for her. I'd have to pick up a phone to find out. In the end, I stewed. Whatever happened to faint heart and all that? Those issues managed to keep the guitar in its case and the harp in my pocket. Throughout, Lowell turned out to be a pal, watching me a lot.

Harry Love hadn't been over-the-moon when my background investigation on Johnnie G turned up nothing. I might not be hearing from Harry again. The single piece of good fortune was the extortion case. No more word from the traders. I assumed that was good news.

Lowell's chase after me at the side of the road was looked on by both of us as his morning walk. When he got to my office, his first and only priority was to lie down in the corner. Mid-morning brought an unexpected call from Harry Love and another job.

'Sorry about the last one, Harry. Nothing to find.'

'Let's hope this one has a skeleton rattling. And invoice me.'

Harry L gave the details, and I told him I'd get on it right away. If there was anything he could use, a couple of phone calls would find it.

Nineteen

Three things caught Eadie Renaldi off-guard.

The first was her mother's enthusiasm, her energy, and yes, it had to be admitted, an unexpected talent for detail. The second was "those goddamned piano lessons," to use her mother's description. Eadie was astonished to discover she actually could play a bit. Nothing great, but not bad. Amazing, considering she hadn't touched a keyboard in over twenty years. She found herself able to anticipate the chord changes without effort; busking.

But her mother's voice was the big surprise. Listening to her sing, Eadie realised there must have been a time when it had been very fine indeed.

'The immediate task is to get our Katie some stagecraft.'

'How will we do that?'

'By singing and dancing. Watching and learning.'

'We aren't preparing her for Las Vegas, Mama.'

'Is that right? Let me ask you a question.'

'Okay.'

Eadie wasn't sure where the conversation was going.

'How good do you want her to be?'

'Well, it's only a kids' pageant. Let's not get all Broadway about it.'

'All right. So how good?'

Eadie flustered. 'Good enough. I don't know. It isn't something I've given any kind of thought to.'

'I can see that. So, same question: how good?'

Katie's mom caved in. 'I honestly don't know, Mama. You tell me.'

'The best she can be, that's how good. Anytime Katie wants to stop entering these events, you'll get no argument from me; my view hasn't changed.'

'But she's a kid. She won't always want to practise.'

'Of course she won't. We'll all agree on times. How often and for how long, and we'll stick to it.'

Eadie Renaldi wondered what she'd unleashed.

'Are we agreed? Good. I think we need three or four sessions a week. Anything less won't produce much.'

There was no stopping the older woman now.

'We don't compete until we're ready – three to four weeks from now, I'd say.'

'Remember, Katie's got to have a childhood.'

Mrs Russell ignored that observation and moved on. 'The first few weeks, she'll sing and dance to everything and anything, build up her balance and her voice.'

'It sounds like boot-camp, Mama.'

'It'll be fun. In the end, Katie might not win, but she'll have done her best. That'll be good enough for all of us.'

'Any songs in mind?'

'A couple we'll try out, I'll tell you later. When we make a decision, we'll see about getting the backing-track on disc in Katie's key; that's how it's done.'

'I know.' Eadie smiled. This was a side of her mother she'd never dreamed existed. 'It would be better if we chose something modern, Mama.'

'Really?' Mrs Russell's sarcasm was laid on thick. 'You mean like "Hard-Knock Life"? That kinda modern?'

Her daughter laughed. 'Sorry, Mama.'

'I should think so, too. Cut me a break, Eadie. I understand how it goes.'

'What about after school three times a week? When I collect Katie, we'll come right here.'

'That sounds fine, if it's all right with Katie.'

They called Kate downstairs and put it to her.

'Listen, honey, your Gran and I are talking about the pageants. You still want to do that?' The child nodded. 'Well, we're thinking that some nights after school, we'll come to Gran's to practise. That okay too?'

'Can I have a nice dress?'

'It's called a costume, baby, and we intend to get you whatever goes with the song we pick. The important thing is, if we say we'll practise three times a week, we have to keep our word. If you don't want to do …'

'I want to.'

'Three times a week?

'I want to.'

'She wants to,' Eadie said.

'All right, that's good. This time, we'll show them what Katie Renaldi can do. And by the way, we don't practise. We rehearse.'

* * *

Joe Johnson was met at the door by a smiling Mia wearing a dress for a change. Her hair was swept back off her face. She looked the way she'd looked in the days when they were on the same page. Joe remembered why he fell for her so hard. Back then, they'd sit up late and talk about what they would do and where they would go, before tumbling into bed to make long, lingering love to each other. A wave of sadness broke over him. Where had it all gone? And what did Mia want now? Well, whatever it was, she could have it. He was done.

'Joe. Hi Joe.'

His wife always had the ability to behave like nothing was wrong between them. An admirable thing, if it wasn't for the fact that Joe knew from experience the clean-slate routine was a precursor to another crazy idea certain to cost more than they had. Perhaps Mia wasn't so different from other women, forever thinking up things their life needed and couldn't do without. Where was the limit? Where did it end? The only money they had was the cash in their pockets; all their credit cards were maxed out.

They'd missed two out of the last five mortgage payments. It wasn't that they didn't have it coming in. The problem was how fast they went through it. They'd had their belt-tightening discussions, too many to count. Nothing ever changed.

Mia threaded her arm through his, as happy as she'd been the day her first new car was delivered. That vehicle had been replaced several times since, always for something bigger, showier and more expensive. Now they were back where they started: a one-car family, the one car being the work's van. They didn't have a vehicle of their own anymore.

When were they going to get one? How did he think that looked?

On the evidence of their last bank statement, the answer to her first question was never. The second wasn't worth a reply.

'Jolene and I have something we want you to hear,' Mia hung on his forearm, gazing into his face. 'Right now, before dinner.'

Joe didn't ask what, he could guess. His wife marched him past the front door and left into the garage. In the middle of the floor, two plastic outdoor seats sat side by side facing the stage. Joe remembered the argument they'd had about that.

'A stage in the garage? For fuck's sake, Mia.'

She had been sitting at the big country table in the middle of the kitchen. Waiting for him. They'd looked at each other. Finally, Mia said, 'She needs it. It'll help her. She needs as close to the real deal as we can get. Practisin' takes ten hours a week. At least. It'll be more fun if she can be on a stage. She'll love it, Joe.'

Her hand tried to find his. He pulled away, refusing to share in her vision.

'Say somethin'! It doesn't cost so much. I got a deal.'

She leaned towards him, gripping the edge of the table, knuckles white, bottom lip trembling.

'Joe! Joe!' Mia had pleaded. 'All that matters is that Jolene's happy, isn't that right? If she's happy, we're happy. That's what you always say. Right, Joe?'

She broke down. 'Right, Joe?'

Mia started to cry. 'Say that's right, say it, Joe.'

Joe recalled how flat his voice had sounded. 'The stage isn't the problem. Fact, I like the idea.'

'So, it's all right? You're not mad?' Mia's eyes blazed with hope. She sniffed away the last of her tears.

'Maybe I don't communicate too well.'

'No, Joe,' Mia reached across and grabbed his hand. 'You communicate fine. Just fine.'

'Well, how come nothin' I say ever gets heard? How come I'm talkin' to myself night and day?'

'Joe …'

'Don't "Joe" me, Mia. We'll carry on, for a time at least, for Jolene's sake. Soon as she doesn't need us anymore, I'm gone.'

'What're you sayin'? We can go at each other hammer and tongs. It don't mean diddly. Never did.'

'I'm sayin' it's over, plain and simple. Over. All that needs thinkin' about is the when.'

His expression told her he was serious.

'How much to build the stage?'

'What? Oh … six hundred dollars, includin' the carpet.'

Joe's eyebrows arched. 'Good price,' he'd said, and went through to his room.

But his wife was a determined woman, so here they were again.

Mia said, 'Now, Joe, you just sit there while I turn the music on.'

Her husband allowed himself to be treated this way because he recognised the effort Mia was making. He was too far down to respond. Even the guys at work commented on it. Whole days passed without him saying anything, other than just enough to get by. The depression Joe Johnson had fallen into hadn't been diagnosed, yet it was there, drawing him deeper every day. He was a man going through the motions of living.

Mia Johnson fussed over the disc player, then shouted, 'Okay, honey, here we go.'

The music began, and Jolene strode on to the stage in her cowgirl costume.

A line into the song her mother began giving Joe a running commentary.

'Her breathing's better, don't you think?'

Joe didn't reply.

'Breathing gives a performer confidence, Miss Wilson says. I think it's true. Does she seem more confident to you? She does to me.'

Jolene twirled the toy gun. Her eyes never once left her mother, and her brain juggled the messages.

Chin up! Eyes on the judges not on the ground!

Big breath.

Big breath. Out slowly. Slowly.

Smile. Keep that smile going.

Joe's wife whispered in his ear. 'She's getting there. This is better, it really is. Don't you see a big improvement? Look at her face, she's enjoying herself.'

Was it better? He didn't know. He thought again about the suitcase at the back of the wardrobe, packed and ready to go. Whenever he was certain his little girl no longer needed him, he'd take it out, disappear and never look back.

That was the plan. Right now, he just wanted to sleep.

Twenty

Another weekend and another bust.

No competition and no Stella. I missed her laugh and the quiet way she managed me, thinking I wasn't onto her. Of course I always was.

Make that sometimes was.

I wanted to call. I can be mule-stubborn at times, so I didn't, and suffered my way through another day. Good decision, Delaney. Later, I did something unusual for me: started drinking before the gig. By the time I got to Mr MaGoo's, my mood was dark. A few more shots of Jack during the first set didn't help, and by the time the break came around, I was in bad shape.

Fitzpatrick sat beside me at a table near the back of the room and tried to lift me out of it. He pointed to the glass in my hand. 'That won't help.'

My reply was sullen. 'You don't say.'

Fitz stayed with it. 'I do say. I've always admired you, Delaney. Want to know why?'

I snorted my contempt for his judgement. 'I'm guessing you're gonna tell me.'

'You've never been afraid to be who you are. The bike, the harp – even talking to a dog. No matter how crazy it looks from the outside, if it feels right, you do it, and to hell with what people think. When the department let you down, you quit. Other officers would've stayed and let their resentment fester. Not you.' He made a gesture in the air with his arm. 'You were gone.'

I swirled the bourbon in the glass, unimpressed. 'And your point is?'

'You've got character, my friend. Don't forget it.'

He got up to leave. The rest of the band were already onstage. Fitzy leaned towards me, put a hand on my shoulder and whispered in my ear. 'Did I mention you can also be an asshole?'

The pity-party was over. For the rest of the gig, I left the booze in the bottle and put how I was feeling into the music. Played a storm, even if I say so myself.

On Sunday, I stayed home nursing the hangover I'd paid good money to get. For once, Catherine didn't protest too hard about not seeing me. I watched the game on TV by myself – the Broncos won 27/15 – but to tell the truth, most of it passed in a haze. After that, I mooched around, kind of cleaned the house, picked up the guitar, put it down, fed my dog, picked the guitar up again; made myself a sandwich and couldn't eat it, poured half a glass of milk I didn't drink, and fell asleep on the couch. The only living soul I'd spoken to all day was Lowell. As conversations went, it wasn't the best. He made it clear he blamed me for Stella.

When I woke up, it was almost eight o'clock at night. Cornflakes for dinner. On a shelf by the fireplace, two books caught my eye. To be on the safe side, I started both of them. An hour later, they were out of my life. I let Lowell out into the garden because I couldn't be bothered taking him for a walk. Somehow, he understood it was the best offer he was gonna get and took it. For the next I-don't-know-how-long, I flicked through the never-ending selection of television channels, amazed to find nothing of interest.

Finally, I pressed the big red button and went to bed.

And I still didn't call her. What an idiot I could be sometimes.

* * *

Death came unexpectedly to Clyde Hays. He'd been surprised to see the two men come into his shop and instinctively understood it wasn't good news; they didn't say a word. Was it starting again?

One of them turned the open sign to closed and pulled down the blind. His friend stepped behind the counter and knocked the old black man to the ground. He coughed blood and felt a tooth loosen. The thugs hooked their hands in the collar of his shirt and dragged him into the back. Then, they got to work.

Clyde's wrists were tied behind his back; a gag bit into his mouth. When he felt the rope go around his neck and tighten, he realised they weren't there for money and started to struggle in earnest.

Too late.

His feet left the ground. Pain like he'd never known made him blind; he couldn't breathe. The men hauled him high and used a grain barrel to tie-off the rope. They watched his legs kick until they stopped. It didn't take long. Satisfied with what they'd done, they raised the blind, turned the sign to open and left.

* * *

I spent Monday in the office on behalf of Harry Love. The place was quiet. Just me and Lowell. He had concluded I was beyond his help. Or maybe he'd caught some of my mood. Either way, he gave me a wide berth, except when he needed me to walk or feed him.

A black cloud hung over New Orleans: a thunderstorm building. It would probably break later tonight. It was hot, not as bad as the previous months but still in the 80s, and humid. Around eight, I was sitting in a bar waiting for the Monday night football to begin when my cell bleeped. I had a text. It was from Stella.

Meet me @ 9. Le Petit Chemineau. S.

I had to meet her, I knew that – but what could I say? Nothing had changed. Julian Boutte was still out there somewhere, and my life still attracted the wrong kind of people.

I ordered another beer. When it came I took a sip, swung myself off the stool and strolled outside for some air, feeling bluer by the minute.

Meet me @ 9. Le Petit Chemineau. S.

The night was unnaturally dark, and the street almost deserted. All around, static air waited to be cleansed. Then, it began. No more than a steady drizzle at first, bathing New Orleans. There were no sounds, other than the hypnotic rhythm of falling rain.

I called Stella's message up again and re-read it just as a flash of distant light split the night, signalling the beginning of the deluge. Down it came, changing the colour of everything in an exhibition of raw power.

The phone rang. I moved inside to the relative quiet of the bar.

She spoke without preamble. 'Meet me. Jackson Square. Nine o'clock.'

The line went dead.

I had two people to meet at the same time: nine o'clock. One of them was going to be disappointed, though not more disappointed than me. I tried to reach her. Her cell was off. This was bad.

"Meet me. Jackson Square. Nine o'clock."

I knew which appointment I had to keep.

Stella was still unobtainable. I started to write a text message and stopped. What would I say? Sorry. Can't make it, something's come up?

I wouldn't be meeting Stella at nine.

The fear in her tone brooked no denial. The telephone number was new; the voice was all too familiar.

"Meet me. Jackson Square. Nine o'clock," Cilla Bartholomew had said.

And I'd be there.

It wasn't a request.

Twenty-One

Torrential rain reduced visibility and made driving almost impossible.

At eight-forty-five, I pulled up near the site of Indian fighter and future president Andrew Jackson's "glorious victory" over the British in the Battle of New Orleans in 1815, and got out. Within seconds, I was soaked to the skin. Hard to believe it could get much wetter. After half a block, I knew different. My clothes stuck to my skin, water filled my shoes. I sheltered under an awning on Wilk Row, where I could see across the Square. It was deserted. I waited, wishing I was sitting in Le Petit Chemineau with Stella, instead of shipping water out on the street, certain something bad was about to happen.

Five past nine. No sign of Cilla Bartholomew. Then, she appeared.

At first, I didn't recognise her. When I did, I stepped into the near-vertical torrent of water, lowered my head against the night, and made my way towards her. She was surrounded by an unearthly calm as she moved from Madison Street at the other side of the French Quarter. Off to the side, the Saint Louis Cathedral was like a ghost ship broken on the rocks.

She walked in small steps, advancing in slow-motion. Her head was uncovered, and she stared at me. Even in those awful conditions, I could see a difference in her not brought by any elemental force. She looked smaller than before, more fragile. Rain cascaded down her face, past the sunken eyes of someone who has cried for hours. She looked at me without speaking, bloodless lips pressed together. Lightning flashed behind her, the wind fell to nothing, and the rain fell and fell.

'Clyde's dead.'

'Dead? How?'

She shook her head, unable to answer, deflecting drops of falling rain. 'They hung him. In his back shop.'

'Fuck! Who did?' I already knew the answer.

Bitterness helped her find her voice. 'They did!'

'Tell me what happened.'

Jackson Square was covered in pools of water inches deep, and still, the heavens raged. A peel of thunder, then another, broke over New Orleans. A flash of lightning lit her for a fleeting moment. She wiped tears away. Or maybe it was rain; I couldn't tell which.

Another flash of electricity washed the dark from the sky then the night plunged even deeper into black. And all the while, Pricilla Bartholomew stared balefully at me through the suffocating rain.

'This morning, two new men arrived to make collections. Imagine our horror, our disappointment. It wasn't over. It wasn't over at all. Henry Duke was in his hardware store and refused to pay. But the men made no threats. All they said was, "We've got a message for you. Two messages. The first is in his back shop. The second is more important. No more Delaney. No more cops." When they left, we found him.'

The rain still fell, and the thunder roared, but I didn't hear. Only Cilla Bartholomew and her horrific tale existed. I was too stunned to speak.

'Mr Delaney, I trusted you, but I was wrong. Do you remember our one request, our one condition?'

I remembered.

No police, we don't trust them.

'But we agreed …'

She cut me off. 'Clyde paid for doing it your way. We'll all pay. I came to tell you to stay away from us. Before you read about Clyde's suicide in the newspaper, I want to say stay away. Far, far away.'

Her hair was flat against her head. She drew an elegant finger under her eyes and smiled the saddest smile I ever saw. 'We made many mistakes, Mr Delaney. You were the biggest.'

On my way back to the car, I didn't try to shelter from the river of water raining down on me. Cilla Bartholomew was right: the death of Clyde Hays was on me.

I had to make this right.

Part Three

That's What Friends Are For

Twenty-Two

The storm lingered into the next day. It fitted my mood all too well. Lowell and I spent time on the rain-washed Moon Walk beside the river watching its swollen progress. What a mess I'd made of everything.

The only people who knew about my involvement were the storekeepers – and there were plenty of them – Cal Moreland and me. I'd said nothing to anyone, not even Danny. That narrowed it to the traders or Cal. Maybe a trader had talked, or perhaps Cal told someone he thought he could trust. Either way, whoever was behind this thing knew all about me.

But what if it wasn't down to some slip up?

That would mean a trader on the wrong side or that Cal was involved. No other options presented themselves. The shopkeepers were the victims. End of story. But surely it couldn't be Cal? I'd known him most of my life and had no reason to suspect he was dirty. Except Hill and Clark had worked out of his district. Did they really get caught up in a drug bust that went wrong?

'Convenient, or what?' Cal had said. Could Hill and Clark have been sacrificed to leave the trail cold and allow the extortion to start again, reinforced by new threats and Clyde's murder? If so, we were looking at three homicides. The racket drew down big money. Big enough to warrant triple murder?

Absolutely.

Julian Boutte never crossed my mind. Not smart, though I didn't care anymore. He could bring it on any time he liked.

On Friday, I went to the office and left Lowell at home. I asked Mrs Santini, the widowed lady next door, to look in and make sure he was okay. Rosa Santini was a tiny woman and a dog-person, with three of her own. The family had emigrated from southern Italy three generations earlier. Her grandfather hadn't liked New York – too cold – and moved to Louisiana. By the time Rosa came along, they were New Orleans republicans, running a restaurant in Marrero. Her husband, Alberto, had died years earlier. Alberto must've been quite a guy to keep up with her. She had a talent for asking questions which shouldn't be asked, and expecting an answer. Rosa was nosey and rude, outrageous and generous, and the best neighbour anybody could have – my go-to girl whenever I had to be out of town and couldn't take Lowell with me. Every female who came to my house got marked out of ten. Low scores and unflattering observations were the norm. Stella was the exception; Rosa liked her and was convinced she was too good for me.

'Saw that girl (with Rosa Santini, anybody under fifty was a girl) 'round again last night. When you gonna do right by her, huh?'

I laughed. 'Won't have me, Mrs Santini. Believe me, I've tried.'

She nodded, as if she understood, which didn't do a lot for my self-worth. In her estimation, every single man was doomed until the right "girl" came along to save him from himself. She might just have a point.

Occasionally – when the morning mass gossip mill was having a slow day – Rosa would bring food and stay to watch me eat. It took months to realise the visits were fishing expeditions. The only topic she wouldn't discuss was how old she was. On her seventy-sixth birthday – information that had slipped out one evening on my front porch thanks to a couple of glasses of red wine – an attempt to congratulate her was met with the flinty wisdom that was her trademark. 'Age is just a bunch of numbers, Delaney.'

'I'm complimenting your energy, Mrs Santini.'

'I know what you're doing.'

'It's called conversation.'

'Yeah. Heard there's an art to that.'

But with Lowell, we found our common ground. In this weather, if Lowell came with me, he would get filthy and leave mud everywhere.

The way I felt, I was better by myself. I had to think. Whenever I remembered that night, my spirits sank. Guilt about what I'd done to Clyde and the traders, regret about Stella, and suspicion about Cal Moreland overwhelmed me.

And a paralysing fear that gripped so hard, I could barely breathe.

Because I'd no idea what to do next.

* * *

Today's competition was in Kenner, out near the airport, and while Ray and Catherine registered, I took a look round, glad to have something to occupy my mind.

I recognised a few faces from other pageants, but the harder I looked, the less I saw. What was I supposed to be looking for, anyway? Some guy with "psycho" tattooed on his forehead? It wasn't going to happen. Until now, I hadn't been even close to the crime scenes. I wasn't likely to help catch this guy if our paths never crossed. All I could do was stay with it.

'Hello again.'

I didn't recognise him at first.

'Hey,' I said, struggling for a name.

He supplied it for me. 'Peter Roy. My wife introduced us.'

'Of course. Vince Delaney.'

We shook hands.

'I know,' he said.

'Peter, yeah. Where's your wife?'

'She's with Labelle. I stay clear of form-filling. Can't stand it.'

'Luckily, I'm only the cheerleader on our side.'

He was wearing the same clothes as last time; the cardigan, the button-down shirt and the jacket with the leather patches on the elbow.

'We almost didn't come today. Labelle isn't feeling well. Tummy ache.'

'Hope she'll be all right.'

'Thanks, I'm sure she will. Any recurrence of the symptoms and we're going straight home.'

'Yeah. Always other competitions to go to.'

'Yes, there are, though I think this might well be our last year. Labelle's had a good run. Won here and there. There comes a point where it's better to retire gracefully and move on.'

'You won't take her up into the young-teens events and beyond?'

I sounded as if I knew something about how it worked. In truth, all I knew about pageantry was what I got from the Internet.

'No. Reba and I are in agreement. It's been fun for all of us, but it's time to let it go. Almost.' He smiled. 'No doubt Labelle will give us a hard time. She'll be a teenager soon. From what I hear, that's their number-one priority.'

Over Peter Roy's shoulder, a man was watching me. Even at a distance, he seemed on edge. I'd keep an eye on the guy.

'I read somewhere they can't help it, something to do with hormones.'

Peter said, 'That makes me feel a whole lot better.' He held out his hand. 'I better go. Look, if you don't see us later, assume Labelle didn't make it. We'll meet again. And tell Molly good luck, although she hardly needs it.'

'Sure, Peter.'

Peter Roy had distracted me. When I looked again, the guy was gone.

* * *

It was good to feel apart from the herd. Different from the masses. What could be worse than being just another walking number on the earth? Thank God that wasn't the way of it. Society saw it otherwise, of course, that was to be expected. Closed minds.

A woman passed with a child dressed in top hat and tails. Fred Astaire? The kid was bawling something impossible to make out, its small face distorted in an anguish that would cease the second the mother relented and let it have its way. When children acted like that, they were almost as unattractive as the adults who spawned them. Well, the mother could relax; her whining offspring was safe; repulsively secure.

No matter, there were plenty more.

Lots and lots and lots more.

Where to begin. The biggest question. The answer would dictate how the rest of the day would go. This was a moment to be savoured. The trick was not to wait too long. That was dangerous. Anxiety about missing-out produced poor-quality decisions. Risk was all very well so long as the thrill allowed for escape.

It was all about timing.

A lost-looking girl came close. Pretty, but pretty wasn't enough. There were many here who out-scored her on that, boys as well as girls, it didn't matter.

Cute. Cute. Cute. Nothing but cute.

'Darleen! Darleen, honey!' A woman bent to scoop up her daughter.

Mother and child reunion.

Time to make a move. But what was the rush? There was a whole day ahead.

All day. All day, every day, if need be.

Twenty-Three

The second time I saw him was during the mid-morning interval. He stood apart from the crowd in the corridor outside the main hall, preoccupied with the people coming and going, and didn't notice me. He was searching for something. And he seemed to be alone. That figured. His eyes darted over every face; his own held an expression of cold excitement. Then, he was gone; he just disappeared. I tried to control the panic that rose in me, without letting Catherine or Ray know how I was feeling or why.

Although I never stopped looking, I didn't see him again until the afternoon, standing off to the side, inside the hall this time. He stuck out – at least he did to me – hardly bothering with the stage, preferring to watch the children beside their parents. When I saw him, I got up. He must've known I was onto him because he made for the door. Onstage, the usual, super-smoothie incongruent in a dinner suit, was making an announcement. It hardly registered.

'And the winner is … Jolene Johnson!'

A woman jumped in front of me applauding and whooping, clapping her hands above her head. The mother. It only took seconds to reach the door at the back of the hall, but I wasn't quick enough; there was no sign of him.

A voice I recognised spoke to me. 'We're going home, Delaney. It hasn't been a good day. Labelle isn't very well again. She's out in the car with her father. I'm on my way to collect her things.'

'Sorry, Reba. Hope she's going to be okay.'

'Oh, she'll be fine, just not today, is all.'

I cut her off. 'Okay.'

'Are you all right?'

'Fine.'

'Well, bye.' Said in the delightful gentle drawl that made her so likeable.

I would get a chance to explain my odd behaviour another time. Right now, that didn't matter. I had a killer to catch.

But my man was nowhere to be seen. The hall was still busy, even though many of the kids who'd lost had gone home earlier. I narrowed my eyes trying to spot him. And I did, at the end of the hall. He was medium height, wearing a dark-blue suit with a white shirt; his hair neither short nor long, with a face that made him appear younger than he was. My earlier guess had been late-twenties; I revised that estimate up.

We both started to run at the same time. This was our man. He ran into a part of the building not in use today, down another long corridor. Our footsteps echoed together, keeping me fixed on catching this guy, aware this could be the one and only opportunity I was ever going to get.

He was always just too far in front, always just round the next bend, racing to wherever it might lead. An alarm bell drowned the sound of my breathing. Another sound, farther away, the sound of brakes squealing on tarmac.

When I rounded the final bend, I saw a set of alarmed doors at the end thrown open. Out in the street, a small group of people gathered round the front of a dark-grey ford Transit. I ran, hoping I wasn't going to find what I already knew was there. People stared at the man on the ground. Someone took off a coat and placed it behind his head. Blood trickled from the side of his mouth, vivid against the deathly pallor of his skin; it was him. And he was unconscious.

Behind the wheel, a young black guy sat rooted to the seat. In the heat of the moment, he'd been overlooked, the forgotten victim of the accident. I opened the door. He wasn't aware I was with him.

'Guy just ran out,' he said. 'Never had a chance.'

'I know. It wasn't your fault.'

He lurched to the side, falling out of his seat, and vomited on the ground in a long continuous stream. The poor guy was in shock. He'd been driving along, minding his own affairs, when his weekend plans changed. In fact, he'd done well to keep the vehicle from running over the man I'd been chasing. Right now, he wouldn't believe that.

A finger tapped me on the shoulder, a uniformed cop. 'I'll take it from here,' he said.

'How is he?' It was a stupid thing to ask.

'Bad, I'd say. Ambulance'll be here soon. Least it better be for his sake.'

I took out my cell, called Danny and gave him the short version of what had happened.

'Okay, Delaney, find out which hospital they're taking him to and call me back. I'll meet you there. Is he going to make it?'

'Doesn't look great, but he's still breathing.'

Yards away, the driver sat on the sidewalk wrapped in a blanket, alone and disbelieving. He'd never be quite the same again. If only he'd been a couple of seconds earlier or later.

A couple of seconds either way.

* * *

My, my. What have we here?

Hello, beautiful. What are you doin' all alone.
Mommy thinks she's the star.
But it's you, isn't it.
Let me see your certificate. Well, isn't that nice?
Tell you what, let's me and you go for a walk.
Not far. Not very far. Nobody's gonna even notice you're gone.
Don't appreciate you, not the way I do.
Nothing like.
Nothing like.

* * *

Mia Johnson had never known anything like it. One minute, her heart was bursting with excitement and anticipation, the next, it overflowed with the joy of realising the dream: Jolene had triumphed, just the way her mommy always knew she would.

What does beat the band mean, Mommy?

A surge of energy electrified Mia when the announcement came.

And the winner is ... Jolene Johnson!

She leapt into the aisle, falling against a man hurrying past. She didn't give him a second look: all the time, all the work was worth it. What could Joe say now, except admit his wife knew what she was doing? As for the money? To hell with it. Nothing was more important than this. Nothing. The sense of elation that engulfed Jolene's mom rose and rose inside her, never close to peaking. Five minutes later, in the lull before the next final began, Mia was still buzzing.

Jolene broke away from the procession on its way back to the changing-area when she saw her mother and ran into her outstretched arms.

'Yes, baby! Yes!' Mia squealed and hugged her daughter to her. 'We did it! You and me!'

The child looked out from under her blonde wig piled high the way those country-music gals liked to wear it into the glowing face of her star-struck mother. The big hair looked fake and ridiculous on the small head. Mia liked it; liked it enough to part with two hundred dollars. She untied the red ribbon round the scroll and read:

'This is to Certify ...'

Her eyes brimmed with hot tears of pride. The surname written on a dotted line in the centre of the page included the letter t, making Johnston. Mia didn't care. They'd done it: her and Jolene. From now on, if Joe didn't like it when she splashed out on something essential for the performance, he knew what he could do. Mia was done with lies and deception. Joe needed to back her judgement without resentful questions and grumbles, maybe even give her a lick of praise for her efforts once in a while. He had better watch his step, or he might be in for a surprise one fine day. The win gave Mia an inordinate sense of confidence, the way cocaine used to.

They walked hand-in-hand through the hall, conscious of their new-found celebrity. 'Well done, Jolene,' a woman said.

Mia basked in her moment in the sun. 'Why thank you.' She offered her hand. 'Mia Johnson. Jolene's mom.'

'I just thought Jolene looked so sweet in her costume. And her hair …'

'Well, do you know, I agonised over that for so long. We were in and out of that shop five or six times, before I let myself go with my instincts.'

'Your instincts are good,' the woman said.

Mia laughed a sad laugh. 'I just wish my husband Joe could hear you say that.'

Jolene didn't need to disengage from the conversation; she'd never been part of it. She let go of her mother's hand. When Mia reconnected with her responsibilities, she was gone. At first, that didn't mean much; she could be anywhere – back at the changing-area, in the john, showing-off her award to some envious kid. Frustration was the first response after ten minutes of searching. She muttered to herself, asking where her daughter might be, then anger because the good feelings were ebbing, making way for a fear the like of which she'd never known.

* * *

Why did you do that?

Because it was fun.

It's dangerous.

Too dangerous.

Crazy dangerous!

But it was fun.

Will waiting on death-row be fun?

Might be.

Don't be stupid! Don't be fucking stupid!

You don't get it. None of you do. It's a game. I've told you. How many times?

But I liked it. I liked it a lot.

We all like it, we love it. That's why we do it.

But you're gonna get us caught,

No, they can't catch us.

Why not?

Because they're dumb and we're smart, that's why.

Twenty-Four

This is stupid! It's stupid!
Dumb! Fucking dumb!
Why take the chance?
You're crazy. Crazy! Crazy! Crazy!
Who the fuck are you calling crazy? Don't ever call me that!
I give up. Why must you only listen to the others?
I like what they tell me better.
Safety first, you asshole!
You're going to lose it for certain.
That'll never happen.
Never happen.
We make life worth living.
Life in jail? You mad bastards!
It's a game! I like games! I'm good at playing games!
But he's a cop! That makes him dangerous.
That's what makes it fun. Fun and games.
We're smarter! Smarter than any cop!
Smarter than anyone!
Pigmy-brains!
Too many chances. He's getting closer.
He's a million miles away. He'll always be a million miles away.
He's a cop. A detective.
He's a dick, don't spoil the fun.
You're crazy!
I told you never to call me that! Shall I let the others deal with you?

The voices stopped chattering. One commanded the others.

Kill that coward! Kill it! I don't want to hear it again! End it!
Of course.
Our pleasure.
Literally.

Twenty-Five

My cell rang. I fished it out trying to hear above the wailing siren. The flashing red lights above me lent an unreality to the call. It was Catherine, probably wanting to know where I was. It didn't matter anymore; it was time for the truth.

'Delaney, where are you?'

She couldn't make out what I was saying. The news she had for me was the only thing in her head.

'A little girl is missing. They don't know where she is! The pageant's been called to a halt, and everybody needs to stay! The police are on their way!'

She shouted to be heard above the din from my end. I could only make out the occasional word. Enough to get the drift, and a cold hand closed over my throat.

I faked calm. 'Is Molly all right?'

'Molly's here with us.'

'I'm in an ambulance on my way to hospital.'

Her voice boomed and cracked down the line.

'I'm all right. I witnessed an accident. I'm needed at the hospital to talk with the police. I'll get back to you as soon as I can.'

Flimsy stuff. All I had.

We had travelled to the event as a family in Ray's car, so it wasn't possible to go with Fitzpatrick's instruction and follow the ambulance. I explained to the officer-in-charge that Detective Danny Fitzpatrick was meeting me at the hospital, and that I had to be there. I had information he required. He offered me a ride in the squad car, clearing a fast route ahead. I elected to travel in the ambulance. I wanted to have a closer look at the man fighting for his life.

Something wasn't right. For this guy to be the killer, he had to commit the crime before I saw him. Abduct a child and stick around. It didn't work.

* * *

Danny was there when the ambulance killed the siren and pulled into the ER. We stood while the medics secured the unconscious man to the trolley, rolled him out and wheeled him inside. A doctor appeared from nowhere and began examining him, at the same time issuing instructions. It was bad. The body language of the team attending him shouted it.

The doctor approached us, his face a study in neutral. 'I'm afraid whatever business you have will have to wait. Preliminary examination shows massive internal injury, his blood-pressure is critically low. He's headed for surgery this minute. When we open him up – if he survives that long – we'll know more.'

Danny started to ask something.

The doctor raised a hand. 'Please, there really is nothing more I can help you with.'

* * *

Two hours passed, and they still hadn't found the little girl. A team of police officers combed the building while another organised statements from everyone present. They'd be checked and cross-checked. No one involved with the case held out hope of turning up much. Mia was sedated and looked as if her bones had been crushed from the inside. The blanket round her shoulders drowned the shrinking figure under it.

The janitor claimed to have seen nothing of Jolene, even the cowgirl costume passed him by. But when a female officer mentioned the too-large blonde wig, something went off in his memory.

'Oh yeah,' he said, 'I do recall that kid. Barbie-Goes-Way-Out-West I thought at the time. No idea where she went though.'

Five minutes later, a young beat cop on his first homicide case answered that one. Officer Zachery Brown entered the boiler room and saw nothing except a concrete floor with a wire-mesh cage guarding the propane gas cylinders needed to supply the kitchen upstairs. Across the cheerless functional divide, a broom rested on one of two large plastic tanks smelling of oil fumes. The rookie unscrewed the top off the first one and shone his torch inside. The oily-black reservoir reflected the torch light and his face. He resealed the lid and moved to the next one. It was the same, except for the floating piece of strawberry-blonde hair, streaked and matted and black, like a bird caught in an oil slick.

He'd found Jolene Johnson.

* * *

When his boss had offered the chance of extra hours at the sawmill, Joe grabbed it. Only half a day, but still.

When he got home, the house was quiet. At first, he didn't like it; he was used to the constant yammer from his wife and daughter. The silence unnerved him. After he'd showered, made himself a couple of bacon sandwiches and downed three cups of coffee he began to appreciate the peace. He'd be out again at the crack of dawn tomorrow for more of the same. All day, this time.

He didn't crack a beer or switch on the TV sports. He was happy just to sit in his living-room, letting the silence soothe him. Later, he wouldn't remember how he'd spent the day. The knock on the door woke him.

'Mr Johnson?'

'Yes.'

'Officer de Mille. Can I come in?'

'Yeah. Sure. What's wrong?'

'I'm afraid I've some very bad news, Mr Johnson. Some very bad news. Maybe you'd better sit down.'

Joe didn't sit down. He stood and listened to how the life he'd known had ended. Through the awful tale, he remained calm. The officers looked at each other.

'Do you understand what we're telling you, Mr Johnson?'

'Yes.'

'Do you want us to take you to your wife?'

Joe didn't answer. Jolene didn't need him anymore.

'Mrs Johnson's with the doctor. It would be better if you were there.'

Joe Johnson wasn't a cold-hearted man; he just had nothing left to give. 'I don't think so,' he said.

The officers turned to go. One of them tried again. 'Is there anything we can do for you, sir? Anything at all?'

'Yeah. There is.'

He left them in the living-room. When he came back, he was wearing an overcoat and carrying a suitcase.

'Can you drop me at the bus station, please?'

Twenty-Six

'Tell me what happened again,' Danny said.

So I did, starting with the guy's strange behaviour at the pageant, his flight when he realised I'd spotted him, the pursuit along the corridors, and the sound of the accident. When I had finished, he opened his hand. In it was a wallet.

'He isn't our man.'

'You sure?'

'A uniform found this near the scene. Four credit cards and a driving licence, all in the same name.'

I began to feel uneasy.

'Who is he?'

'Tom Donald.'

'You've lost me.'

'Tom Donald. Timmy Donald's father.'

'Timmy Donald. Baton Rouge?'

'The same. If we accept that Lucy Gilmour was the first victim, Timmy was the killer's fifth.'

'What was he doing there? Why did he run?'

'Good questions, Delaney. Wish I had the answers.'

* * *

Danny called to update Delaup. The Captain was at the crime scene, and the conversation was short. I called Catherine to make sure they were all okay and to cancel my visit the next day. She'd have none of it. She wanted an explanation, preferably a good one. Unfortunately, I was fresh out.

We got to our feet when the surgeon approached, a mask still hanging round his neck. He introduced himself and explained.

Tom Donald was in bad shape; a broken arm, broken legs, fractured ribs, and, more serious, a ruptured spleen.

Fitzpatrick asked, 'Will he live?'

'Impossible to say at this point. We haven't established brain injury. Until he regains consciousness, we can't be certain.'

'But he has a chance?' The desperation in my voice was clear, even to me.

'Of course he has a chance. Though it may depend on how much he wants to live.'

He shrugged. 'I mean, does he have a good reason to put up the kind of fight he'll need to make?'

Another good question. I wouldn't bet the farm. My colleague felt the same. A uniform would stay with the injured man and call when he regained consciousness.

Fitzpatrick pulled up outside my house. 'I'll call you if anything changes.'

'Right.'

Fitzy wasn't blaming me – experienced cops know better. Still.

He put his arm round me. 'Listen, Delaney. I know how you react. You shut down. Go into yourself. My advice is to cut yourself a break. Shit happens.'

Easier said.

Inside, Lowell leapt on me, licking my hands and face. When I took his lead off the hook on the wall, he raced a couple of laps round the room, excited to be re-joining the world outside. I wasn't the only one who'd had a long day.

The night air was cool and fresh. A million stars shone down on New Orleans, helping me gather my thoughts. But they weren't good thoughts. So far, the killer had called the plays; the latest victim had been abducted and murdered right under my nose, taking the body count to eight. I talked it through with Lowell. 'How's he doing it? What's his disguise? They know him, don't they, boy?'

Lowell stopped at a tree and tilted his head towards me. We were onto something, and he knew it. I threw questions at him that lacked answers. 'How can you breathe the same air as a maniac and not recognise the madness in him? How can that be? How does he blind them to what he really is? Kids, maybe, but what about the adults; the parents? Isn't there a vibe? A suspicion? Some sense of unease about the guy standing next to them?'

Except, there hadn't been with me.

Above our heads, an owl flew noisily out of a branch and disappeared into the black sky. Usually, Lowell would chase after it. Not tonight. He stuck with me. In my head, an idea was forming. Just like with the Word Jumble, Lowell let me get there by myself. 'It's about trust, isn't it, boy? They trust him.'

His tail beat the grass, and he nuzzled against me.

'Yeah. It's all about trust.'

* * *

Danny called to cue me for a seven-a.m. meeting next day. 'Think yourself lucky you're out. It's a fucking circus here. Every clown up the chain screaming for results and pushing each other out of the way to get their face on TV. Nothing on Tom Donald. Still critical.'

'Hope we get a chance to speak to him soon.'

'Mmmm. See you tomorrow,' he said and hung up.

I got a big welcome at Catherine's from Molly, a story about a bad man and exaggerated descriptions of his evil works. Her eyes grew large. 'And there was a helicopter. And there was a camera. Mommy says I might be on the television.'

She warned me of the dangers that lurked in the world. I promised to be careful, especially at night. Her parents' reception was less fulsome. It couldn't be avoided forever. I hung out with the junior member of the family as long as I could. Once Molly was off the carpet, Ray got up and poured everyone a drink, guessing we'd need one. Good guess.

Now the game was over: time to 'fess up, and after a hesitant beginning, I managed to get it out.

'I got a call from Danny Fitzpatrick telling me my old boss wanted to speak to me. Anyway, when I met Fitzy and Delaup they filled me in on a serial killer working his way back and forth across the South. Because of the nature of the crimes and the geography, it was a federal case.'

They listened, every reaction held in check.

'Long story short, they persuaded me the investigation would benefit from my involvement, though I no longer carry a badge. I agreed, and I've been working on it since.'

I was happy to leave it at that. No dice. Ray was a bright guy: too bright. He nailed it in one. 'Why did they want you?'

I couldn't lie to them anymore. But I tried, hoping to keep the full extent of my involvement from them: a doomed strategy. 'The nature of the crimes led them to think I might have something to offer the investigation.'

'How? What made them think that? What was the nature of the crimes?'

He already knew the answers.

'The killer. His victims are all children.'

The skin round his eyes creased. 'And you could help because of your experience with that kind of criminal?'

My sister couldn't look at me.

'No, Ray. I'm someone who can go where the killer goes, without attracting attention.'

They were at the end waiting for me. They knew.

I stopped running. Let the chips fall where they may. 'This killer had murdered five children when they asked me in. Five children over five states. Now, the total is eight kids in seven states. The serial aspect of the attacks was played down because we wanted to catch this guy. If we'd broadcast we were onto him, he'd have disappeared like smoke. Not forever, just until the trails were cold.'

I took a pull on the drink Ray had poured before we started down this road. If ever I needed to find an extra gear, it was now.

'Why they asked me was simple. You'd told Fitzpatrick about Molly. About the pageants and how I was against the whole idea.'

The contempt in Catherine's voice shook me. 'You were prepared to put Molly's life in danger? Our daughter, your own flesh and blood?'

When I heard it put like that, I wanted to be sick.

But that wasn't how it had been.

In or out, Mr Delaney?

Did I care enough to put aside my own feelings? Yeah, as it turned out I did, because it was the right thing to do. I didn't add that in spite of everything my reply to McLaren wouldn't alter.

In.

'The option was to do something or do nothing. Cee, I love Molly. But other people have their Molly. Just as important. Just as loved. My choice was to try to stop them losing their child. As for the pageant thing, you didn't realise it was a serial, but you knew about the kid in Baton Rouge. And once you were going, I was going too. And you were right. I can't ever *not* be a cop.'

My passionate defence changed the atmosphere.

Catherine said, 'What happened yesterday? Were you chasing somebody?'

After all the shit about a cop's instinct and being in a unique position, able to go where the killer goes without attracting attention, it would've been good to report how it all had paid off.

'Yesterday was a new low for me. I picked up on a guy acting strange. When I tried to talk to him, he took off. I raced to the other side of the building and caught up to him seconds after he'd run into a moving vehicle. Now, he's close to death.'

'But you've stopped him. It's over.'

'No, it isn't. There's little to no chance he's our guy.'

'How? How can you know that for sure?'

'Because the man I chased is Tom Donald. His son Timmy was one of the killer's victims.'

'So, what was he doing there? Why did he run from you?'

I held my arms up and out in a gesture of defeat.

Catherine spoke again, to herself this time. 'And while that was happening, the murderer took that poor girl. She'd just won, too. Her mother looked pleased as punch. It was a big thing for both of them. It was horrible. Really horrible. There were cops everywhere, then, when they finally let us go, there was the media shoving microphones at us, shouting questions we wouldn't have answered, even if we could.'

Ray said, 'How do you get over something like that? What is there to make you want to get out of bed ever again? That's the end of contests for us. We're done.'

It wasn't the end of anything for me. The madman was still out there. That was where I needed to be, with or without my family.

'I'm sorry I wasn't straight with you two.'

They didn't tell me it was all right, but they didn't throw me out.

That was something.

Twenty-Seven

The team assembled for the Monday morning meeting long before seven a.m. The latest attack only made me more determined to bring this guy down. Everyone felt the same.

At one minute to seven, Captain Delaup banged on the table, and conversation ceased. Never a comedian, today, his face was stone. The feds shared his expression. I could only imagine the pressure these guys were under to get a result.

'All right. First, the bad news. On Saturday, Jolene Johnson became the eighth victim right here in Louisiana. Her body was found hidden in an oil reservoir in the boiler room of the venue where she was performing. Jolene was drowned.'

He gave us a minute to imagine the horror of drowning in oil.

'Before anybody asks, no clues and no witnesses. In fact, the usual with this guy, even though the circumstances increased the chance he could get caught. Nothing.'

He cast a baleful look over the assembly.

'She was six years old. We thought we had him; we were wrong. More on that later.'

Agent McLaren took over. 'Eight victims now. Unless our killer makes a mistake, we're going to be hard-pressed to stop him.'

As law enforcers, that was unacceptable.

'Agent Rutherford will pass out the autopsy findings. Bottom line: we missed him again.' He glanced in my direction. Danny's jaw tightened.

'Mr Delaney chased a man acting suspiciously. The guy's behaviour supported the assumption he could be our man. When he was spotted, he ran – into a passing van. He's in the hospital, unconscious and critical. It hasn't been possible to interview him. Turns out, he's Tom Donald, father of Timmy Donald, victim number five, murdered in Baton Rouge. We guess he was doing the same as us: looking for his son's killer. So why run? As soon as he wakes up, we'll ask him – if he ever does.'

What he said next didn't make me feel good about how Saturday had ended.

'Mr Delaney was undercover at the pageant looking for the kind of behaviour shown by Tom Donald. It may be the killer seized his opportunity to attack Jolene, knowing our man was going in the other direction. We think Delaney's presence forced him to hurry and change his modus. That would account for drowning. Nothing like as intimate as strangulation. No time to savour the breath leaving the body.'

McLaren stopped to sip some water, then said, 'He's laughing at us, people. And with reason. For all our work, what we've achieved is easy to quantify. Marginally more than fuck-all!'

The veins in his neck threatened to burst through his skin; cords of frustration, ugly against the pristine whiteness of his shirt.

'He's laughing because he knows we've no idea who he is. If he decided to stop, even for a while, we'd be left with zip. Nothing but eight dead kids.'

He turned to Diskins. 'Anything to add, Charlie?'

Diskins shook his head. Coming second to this psycho was dragging everybody down.

Delaup came in. 'There has to be something we're missing. Has to be. Everyone. Go over it again. Get to it as soon as you leave here. There's all kinds of heat on this. One dead child was bad enough. Two is unacceptable. All overtime is cleared and, I might add, expected.'

The troops didn't argue; this was the reality of police work: drudgery, disappointment and still more drudgery.

Charlie Diskins found his voice. 'Captain Delaup's right. There's no such thing as the perfect crime. The evidence is out there. We're looking at it.'

Diskins was trying to boost morale; it was going to take a lot more than that. Agent Rutherford contributed nothing, looking more unwell than the last time I'd seen him. When the meeting broke up, I stayed behind with Danny and the boss.

Fitzpatrick said, 'Don't blame yourself, Delaney. On another day, you might've been right.'

'But I wasn't. And things have changed. Ray and Catherine know I was using them as cover.'

'How did they take it?'

'Weren't thrilled. That isn't the point. The killer must've seen some of what went down, which means my cover's blown.'

'Do you want out?'

'No. When I said I was in, I meant for the full term. I want to get more involved in the investigation. With my uncle-disguise in the wind, I can operate out in the open.'

'What do you have in mind?'

'I'll start by going to the three crime scenes in this state. Talk to some people there. Maybe shake a memory loose. We all agree there's no perfect crime.'

'Anything else?'

'Yeah, as a matter of fact. The motive we know from Charlie Diskins. But do we? Back at the start, he reminded us these crimes were about power. Okay. So how does he choose his victims? The place's full of potential marks. Why settle on the ones he takes? What attracts him to them?'

'Do whatever you have to. You'll keep going to the competitions?'

'Yeah, though the odds against ever being at the same one as the killer again are long.'

Danny said, 'Could be you're just the incentive he needs. Got more crimes here than any other state. First time he's doubled back. What if he's decided to put himself up against you? What if it just got personal?'

'Fucked up or what? I still have to decide where I'm going next weekend. The Jolene Johnson murder's all over the news.

Maybe Saturday was the psycho's last hurrah. Hell, maybe there won't be any more pageants. Hearing a lotta noise about shutting them down.'

Delaup said, 'Let's hope not. We need this guy to keep operating. Anything less kills our chances of catching him. But Danny may be onto something here. I'll pass it along.'

He walked me to the door. 'Do what you do, Delaney. What you always did.'

What I always did. What had that been again? Keep on keeping on. If that was what Delaup meant, he could relax, except it would take more than spent shoe leather.

* * *

I got a call about Harry Love's client. I listened, smiling to myself. What I'd been told would guarantee the lawyer's business kept coming my way.

I needed to take stock: Clyde was dead, and the victims had warned me off. The victims, not the perps. They blamed me. So, did I. I couldn't let it go.

And there would be no cops – not Cal, not even Danny.

Tomorrow was Tuesday. I'd start at the beginning and try to get it right this time.

Over at the other case, my remit had been extended to something akin to my old job. Well and good, except it was a poisoned chalice. Our only potential lead lay in intensive care. What Tom Donald did or didn't know might still be denied us.

Do what you always did.

Delaup's memory was better than mine, or he was clutching at straws like the rest of us. Either way, my approach needed to alter. "Back to basics" was a phrase I hated. But that was where I had to go, beginning with a whirlwind tour of the Louisiana crime sites later in the week and an overt appearance on the pageant circuit. I might get lucky and get close to the killer again, though I wouldn't be holding my breath on that one.

I was sure what I was missing was right in front of me.

Much later, I picked up the phone and called Harry Love.

'Delaney. How are you? Got something for me already?'

'Maybe, Harry. What does the witness say against your client?'

Building up my part.

'Eye-witness. Strong stuff. Definite he saw my client's car leaving the scene.'

'Kind of car does he say it was?'

'The right kind for the prosecution: a blue Audi. So, what've you got?'

'Good news. The witness had ambitions to join the NOPD. It never happened.'

'Why was that?'

'New Orleans' finest turned him down.'

He sensed a break coming his way.

'Failed the medical.'

'Really?'

I put him out of his misery. 'Hard for him to positively ID a vehicle, Harry. He's colour blind.'

* * *

The Julian Boutte I'd known couldn't have waited to come after me. So, unless he'd changed, he was gone.

Since the night of Cilla Bartholomew's bombshell, Stella's cell had been off. It was me she was keeping out. The shop was still open. No "For Sale" sign hung in the window.

Inside was cool and fresh. A couple of female customers browsed the racks. Stella saw me and looked away. I waited. When the women left, I followed them to the door, put the Closed notice in the window and turned the key. I needed Stella to listen.

She looked so good, I wanted to make love to her right here.

'Hello, Stel. We need to talk.'

She shook her head.

'All right, I need to talk. Just hear me out.'

Her eyes softened when I told her about Cilla Bartholomew and our meeting in Jackson Square – the reason I hadn't made it to her. I blurted out my guilt. 'I want to be with you, Stella. I don't want you to go. But I can't let you be part of my craziness. I couldn't let you walk out of my life, thinking I don't love you. I'm doing this because I love you.'

'I'm not going, Delaney. I know. About Ellen.'

I stared. 'How?'

'Danny told me everything. And before you butt in, it's not your decision to make. It's mine, and I've made it. I just needed you to reach out to me, and you have.'

She came towards me, put her arms around my neck and kissed me, hard. I kissed her back. When we came up for air, she said, 'No more wasted time. I want us to be together.'

'Got some catching up to do.'

'So, your place or mine?'

I pulled down the shade. 'What's wrong with right here?'

Stella seemed surprised. 'Nothing. Except I was talking about where we're gonna live.'

Twenty-Eight

The next day, I headed to Baton Rouge. Lowell wanted to come. I told him about Stella and me, and the downer he'd been on passed. He lay on the front seat, which meant he was up for listening to the radio. When they played a song he liked, he howled until I turned the volume up.

On the outskirts of the city, I pulled into a diner for coffee and a last read at the thin file. The coffee was the worst I'd ever tasted. A second cup confirmed my opinion, while I studied what was known. Apart from the now usual forensic blank, nobody interviewed had anything to add. The killer was invisible, leaving no trace, except for the broken bodies of his victims.

A waitress approached with the offer of another top-up. I smiled the freebie away; I'd learned my lesson. Back in the car, I nosed through city traffic, looking for the offices of Mad About U. Baton Rouge is the second city of Louisiana, with a population of around a quarter of a million. I wasn't anticipating any problem finding 517 Sinclair and Claudine Charlton. Wrong again. Twice I had to ask directions from passers-by before I made it to the event company.

From the outside, it didn't look promising. The building was painted a tan colour that wouldn't have improved the look of anything it came in contact with, though it was a perfect partner to the grills on the windows and the grey roller-door. A cracked sign told me Mad About U was on the third floor. I got the impression they were the only tenant. Business life had moved on from here some time before. With the exception of the people who organised and ran the Little Louisiana Pageant, where Timmy Donald had died.

At the top of the stairs, I pressed a grubby intercom button and was buzzed in without any questions about who I was or what I wanted.

A voice called, 'In here.'

I followed the sound down a tight corridor lit by a single low-watt bulb. At the end, a blonde woman was reading a magazine. 'Delaney? Sit down.'

I cleared a pile of unfiled papers off the only other chair and threw in a smile that got me nothing. It had been a long time since Claudine Charlton had been impressed by a man. She raised an eyebrow when she saw Lowell. 'What can I do for you?'

I handed her my card. 'I'm part of the police team investigating the death of Timmy Donald. I operate in the private sector these days.'

'But you were a cop, right?'

'Right.'

I'd become more interesting. I returned the scrutiny, seeing the blunt features of a woman who'd turned more than a few heads in her time. A lady who dispensed with charm the minute it was unnecessary.

'And how can I help you?'

She lifted her legs onto the desk, giving me a good look at the worn-down heels of her cowboy boots. This gal made alright money, though it wasn't going on anything here, including her. Maybe she had an unnatural fear of rainy days.

'You've already been through all this, I know. I'm trying to find something, anything, we missed first time round.'

She glared at me. I'd taken away her first objection. The office walls hung with posters of events past, tired and faded with time and the air coming from the portable heater next to her chair. Claudine Charlton would like me to believe she'd somewhere better to go. The film of dust on every surface told a different story.

'Tell me about your business, Mad About U.'

'Nothin' to tell. We run different pageants through the year, once or twice a month.'

'Do they always feature children?'

Her jaw tightened. 'Of course not. We run a variety of events for all ages.'

'All ages?'

'All young ages. How much do you know about the pageant business, Mr Delaney? Not much, I bet.'

'You're right, not much. One reason I'm here. Tell me about it.'

She found a spot on the damp-stained ceiling to focus on. 'Here in the South, pageantry's a living tradition.'

'What's the appeal?'

'For a few, it's the first rung on the ladder that'll take them all the way to Miss United States, even Miss World. For most, it's a chance to get out there and shine ahead of the rest.'

She took her eyes from the ceiling and bored them into me.

'A university degree's all very well. If the girl's a former Miss Texas, you're gonna bet on her getting the job.'

'And for the others?'

'A day out for the family. They hope it'll round out Juliet and help her confidence. Who knows?'

'What about the parents?'

'All of the above, plus it makes them happy to see their little darling doing things they'd have liked to have done but never got the chance.'

Claudine Charlton had no interest in the motivation, only the money.

'Must have hit your operation pretty hard?'

'Yeah, you'd think. But it was business as usual after two weeks.'

'Do you have an opinion on the very young taking part?'

'Nope.'

'The day Timmy died, where were you when you heard there might be a problem?'

'Don't remember.'

'All right. What was the first thing you did?'

'I went to the stage manager, Alec Adams. He said they were looking for a boy.'

'Then what?'

'I was concerned the audience know nothing was wrong.'

'So, what did you do?'

'Went to the judges.'

'Why?'

'We needed a new result. That little guy had a Chaplin routine that was way ahead of the others.'

'But if he was missing …'

'Somebody needed to take his place.'

'Any men acting suspiciously?'

'Mr Delaney.' She gave my name a hard edge it didn't have. 'In my experience, men don't behave any other way.'

'The stage manager Alec Adams, what do you know about him?'

She sneered. 'More than I want to. He's my ex-husband. There're plenty of reasons for that, but he's straight up and down hetro.' She gave a bitter laugh. 'If he wasn't, we might still be married. Look Mister, Alec's a lying snake, and the world's worst husband, but he isn't who you're after. A loser, yes, a killer, no.'

I asked about security. Nothing new came out. On the drive back to New Orleans, I stopped at the diner I'd been in earlier; bad coffee must be addictive. Something Claudine Charlton had said stayed with me.

That little guy had a Chaplin routine that was way ahead of the others.

I'd wondered how the killer chose his victims.

Now I saw it, plain as day.

Twenty-Nine

When I got home, I went through the files again, and for the first time, felt confident I'd get this guy. Unearthing the link between the victims had given me hope. I popped a beer and settled down, more relaxed than I'd been in a while. Lowell sensed the change and lay on the carpet, staring up at me.

'He's thinks he's clever. Smarter than everybody else. But he isn't, is he, boy?'

I leaned forward and ran my hand through his coat; he was pleased for me but afraid I'd get ahead of myself and do something rash.

'Don't worry, I'll be careful.'

That seemed to reassure him. He put his head on his paws; still listening.

'But how does he get away with it, eh? How? What's his secret? What's his secret, fella? Does he use a disguise? What do you think?'

Talking it through with a friend helped; it always did. Peace washed over me, and I knew it was gonna be all right.

Spending time in front of the TV wasn't something that happened too often. Trying to find a program reminded me why. Given a choice, Lowell would always go for one of the music channels. Eventually, we found an old documentary on the Doobie Brothers and watched it to the end. When they played the final song – "Long Train Running" – he was on his feet, over at the screen, tail beating against the carpet.

Say what you like about him: the dog knew his music.

After the show finished, he went to sleep, and I started a book Stella had recommended. The house was quiet. After a while, I went outside into the warm air, heavy with moonflower and jasmine. Above me, the sky was black, and the street was deserted, apart from a car parked further down, beside an old sycamore tree. Nobody was going anywhere, including us. I locked the doors and returned to the story.

Time passed. With adrenaline fading, I felt exhausted. Just as I closed my eyes, a sound brought me wide awake. Lowell sat up and let out a low growl. I patted his head and reached for my gun. Every thought in my head boiled down to two words: Julian Boutte.

I killed the lights, crept over to the kitchen and listened. Footsteps crunched on the gravel I'd covered the yard with the summer Ellen had called off the wedding and left me with a property I didn't want and a mortgage I couldn't afford. The footsteps stopped. Lowell was beside me, his ears back, like me, imagining the intruder on the other side.

I whispered, 'Easy boy. Easy. It's all right,' and failed to convince either of us.

Suddenly, the room filled with a blinding light, throwing jagged shadows on the walls. I shielded my eyes, crawled back to the window and looked out. On the lawn, Danny Fitzpatrick was hunkered behind the driver's door of a police cruiser, his service revolver in his hand and his face an expressionless mask.

Fuck! Boutte, it had to be.

I opened the front door. Danny waved me back. 'Stay inside, Delaney. He's here.'

I wouldn't hide. I'd waited as long as Julian Boutte had for this moment. At the back door, the gun felt heavy in my hand. If I had to use it, I wouldn't think twice. The key turned silently in the lock. I eased the handle open and stepped into the night. There could be only one reason Boutte was here. He'd come to kill me. Or die trying.

Let it be.

It took a second for my eyes to adjust. When they did, I saw him, crouched with his back to me. He seemed smaller than I remembered; slight even. He'd lost weight, and with it, his edge. Seven years in Angola must've made him careless, because Juli didn't realise I was there. I edged towards him, expecting him to fire. At this distance, the chances of missing were low. I'd get a couple off as well. We both might die. It occurred to me to just shoot him in the back and end it – why not? He wouldn't hesitate – except tomorrow and every day after, I'd have to live with myself.

Under my foot, stone grinding against stone gave me away. Julian realised he wasn't alone and rounded on me. I dived at him and brought him down, punching and kicking. We rolled on the ground in the darkness, until I managed to work myself free and cracked his skull with the butt of my gun. He stopped struggling and lay still. Two men appeared at the corner of the building, a guy I'd worked with when I was with the department and Danny Fitzpatrick.

Danny looked at the unconscious man and back to me. 'You okay, Delaney?'

'Yeah, I'm okay.'

The plainclothes cop knelt beside the body and turned the face towards me, shaking his head. For a moment, I thought he was telling me I'd killed him. Wrong. The figure on the ground was a boy, a white kid – fourteen or fifteen years old at most. They hauled him to his feet, cuffed him and marched him to their car.

This might've been his first step down a rocky road which would end when the gates of Angola closed behind him. Or maybe he'd learnt his lesson, and attempted burglary was as heavy as it was going to get. I'd never know. But one thing was certain: he wasn't Julian Boutte. He was still out there.

* * *

Stella called the next morning to say hi and have a good one.

I kept it light. 'That's the plan, Stel, that's the plan.'

I told her about the false alarm and passed it off as a joke. Bad decision. She wasn't amused and rang off, angry at me for not taking a madman's threat seriously. Then, it was Mrs Santini's turn. She'd witnessed the drama the night before and made a special trip to hassle me. 'No shortage of excitement when you're around, is there, Delaney?'

I tried to apologise and didn't get far. 'A burglar made an …'

'Used to be a quiet neighbourhood when my Alberto was alive. Not anymore.'

'Sorry about that.'

'Lucky the police happened along.'

'Yeah, it was.'

Rosa was a wily old bird. She folded her arms across her chest; unconvinced. 'Thought the NOPD was short on manpower. Didn't seem like it last night.'

It was the wrong moment to ask. I didn't have a choice. 'Since you're here, Mrs Santini, I need a favour. I'm working an important case. Might be away a lot. Would you keep an eye on Lowell?'

From the look she gave, she'd be keeping an eye on a lot more than the dog.

Around ten-thirty, I met Fitzpatrick and Delaup. The night before didn't rate a mention. We both knew that if the roles were reversed, I would've done exactly the same.

I got right to it. 'Okay. I'll keep it short. Nothing until Baton Rouge and Timmy Donald. Claudine Charlton, the organiser, said something that only connected with me later. She told me, "That little guy had done a Chaplin routine that was way ahead of the others."'

'So?' I'd lost Delaup.

'"Way ahead of the others." The result had to change. Timmy was missing. They were about to announce he'd won.'

Fitzpatrick shook his head. 'What does that tell us?'

'He was the winner. That's what made him special. That's what got him killed.'

I moved to the pictures pinned to the wall in chronological order and pointed at an image of a smiling Timmy Donald.

'Timmy was the winner. Billy Cunningham – Supreme Mini-National King.'

They wanted to be convinced. They weren't.

'Jolene Johnson, the latest victim. Another winner.'

They shifted their eyes from me to the photographs and back. I was alone on this one. Danny said what they were thinking. 'It doesn't work, Delaney. Three out of eight isn't a consistent pattern.'

'But it isn't three from eight. It's the three obvious ones, that's all. We haven't been looking for that connection before, so we haven't found it. All we know about Lucy Gilmour is she went missing from a pageant in Panama City Beach, Florida, and that her body was never found. What happened at that event? How did she do? I'm betting we're going to find Lucy won.'

They were listening, no more than that.

'Dorothy Dulles in Alabama. The details of her death are in the record. Did she win?'

My delivery started to pick up speed.

'Mimi Valasquez.'

My finger tapped the shot of an innocent child who'd been unlucky enough to be born with some singing ability.

'Agent McLaren called to tell me about her. The mother left to collect her brother. Mimi had got through to the final. An outstanding performer for her age. "A real talent," that was his phrase.' I was on fire. 'Let's check Lucy, Dorothy and the others. I know what we'll find. Winners: all winners.'

Delaup said, 'Let's do that.'

Danny bent over his case-notes, speed reading. 'Here it is. Andrea Hassel came first in her age group in the Modern Miss Mobile Pageant.'

'It fits.'

'No, it doesn't, Delaney. It doesn't fit.'

Danny walked to the wall and singled out one of the victims. 'Pamela White in Texas wasn't in the competition. She was only there to support her sister, Donna.'

'How did Donna do? We need to find out about her, as well as the first two. My guess is when he couldn't reach Donna, he settled for the next best thing: her sister.'

Delaup said, 'Suppose you're right, what would that prove? How does it help us?'

These guys must have missed their morning cup of Joe. They were slow to catch on.

'It reveals the connection between the victims. He goes for the winners, or someone close to them. That doesn't narrow who we're looking for. It sure as hell tightens the focus on who we're trying to protect. And it tells us something about the perp. Charlie Diskins might make something of it.'

Fitzpatrick was already on the phone talking to the FBI. Soon, we'd have the information we needed to fit another piece of the puzzle together. I felt good, because if I could dig out how the victims were chosen, I could go all the way.

It wasn't over, not by a long shot, but at least we were in the game.

* * *

I hung around until confirmation came through. Before she disappeared, never to be seen again, Lucy Gilmour had won in Panama City Beach; Dorothy, too, in Alabama. The information on Donna White took another hour. It fit with the rest. Donna was collecting her scroll and a check for fifty dollars when her big sister, Pamela, went missing.

Eight out of eight.

The killer preyed on winners. Molly had won. Our family had been lucky, though I wouldn't be telling Catherine or Ray. Delaup said the FBI considered the connection between the victims important. Charlie Diskins would work on it. Try to tease it into something helpful.

The Captain patted me on the back. 'Good work, Delaney.'

I doubted my name had been mentioned to the Feds. What did that matter? I was a team player, wasn't I? The only important thing was the result.

Danny caught up with me out in the corridor. 'Don't want to rain on anybody's day, but we're still miles away from stopping this crazy. Diskins may well come back with something we can use. I doubt it.'

We sat on a big old cast-iron radiator. Fitzpatrick was subdued, his mood was off.

'We'll get him, bud. I know it.'

'Hear about Rutherford?'

I hadn't.

'He's out of it, at least for a while.'

'What happened?'

'His wife left him. He just snapped.'

I remembered Jim Rutherford the last time I'd seen him, withdrawing into himself as his professional life and his real one collided before our eyes. Some can juggle the pressures and priorities for years without the cracks showing. Too many crashed and burned. It was a hard life to lead and an even harder one to leave.

I said, 'We need to talk.'

'What about?'

'Can't tell you yet. I think I need your help.'

He nodded. 'Sure thing.'

'Can I trust you?'

He reacted like I'd slapped his face. 'Fuck off, Delaney!'

I relaxed. It was the right answer.

Thirty

Stella surprised me with a visit and a bottle of something cold. Next morning, she left before eight a.m. After she'd gone, I lay for a while, thinking things over. I had a plan to help Cilla Bartholomew, one that didn't involve the cops. Danny Fitzpatrick was a friend before everything else. I'd asked a friend for help, and he'd said yes. That's what friends were for.

The serial killings were more difficult. My job was to stay with it. The break would come.

I padded through to the kitchen to put coffee on. The soles of my bare feet slapped where the floor was tiled. Halfway there, Lowell sneaked up on me, almost knocking me over, letting me know I hadn't spent nearly enough time with him.

'Easy boy.' I patted his side to quiet him down.

The coffee was good and strong, reviving me enough to send me into the shower whistling. After that, I took Lowell out and played with him, throwing an imaginary stick for him to catch and racing against him. You needed to be a dog lover to get it.

When we got back, I fed him and went over my arrangements for the weekend. For a change, the band didn't have a gig. That suited. Tonight, I could give Stella my undivided attention. Tomorrow, the Saints were at home to the San Francisco 49ers. Cal and I would be there. I'd keep my arrangement with him, though I didn't want to. Anything else wouldn't look right. Then, I'd go to my sister's and hang out. This morning, the long-shot search for the child-killer would continue at a small pageant not far from the city.

The phone rang. It was Catherine. 'Hi, how's it going?'

'Hi, sis. Everything's fine at my end. You?'

'You'll be over tomorrow as usual?'

'Sure will, right after the game.'

'Good. There's something I want to tell you.'

'Something good?'

She laughed. 'We'll see. It's a surprise.'

'I'll be straight over.'

'All right. Think those Saints can get enough points on the board?'

'I live in hope. I live in hope.'

'Okay, see ya.'

If there was one thing I hated, it was a surprise. I preferred to be in the dark until the last moment. Better still, forget surprises for me. The phone sounded again, and my plans went down the pan.

Surprises. Who needs them?

* * *

Tom Donald was still in the ICU. A uniform stood by the door. The news that Timmy's father was regaining consciousness meant everything else went on hold. A white-gowned doctor laid out his priorities; priorities very different from ours.

'Mr Donald keeps slipping in and out of consciousness, and really, it would be in his best interests to leave him undisturbed. Your boss – Delaup, is it? – assures me my patient may hold vital information.'

We didn't respond.

'This man is very, very ill. Anything that tires, excites or weakens him reduces his chances of coming out of this alive. Do you understand?'

We did.

'A few minutes, no more.'

No matter how important we believed our business to be, it came a long second to his. We sat down next to the bed. Life-support mechanisms droned away.

Fitzpatrick spoke, 'Mr Donald? Mr Donald, can you hear me? I'm Detective Danny Fitzpatrick of the NOPD, and I'm trying to find the man who killed Timmy. Help us.'

Tom Donald didn't stir. Fitzpatrick tried again. The figure of the doctor loomed in the doorway ready to call time.

'You try,' Danny said.

The doctor looked at his watch; the chance was almost gone. I leaned forward, the damaged face, pitiful under wads of bandage and gauze.

'Mr Donald. Mr Donald, why did you run? Why did you run from me?'

The head moved a fraction. The cracked lips parted. I bent low, my face turned so my ear was close to the injured man's mouth.

And he spoke. Almost. I felt Danny rise from his seat. A tortured sigh escaped Tom Donald. A ghost word slipped out into the world and away. I leaned closer. His breath brushed my face. I thought I made out "ann." And "hatch."

Danny willed me to capture the precious clue. I couldn't.

'Mr Donald,' I tried again, 'why did you …'

'Enough. That's enough.'

The doctor ended it before it had even begun. He stood between us and his patient until we headed for the door.

The noise from the bed made us all stop and turn.

'Man,' Tom Donald forced the clumsy sound past his tongue, weak and guttural, barely audible. 'Man … match …'

Timmy's father faded into the comfort of unknowing.

Thirty-One

'So, you're sure?'

'Sure? No. That's the best I could get.'

Delaup repeated the words to himself. '"Man" and "match."'

It was after ten o'clock at night, and the three of us were in Delaup's office. The Captain wrapped the bowtie he'd been wearing at the black-tie dinner around his fingers. When Danny called him, he'd left and joined us. About now, a taxi was dropping an unhappy Mrs Delaup home. 'Will he live?'

Fitzy supplied the same unacceptable answer. 'Who knows?'

'Maybe we can get another crack at finding out what he was doing at a kids' event by himself.'

'If he recovers. Meantime, the killer walks free.'

Fitzpatrick added new information that brought little relief. 'Called McLaren on the way here. No new attacks. That's something.'

Delaup nodded. 'Yeah, it is. No thanks to us. The perp's still picking and choosing, still in control. We'll get a break when he gives us one. Which means he gets to decide who lives and who dies. Write up what happened today. Present it to the team.'

Delaup got to his feet, his face full of tiredness. He called the front desk for a car to take him home. We took the elevator to the underground garage. Danny drove in silence. The morning's optimism was far away.

Do what you do. What you always did.

Danny tried to cheer us up. 'If Tom Donald pulls through, we'll have a shot.'

'"Man." "Match." It's in there somewhere.'

I played the game. 'He definitely said "man." No question. He was following somebody. But "match"? I've no idea.'

'Unless that wasn't it.' Fitzpatrick kept his eyes on the road. 'Match – batch, hatch, latch, patch, thatch, scratch.' He bit his lip. With nothing new to contribute, I stayed quiet.

'Delaup would like this one to come through,' he said.

'I know.'

'High-profile. Working with the Bureau. Make him look good. He gets to look good, we get to feel good.'

'I'll take that deal.'

'You'd better. It's the only one on offer.'

'It's the only one I want.'

The car slowed outside my house. Danny turned the engine off.

'What was that "can I trust you" bullshit?'

'I need your help, Fitzy. Not as a cop, as a friend. The people involved have already been burned, because I made a mistake. I wouldn't listen. This time, I'm listening. Trouble is, I can't pull it off alone.'

'And do I get to know more?'

'Of course. Next week. Next week we go to work.'

'Doing what?'

'Catching the bad guys. You remember how to do that, don't you?'

* * *

We met as usual for a late breakfast at Cafe Du Monde on Decatur, ate scrambled eggs and croissants, and talked football.

Things had changed for the Saints in the three weeks since they opened their new season account with the win over the Bucs; they had a catalogue of injuries.

In the diner, Cal wolfed through the food. 'Today's a big one. We need a win.'

'Sure do. Still an awful lot of football to be played.'

'That's right, but the charge starts today. 2-2, I can live with. 1-3? No way. No quarter.'

'The games we lost were close, Cal, only seven points all told. We can play better.'

He rubbed a hand over his chin. 'We'd better.'

And that was typical of Cal Moreland: all or nothing.

Because I was leaving to go to Catherine's after the game, we travelled to the Superdome in our own cars. When I came up the stairs, he was already there, standing in the aisle with his cell pressed against one ear and a finger in the other, trying to block out the background noise. I spent a minute watching how animated he was, pacing up and down, turning and turning back again, speaking all the time.

He settled into his usual place. Whatever his call had been about, his mood had changed. Now, he was Mr Positive. He clapped and shouted as the teams came out. It meant a lot more to him than it did to me.

'We can do this, Delaney.'

'By how many?'

'Ten points.'

He held up both hands, fingers splayed. 'Ten.'

'Got fifty on it?'

'Sure do.'

New Orleans needed to find energy from somewhere to lift themselves out of their losing run. At 28-9 early in the fourth quarter, Cal Moreland's prediction was coming true. He beamed and applauded, joking with strangers in the crowd.

The final score was 31-17. Leaving the Dome, Cal raved on and on about the team. That was the way it was. You were either important to him or you weren't; useful to him or not; helping him win or responsible for some loss in his life. He didn't mess with the middle ground.

He said, 'This is our season.'

'You really believe that?'

'Yeah. Who knows where the road goes.'

He laughed and walked off to his car. I watched him go, cutting through the crowd. A man I'd been friends with most of my life and didn't really know at all. The whole time we'd talked only about football; not the traders or the dead cops.

* * *

Catherine's face flushed; a cross between pride and embarrassment.

'I'm pregnant,' she said.

'That's the surprise. Fantastic. You must be delighted.'

'I am. We don't want Molly to grow up an only child. A brother or sister will be good for her, don't you think?'

I hesitated. 'Can't say. You were doing fine 'til I came along.'

She thought about it. 'You're right. I forgot about that.'

* * *

It was hard to remember when the week hadn't begun with the Monday meeting. Now, only McLaren and Diskins represented the Bureau. McLaren sat ramrod straight, revealing nothing of who he might be when ID was no longer necessary and the gun in his shoulder-holster had been set aside.

The same could be said of Diskins, the FBI profiler. All the usual faces were there from our side. The polite protocol, evident in the beginning, was gone. Agent McLaren took over from the off. And if Delaup was annoyed, he hid it well.

'Okay, let's get started. There were no new attacks over the weekend, and for a change, we think we've got the beginning of something. Detective Fitzpatrick.'

Fitzy cleared his throat. 'On Saturday, Tom Donald regained consciousness for a few moments and said two words. As far as we could make out – and remember this man is fighting for his life – Tom Donald said "man" and "match." We're certain about the first word. The second could be wrong. Maybe he was asking us to catch this man. We can't know until Mr Donald improves enough to tell us.'

McLaren moved in. 'Before we break up, I want you to form groups of twos and threes and spend half an hour exploring what those words might mean. Bat ideas around. Nothing's too outrageous. The break we need is there. We need to see it.'

He cued me to speak.

'Mr Delaney's gonna speak, but I want you to know the current thinking. The crimes have concentrated in the New Orleans area since he came on board, so the perp may be using him as a focus. For example, there was no incident on Saturday when he wasn't at an event. Is that just a coincidence? So far, we have nothing except dead kids. We have to consider every possibility, no matter how unlikely.'

I stepped forward and threw in my two-cent's worth.

'Last week, I re-interviewed people who may've seen something. It was a waste of time until Baton Rouge. The woman responsible for the event told me she had ordered the judges to change the result when they couldn't find Timmy Donald. She did that because they were about to announce he'd won. Timmy was going to be the winner. We checked the other victims, and bingo! They were all winners, except Pamela White. Her sister Donna came in first in her age group. The thinking is, he couldn't get to her, so he took the next best thing. That pattern works in all cases. Even Lucy Gilmour, the first victim whose body was never found. The last thing she did before going missing was win.'

I paused and studied the faces staring back at me, willing me to give them something they could use. I believed I had. 'Understanding the thread that connects the victims gets us a little nearer to catching this guy. Before, we were watching every kid there. Now, we can concentrate on anybody taking an unusual interest in the winner.'

McLaren spoke, 'Charlie Diskins has done some work on this. What does it tell us, Charlie?'

'It allows speculation about motive – taking the best may feed the enormous ego we know this killer has – or it might be a reference to something in his past, we can't know. Some disappointment or rejection. Mr Delaney has, I believe, correctly identified the link between the victims that helps us build it into a plan to bring him down. Unfortunately, with scores of these events taking place every weekend, the target area is too wide. That's the main problem.'

Diskins rubbed his chin, sorry to be the one to throw cold water on my discovery. He needn't have worried. I was way ahead of him. The connection was valid, though, in the end, limited. Our best bet was still what Tom Donald had strained to tell us. Understand that, and we had a fighting chance.

I joined a group with a male detective called O'Rourke and Detective Corrigan, the dark-haired woman who had asked a question about the lack of semen at the crime scene. I got the impression she was wary of me. O'Rourke, on the other hand, was relaxed and friendly.

'Good work, Detective.'

I accepted the compliment. He was right; it was good work. Just not good enough for me or the next victim, if we didn't catch this guy soon.

'It's not detective anymore. I'm only drafted for the duration.'

'Yeah. I hear McLaren make a big thing out of the *Mr Delaney*, remindin' you you're the temporary help. Listen, I've been in five years now. When I started out, I partnered Ricky Young.'

'Oh, I remember Ricky. How's he doing?'

'He's in Florida. Says he loves it. I don't believe him. Anyway, one morning we were drivin' past the courthouse, and Ricky points you out. You were walkin' up the steps on your way to testify, I guess. Ricky said, "See that guy climbin' the steps? That's Vincent Delaney. You don't know it, but that's who you want to be: that's a detective." So, it's *Detective* Delaney, far as I'm concerned. Okay, let's bat the ball.'

And we did. For forty fruitless minutes.

Match, catch, latch, patch, thatch, scratch – zip, zero, nada, nothing.

* * *

These two were a whole lot less conspicuous in their behaviour than their boisterous predecessors and still managed to look more arrogant than anybody else on the street.

Trainee gangsters, and loving it.

They made the same stop-offs as the first two, out of sight for a couple of minutes then back, kidding their way through a felony-filled morning.

Eventually, they walked into a Universal Car Parking facility. Five minutes later, I recognised them in a white Honda Civic. I pulled out a couple of cars behind. For all their kings-of-the-hill attitude, these were trained people who might spot a tail.

I hung back all the way out to Crossgates. When they drove off the road down to some derelict ground, I let them go and carried on a few hundred yards until my car was out of their sight. Then, I clambered down the bank away from the road. Now, there were three of them – the two I'd followed and a stranger leaning against the side of a blue Mustang. In the distance, the mighty Mississippi flowed on by. The new guy was wearing shades, a dark coat and a deep-red tie. His hair was slicked back above a pencil moustache and a prominent nose. He was relaxed, chewing gum, and smiling at the two felons. The main man took the briefcase from his colleague and handed it over. Two white envelopes were exchanged. Payday.

I'd seen all I needed to for now.

These guys were confident. Running exactly the same scam in exactly the same way: believing they were beyond detection. They hadn't bargained for Pricilla Bartholomew's anger and shame on a rainy night in Jackson Square, and her need to confront me.

I imagined them laughing in the Honda, fingering the cash and thinking how clever – and easy – it was, while the big money went somewhere else. Tomorrow, I'd know where.

I was close to facing what I'd been unable to discuss with myself until now. And I didn't have to wait until tomorrow. I already had that information. All I needed to do was admit it.

Who knows where the road goes?

Who indeed?

But wherever it went, I'd follow.

'It's gotta be.'

Words I'd heard him say so often.

Thirty-Two

For more than a week, there had been no practice – or rehearsal, as Katie Renaldi's gran insisted on calling it. Katie tiptoed from her bedroom and sat down on the top step. A thin line of light came from under the door. She could hear adult voices.

Talking about her.

Their sound rumbled like a far-off thunderstorm, too indistinct to make much out. She went back to bed and fell asleep. Downstairs in the lounge, Bob and Eadie sat side by side on the couch. Eadie's mother occupied the armchair by the television.

Ray said, 'Well, it looks like you were right, Mama. According to the newspaper, she was drowned. We live in a sick world.'

'Maybe the contests will stop.'

Gran Russell shook her head. 'I doubt it. People never think anything bad will happen to them. It'll be business as usual next week.'

'But how does that affect us? What're we going to do? You said the wrong kind of people gravitate to these events. I didn't want to hear that. Now, look,' Ray said what they were all thinking, 'you've put in so much time, but if being there puts Katie in danger, we have to let it go. Nothing to discuss. What do you think, Mrs Russell?'

Emily Russell took a deep breath. 'I think what I always thought. Anything that guarantees a whole lot of kiddies will be there's bound to gather some weird types. You're right, Bob. It's the world we live in.'

Eadie sighed. 'Poor Katie. She'll be so disappointed.'

'Her safety comes way ahead of any disappointment.'

'Her safety is our responsibility, nobody else's. I've always accepted that,' Gran Russell said. 'I don't just accept it, I welcome it. Who else would we trust?'

'So, how do we do that? How do we keep Katie safe?'

'By never leaving her alone, even for a minute.'

'But the danger is real, Mama. Why would we go anywhere near these events?'

'We can't teach a child to run away every time life throws up a problem. No more singing? That can't be right. Nothing's different. Not really. This killer has been out there all along. Now we know what we have to do to look after Katie.'

Bob didn't agree. 'Katie can sing anywhere.'

'Where, Bob? She wants to sing, that's what all the work's been about, an attempt to change how it was the last time. I think we should allow her her moment. Even just one time.'

'And her safety?'

'Her safety is always down to us. Doesn't matter where.'

Bob Renaldi bit his lip. 'Mama?'

'It's important to get out what's inside us when it's pure and good. Don't let it be suffocated by what other people do. Katie wants to sing. Why don't we let her?'

'So, we're going?'

'To one more,' his wife said. 'Only one. I don't want Katie to keep her music inside. That isn't the way to live.'

'One more. When?'

'Are we ready to do this, Mama?'

'Yes, I think we are.'

'Saturday then.'

Thirty-Three

The next morning, everything happened just as before, the collectors worked both sides of the street and returned to their car. I followed their Honda to the pick-up point. Danny was in position to take it from there. Thirty minutes later, I joined him outside a house in Marrero. The bag-man had been in his sights from the moment he pulled off the wasteland on to the road. His gaze never wavered, even when I slipped into the passenger seat beside him.

'There.' He nodded to where the blue Mustang I'd seen a day earlier sat in the drive at the end of a block. 'Sergeant Miller Davis. Long-time law enforcement officer with the NOPD; dependable, upstanding and dirty as they come.'

Our paths had never crossed. He was a stranger to Fitzpatrick, too, until he'd run a check on the vehicle reg.

'And where do you suppose he's stationed?'

'The Fifth?'

'The Fifth. Same as his deceased colleagues.'

'Don't know him.'

'His mother doesn't know him, Delaney. These guys should be on the History Channel – Secret Lives of New Orleans' Finest. That precinct's a nest of snakes.'

Around six o'clock, Sergeant Miller Davis came out of his house, still wearing his shades and still chewing gum. He got into his car, backed out on to the street and took off. He drove north. I hadn't been here in a long time. But I'd been here.

When he pulled the Mustang over, we parked down the street. He wasn't in a hurry. A couple of minutes passed, before he emerged from the car carrying the briefcase. The door in a white clapboard house opened to let him in. He was expected.

The click, click, click of Fitzy's camera added a dramatic soundtrack. Danny knew what I was feeling. I remembered Cal's outrage in the greasy spoon; the colour washing from his face. He said he'd lost something of himself and had learned to live with it, to adjust. Now I realised what those adjustments had been.

The house looked the same as when he lived there with his mother, in the days when we were buddies hanging out together: listening to music, talking about girls and football.

But that was then.

* * *

When I called, he was upbeat.

'Sure thing. When do you want to meet?'

'Tomorrow some time.'

'Can't do tomorrow. On duty during the day, and later, there's a lady waiting for me.'

I didn't believe him. 'Okay. Friday then.'

'Friday night. Late. For the same reasons. I'll tear myself away.'

'That'll do.'

'So where and when?'

'How about the Algiers Ferry pier?'

A note of hesitation crept into his voice. 'All right.'

'After your date, say one o'clock?'

'I'll be there, buddy. Any clues about why?'

I didn't answer. No need. He knew.

'And, hey, are we on for Sunday?'

'Can't miss that,' I lied.

There was no woman, and Cal Moreland was no fool. Neither was I. He'd been a friend. Now, he was a dangerous stranger, probably a murderer. And something in that last exchange told me he was rattled.

Are we on for Sunday, same as usual?

He was talking about football. I'd answered yes. But the Saints were away to the Panthers, so unless we were flying up to Carolina, I doubted it.

* * *

A crowd gathered to watch the excitement. The police car sat in front of the garage door, its red light flashing. Another squad car was parked twenty yards away with a uniformed officer beside it.

High above the drama, the sky was cloudless and dark, filled with the noise of a news chopper. Two policemen kept the spectators back. Every light in the house was on. Inside, Officers Dimmock and Paterson completed their preliminary inspection and found nothing amiss. Nothing, except the body on the bed.

A wailing siren told the ghouls an ambulance was on its way. When the white vehicle raced into the street, the warning noise was deafening. The crowd watched the medics remove a stretcher. Curiosity outweighed compassion.

Officer Paterson met them and went ahead. There were no unnecessary words. The cops stood aside to let them do their job. On the bed, a woman's naked body lay sprawled across the covers. The medics ran simple tests to establish her status. It didn't take long.

The empty pill bottles on the bedside table explained how. When the body was taken out to the ambulance, the bystanders were rewarded for their patience. Tomorrow, they'd have plenty to talk about.

Mia Johnson's final act.

Centre stage, at last.

Thirty-Four

Drizzle fell from the night sky, the kind of rain that rests on every surface; seeping through clothes and skin, cooling blood, chilling bone, muting the spirit. Perfect conditions for what I had to do.

I arrived at the meeting-point ahead of time and let the car roll to a stop in the lot next to the landing: a featureless tarmac space jutting over the Mississippi, illuminated by spotlights on the terminal roof.

It felt unreal.

The Aquarium of the Americas sat off to my right, a bold, black smudge against the grey sky. It was twelve-fifty. He'd be here soon. I wasn't afraid. I was beyond normal emotions. Cal had said it best: gotta be.

I walked towards the deserted jetty, conscious of the wire underneath my shirt. Danny's idea. At the rear of the terminal hidden in the gloom, a van sat. I ignored it and was glad it was there.

The broad steel barrier was wet and cold on my hands. I leaned against it and looked into the void below. There was only blackness, and at the bottom of it, the Mississippi River rushing to the end of its long journey. I ran my fingers over the out-sized rivets that held the barrier in place, lowered my chin and spoke in a whisper to the dank night air.

'Hope you're getting this.'

At one minute to one o'clock, a car turned off Canal onto the ferry approach. It stopped in the middle of the embarkation area thirty yards from where I stood.

He waved, playing our friendship to the last. Cal wore the same blue windbreaker he had that night in the diner when I'd gone against the traders and told him about Cilla Bartholomew and her friends. I was the one who warned him of the danger he was in. I'd confused his angry reaction with everything good.

'Hi, buddy. What gives?'

His act was old. I'd had enough of it. He was dirty.

'When did it begin?' My voice was flat.

He made a face, pretending he didn't understand. 'When did what begin, Delaney?'

I watched him, still confident in his ability to end up walking away free and clear. It wouldn't be like that. However, it finished for me; he was going down.

'When did what begin, buddy?'

I looked at my watch. 'Right now, Miller Davis'll be wondering who could be knocking on his door at this hour. Boy, is he in for a surprise.'

He dropped the pretence. We'd arrived at the end-game. The fingers of his right hand tensed and stretched. Then, the gun appeared, its stubby charcoal barrel pointing at me.

'You just couldn't leave it, could you? Just couldn't leave it alone.' He cocked the hammer.

'Thought we were on the same team, Cal.'

His lips parted in a grim smile, and I knew we'd never been on the same side.

'That night in the diner, I realised it would take a miracle to shake you off. You've always been a pussy, Delaney. But you're a persistent pussy.'

'So, you killed Raymond Clark and Ryan Hill.'

Hope you're getting this.

'Casualties of war. Low men on the totem-pole. Gotta be.'

'And Clyde?'

'Who?'

The name was unfamiliar to him. He'd killed a man he didn't even know.

'The trader you hanged in his back shop.'

'A warning to the others. Except somebody wasn't paying attention.'

He took a step towards me getting ready to pull the trigger. I felt the steel barrier against my back and moved away from it.

'Why?'

He sneered. 'Why? Money, that's why.'

'Money to do what?'

'Those Saints don't win nearly often enough.'

'Fifty dollars?'

His laugh was a bitter snort.

'Yeah, right, fifty dollars.'

He raised the gun. This man hadn't bet only fifty dollars on anything. Ever.

'Sorry, pal,' he said, and shot me. Twice. I didn't feel myself fall. After the first bullet, I didn't feel anything.

Being able to give good advice is fine. Being able to take it is something else. Danny had thrown the Kevlar vest to where I sat checking the fixings on the recorder.

'And wear this.' It wasn't a request.

'You can't believe he'd shoot me?'

'Wear it.'

My chest felt as if a bus had run over it, but I wasn't dead. I struggled onto one elbow. The scene had changed. At the back of the lot, the side door of the parked van lay open. A figure crouched behind it: Danny. Cal had disappeared.

Then, I saw him walking along the top of the barrier that stood on either side of the landing out over the river.

I called, 'Cal! Cal! Stop! It's over!'

He edged along the width of steel, measuring each step on his road to nowhere. To his right, the last few yards of asphalt slipway still offered a safe alternative. Tomorrow, hundreds of vehicles would use it to board the ferry to Algiers. Tonight, Cal Moreland was alone, inching into the pitch-black night above the Mississippi. Then, I understood his insane balancing-act and, in spite of everything, wanted to help him. It shouldn't end like this.

'Cal! Not this way!'

'Yeah, buddy! This way! The only way!'

'You can cut a deal!'

Cal Moreland laughed. 'The people I work for don't make deals, Delaney! There are no deals with them!'

'Cal! Don't do it! Think!'

He stopped and stared into the blackness below. He had a look about him; the wildness I'd admired all my life.

'Cal! Give them up! Whoever they are! Whoever's behind this thing!'

The rain kept falling. Nobody noticed. The sound of footsteps running towards me got louder.

'Cal! Let's talk!'

For the briefest moment, I thought he'd changed his mind. Then, he spoke. 'Who knows where the road goes? Sorry, Delaney. It's gotta be!'

'Fuck's sake, Cal! Don't! Let's deal! Give me a name!'

Then, he was gone.

He cried out as he leapt into space. Fitzy and a guy I hadn't seen before arrived at my shoulder, eyes fixed on where Cal Moreland had been. Fitzpatrick dragged his gaze back to me.

'You all right?'

I didn't answer.

I'd been shot. I'd survived. But I wasn't all right.

* * *

Friday night became Saturday morning.

Fitzpatrick called for assistance. An hour later, we were back in his office writing our separate reports of the incident and the case. Miller Davis was in a cell downstairs. So were the two collectors, and apparently, one of them was ready to talk. Danny made arrangements for the river to be dragged, but that wouldn't begin until dawn. It was possible Cal Moreland had escaped death when he jumped into the Mississippi. Neither of us considered the idea. When the new day arrived, we were sure we had more than enough evidence to put the extortionists away for a long, long time.

Around 6 a.m., another call from Danny brought in Delaup. We ran through the chain of events with him. He was stunned, of course, not least because, once again, the NOPD faced a scandal.

I told him how it began: the meeting in my office with Cilla Bartholomew and the traders; their fear-filled insistence on no contact with the police. How I'd solicited Cal Moreland's help, and the murders of Raymond Clark and Ryan Hill in the so-called drug bust. He was furious to be party to the information so late in the day.

'Your reason for trusting Moreland at this stage was based on the friendship between you?'

'Yeah. And because Clark and Ryan were from his precinct.'

'You knew that, how?'

I took a breath. 'I asked Officer Fitzpatrick to put a name to the license plate number the first time I followed them.'

'Does Officer Fitzpatrick supply you with confidential information on a regular basis?'

He was making a point about being left out of the loop, not the misuse of department resources.

'You put a lot of store in friendship, don't you, Delaney?

'I guess I do, Captain.'

His eyes bored into me. Then, his anger passed. 'Go on.'

I told him about the racket starting up again, Clyde's murder – still unsolved – coming clean with Danny Fitzpatrick and tailing the two new collectors to their meet with Miller Davis.'

Fitzy spelled me. 'We followed Davis to Moreland's place. The circle was complete. After that, it was about making sure we had enough on everybody.'

'And do we?'

Danny lied, 'I believe so, yes, sir.'

He moved to a table covered in blown-up shots of the collectors in action, the money exchange on the piece of waste ground with Miller Davis, then Davis entering Cal Moreland's house. The raids on his house and Cal's turned up cash. A lot of it, though not the big numbers we knew the scam was producing. The money sat in bundles next to the photographs.

'The traders will identify the two collectors. At least they will, if they're sure it's over. In the face of the evidence against them, both patrolmen will give up Miller Davis. Moreland is gone, but we have him confessing to three murders on tape, apart from his attempt on Vince, which I witnessed.'

'What's the sound quality like?'

'Good. Listen.'

Danny pressed a button and the voice of a friend who'd become a stranger filled the room, an eerie reminder of hours before.

'Hi buddy. What gives?'

'When did it begin?'

'When did what begin, Delaney?'

We listened. Fitzy ran the tape forward.

'... couldn't leave it, could you? Just couldn't leave it alone.'

'Thought we were on the same team, Cal.'

'That night in the diner I knew it would take a miracle to shake you off. You've always been a pussy, Delaney. But you're a persistent pussy.'

'So, you killed Raymond Clark and Ryan Hill.'

'Casualties of war. Low men on the totem-pole. Gotta be.'

'And Clyde?'

'Who?'

'The trader you hanged in his back-shop.'

'A warning to the others. Except somebody wasn't paying attention.'

'Why?'

'Why? Money, that's why.'

'Money to do what?'

Danny Fitzpatrick stopped the recording and looked at his boss.

'Of course, the transcription will be part of the final report, but it's all there.'

Delaup looked ill. A man with more worries than he could handle. 'Okay. Write it up. No mistakes.'

He walked to the door. The clock on the wall said seven-twenty-five. I understood the position he was in and didn't envy him. His skin was grey, his eyes even more hooded than usual. He might've been the one who'd been up all night instead of us.

'Can't wait to tell the super about this one. Good work, by the way.'

Good work? Maybe it was, though, at best, a double-edged sword. We'd solved the cop killer case, the murder of Clyde Hays and the extortion of the traders, but landed the department bang in the middle of another NOPD scandal. No prizes for guessing which would be remembered.

Thirty-Five

We went back to putting the evidence together. Fitzpatrick took time out to introduce himself to Miller and the other two in the cells downstairs. He would question them in earnest later. The tape played the unreal conversation. We stopped and started the machine, checking and rechecking what had been said. When it came to the part where Cal Moreland shot me, I blanched.

'Sorry, Delaney, it's got to be!'

'Fuck's sake, Cal! Don't! Let's deal! Give me a name!'

The phone rang. I pressed a button on the recorder and the tape came to a stop. Danny rolled his chair across the room and lifted the receiver.

'Yes, it is,' he said.

Something was wrong.

'What?'

'Tom Donald died twenty minutes ago.'

The news hit me harder than the bullets from Cal Moreland's gun. If I hadn't chased him, he wouldn't have run. He'd be alive, instead of lying on a mortuary slab. Suddenly, I felt tired.

We'd never speak to Tom Donald now. There would be no explanation of why he ran from me. A moment of clarity cut through. Tom Donald hadn't been running from me, not at first; he'd been chasing someone, until he heard or saw me coming after him.

Match, batch, hatch, patch, thatch, scratch.

My pursuit of an innocent man had let the killer escape. The accident was the final distraction, the icing on the cake. The only one who might be able to identify him had been hit by a car. The perp sure had his own share of luck.

'You all right?'

Danny must've been collecting air-miles on that question.

'I need some sleep. I've got a talent contest to go to.'

* * *

Lowell's eyes clouded with the beginnings of doubt. I guessed he was thinking perhaps he'd hitched his star to the wrong wagon. We both knew taking care of him had fallen to the back of the line lately. And here I was again. Running late, passing through. In the park, I gave him all of five minutes. Strictly business.

I called Catherine and asked her to collect Lowell and take him to her house for a day or two. Pressure of work and all that. She agreed. I fed and watered him, and played Little Feat's Dixie Chicken album loud for him while I showered and changed. The need for sleep was replaced by the need to put events of the previous night behind me. Today, the nearest pageant was in Metairie, not far from New Orleans. Would the killer be there? It wouldn't surprise me. If Danny Fitzpatrick was right, I was part of the game.

* * *

The first thing I did when I arrived at the church hall in Metairie was speak to the organisers, dazzle them with my ID and give them Fitzpatrick's number to call if they doubted me. A blousy woman sitting by the front door doing registration asked me to stand to the side and wait until someone could speak to me. Mrs Rose Sinclair and Chantelle Dawson were the people in charge: in their fifties – ruddy-faced, wholesome, matronly figures. Ladies totally immersed in their community. Their main concern was that their event wasn't disrupted. Of course, they didn't get the real story. I fed them a version invented on my way over about a search for a tug-of-love kid. Long on emotion, short on facts.

'And what makes you think this child may be here, Mr Delaney?'

'I don't think she's here. The last sighting of the father was in the Metairie area. In Atlanta, Susannah – that's the little girl – was involved in all kinds of stuff – tap-dancing, singing. Even did some modelling for children's wear. The thinking is, that to keep her happy, her father might be forced into letting her compete in Saturday events like yours.'

Chantelle Dawson was sharper than her colleague. 'Why don't we check our lists and give you a photocopy?'

And keep me at the door.

'That would be helpful, ma'am, thank you, though sure as hell he'll have changed their names.'

'So, what is it you want to do here?'

Rose Sinclair was getting the idea. I wasn't going away.

'A couple of things. You needed to know who I was, and why I was here, in case I found them, and he tried to make a run for it. Now, if I ask you to call the police, you'll do it. It isn't my intention to disrupt anybody's day. I'll be discreet. I need to be able to drift around checking it out. He's probably changed the way Susannah looks, dyed her hair, had it cut, who knows? All I'm gonna do is look.'

Their reluctance was tangible.

'I understand everybody's on edge.'

The senior woman relented. 'Very well. A list of the entrants will be left here at registration.'

Her friend took a final officious shot. 'And if we call the NOPD, they'll vouch for you, is that right?'

'No. If you call Detective Daniel Fitzpatrick. Not everyone knows about this. Check on me, by all means. Just remember, we're trying to reunite a mother with her child. It's a delicate situation; it requires sensitivity.'

She pulled her shoulders back, bristling with self-importance, but she got the point. I was in. And they never did call Fitzy. Too busy selling prize-draw tickets. At the desk, a couple of women and a man were registering a child.

Cute kid. Weren't they all?

The younger woman did the talking, the older one at her elbow with the girl's hand in hers. The man stood back, surplus to requirements.

'Renaldi. Katie Renaldi.'

The church hall was actually a much bigger building than I thought. Two large halls and a lot of smaller rooms, all with the faint musty smell that comes with old buildings when the heating isn't on often enough, and the windows are never opened because they've been painted shut. It was going to be busy; women and kids were everywhere. Men were outnumbered. The competition had started in the larger of the halls. Music drifted out. I poked my head around the peeling frame of the door. 300 or 400 seats faced a stage where a little girl – no more than a baby really – was muddling through an under-rehearsed version of "On the Good Ship Lollipop."

My heart sank, not from the performance – although that would do it – the kid stood in the middle of an orange spotlight, effective because the rest of the hall was in total darkness.

At the front door, people were still arriving, and a line had formed. The woman at the desk was under pressure. I was about to turn away when I noticed a man and a woman tag on at the end. I recognised the woman, though not at first. The man was a stranger to me.

They didn't have a child with them.

Thirty-Six

What to do didn't stay my decision for long. The woman saw me. I waited. When they reached the desk, the females greeted each other warmly. The couple moved into the building without the interrogation I'd been through. She came forward.

'Well, well? Still on the case?'

Claudine Charlton remembered my face, not my name. The guy beside her looked me over. She introduced us. 'This is Alec Adams, my stage manager.'

It was my turn to do the weighing-up. Adams was six-one, late-forties and balding. He'd been handsome. Now, threads of purple from too much booze etched his face. He shook my hand, pressing hard, holding on longer than necessary in a quiet show of macho bullshit. I didn't like him. Or her, for that matter.

'Pretty far travelled, aren't you?'

'Checking out the talent. My shows work because I try to keep the standard high. Don't always succeed. When I hear about a kid who has something, I want them in my competitions. I operate a good few notches above this level, I'm pleased to say. I intend it to stay that way. This is a field trip. Tough going but necessary. Alec's been with me for years. His opinion's always worth hearing.'

A nice explanation, delivered off-the-cuff, though I hadn't forgotten Timmy Donald died in Baton Rouge at one of Claudine Charlton's events. I didn't consider her or her stage manager could be involved; the attack on Timmy Donald was too close to home. Unless that was their cover.

* * *

Fitzpatrick picked the phone up on the first ring. 'How goes it?'

Seeing Claudine Charlton and her ex had rattled me. I was reminded how little we knew about the killer even after months of work. He preyed on winners: not much, considering the amount of effort that had gone in.

'Everybody wants to talk. Since you left, we've been conducting simultaneous interviews with Miller Davis and the bully boys.'

'Good. Good.'

At least that case had moved along.

'And there's no honour among thieves, I can tell you that. These guys would kick their grandmas, if it helped them out. But we do have a problem. The two thugs only had contact with Miller. Miller only dealt with Cal Moreland. His job ended when he passed the cash.'

I finished it for him. 'And Moreland's dead.'

'Exactly.'

The people I work for don't make deals, Delaney. There are no deals with them.

'Any ideas?'

'None.'

'Where are you?'

'Metairie'

'Why there?'

'That's where the nearest event is.'

'Anything cooking?'

'Not so far. The woman who organised the pageant in Baton Rouge is here.'

'What's she doing in Metairie?'

'She's here with her stage manager, a guy called Alec Adams. He's her ex-husband, and she's supposed to hate him.'

'So, why're they together? What're they up to?'

'Talent spotting, she tells me. Hoping to find some kids with enough going on to step up a gear and perform in her shows.'

'You believe her?'

'No reason not to. Yet.'

There was nothing else to say.

'We should hook-up tomorrow. Go back over the evidence together. See if we can't find an angle on this thing.'

'Let's do that.' I ended the call, closed my cell and looked around at the flow of adults and children, preoccupied with their moment in the sun.

'Hello.' Peter Roy was coming towards me. 'Peter,' he reminded me and took my hand. 'We meet again. Busy, isn't it?'

'Yes, it is. Must be an awful lot of talent in the South.'

'Do you really think so?' He made a face, and we laughed.

'Where's your wife?'

'Getting Labelle ready. You haven't heard our girl sing yet, have you?'

I hadn't bothered to give their daughter a listen. 'When is she on?'

'Supposed to be in an hour. These things rarely run on time. Has Molly done her stuff?'

I decided to tell him; he'd suss it sooner or later. His wife would have got it in one. He raised an eyebrow, understanding the implication of what I was saying. 'They're not here today.'

'Really?'

I'd spoiled his day. Peter Roy was a father and bound to be concerned about the safety of his child. His wife had chastised him in front of me for breaking their agreement. "Labelle is never to be left alone. Not even for a minute."

That day, he pretended to be relaxed about the threat. He wasn't now. The tension seeped out of him, at odds with his middle-aged clothes; the suede shoes, the sweater and the beat-up tweed jacket with the protective leather additions at the elbows that made him look like everyone's favourite uncle.

'I better go find Reba,' he said and hurried away to make sure his family was safe.

* * *

Well, well, well. Once more into the breech, and all that. And such rich pickings today. Might have thought the good folks would be deterred by recent events, but no, here they are. Bright as buttons and ready to go. Hell mend them. They just won't learn.

Careful. Careful.

You've been warned.

He's here.

What does he know? Nothing. Stop! What's wrong with you?

He's here. It's dangerous.

That's what makes it fun. Seeing him try to figure it out. And every time he fails, we win.

But the danger?

Yes, the danger.

That's what makes it fun. It was too easy before he came along.

But now, he's here.

Aren't you afraid?

You must be afraid.

No. Why should I be afraid?

* * *

'Excuse me. Can I give you this?' The woman who had spent the morning taking registration stood beside me. Her voice brought me back from wherever I'd been.

'Oh. Thank you.'

'Mrs Sinclair said you needed it. I'm finishing up, so when I saw you, I thought …'

'Yes. Thanks again.'

I stuck the envelope inside my jacket. There was no tug-of-love child to check on; I'd wasted somebody's time. Without the family, I felt uncomfortable. My watch said eleven-thirty. It wasn't even half over. I bought a coffee and took it to the front door. Instant. Good enough.

I remembered Peter and Reba Roy's daughter and took the envelope out to check when she was due to appear. The list ran to three, neatly typed sheets, segregating the children by age. I scanned the names of the first two groups who had performed earlier, turned over and let my eyes scroll down the second page: nothing. And the last sheet: the same.

Labelle Roy wasn't anywhere. That had to be a mistake. How else could it be missing? Then, it came to me. I'd never actually seen Labelle. I'd heard about her. Often. But she was always doing something, or off with the parent I wasn't talking to.

What had happened to her?

Just then, I saw Peter Roy heading away from the main hall. He was taller than almost everyone there, impossible to miss in his old tweed jacket.

And suddenly, I knew what Tom Donald had been trying to tell us.

Two words. The first was man – we were right about that. The second wasn't match, batch, hatch, thatch or scratch. It was patch. Timmy's father was describing his son's killer. He'd been trying to say "patch."

Like the leather ones on Peter Roy's jacket.

Thirty-Seven

Eadie and Mama leaned forward in their seats, clasping each other's hand. Bob Renaldi sat straight, lips pressed together. His heart pounded. When they heard the introduction – 'Katie Renaldi!' – they clapped; an island of applause in the hall. Katie stepped forward, small and vulnerable, alone on the stage. Her eyes darted to where her family waited, willing her to be good.

Come on, Katie. Come on, baby.

In rehearsals, hitting that first cue had been a problem. From then on, it was easy. Easy-peasy-japanesy-lemon-squeezy. Nursing her along, helping her find timing and confidence. Onstage, Katie took a big breath. When the single piano note played across the count, she caught it and sang the opening lines of "American Pie."

A faint sensation flickered inside Emily Russell, like a trapped bird struggling to be free. She ignored it, chastising herself for being an excitable old fool. Seconds later, she couldn't breathe as an invisible band tightened across her chest. Her granddaughter's singing faded; the noise in her head climbed to a roar.

All Katie knew was the song. The hours of practice paying off with every line. When she reached the first chorus, Eadie began to relax. She didn't see Mama's ashen face or notice the tremble in her hands.

The crowd joined in. Eadie hoped they wouldn't put Katie off. In rehearsals, Mama talked and roamed around while the girl sang, insisting she carry on with her performance.

'As soon as the music begins, you go to Katie's world. And don't let anyone in. Nothing exists but you and the song.'

When Eadie suggested the Don McLean classic, both women knew it was a winner. Katie moved in the spotlight like a pro, the humiliation of the previous ill-starred performance gone. Pride washed through Bob and Eadie. They saw their child, happy, assured and enjoying herself this time. The song ended to generous and deserved applause.

Mama Russell slumped in her seat gasping for air. It had worked, just as she'd hoped. Better.

Easy-peasy-japanesy-lemon-squeezy.

Her eyes closed, and the pain stopped.

* * *

'Peter! Wait!'

He looked over his shoulder. When he saw me running towards him, a feral expression clouded his features. Just for a moment. Then, it was gone.

'Delaney?' he said, once again the urbane, laid-back guy. 'Where's the fire?'

'We need to talk, Peter.'

'Sure. What about?'

I tried a door. It was locked. The next one wasn't. Inside, dust-covered boxes lay on the floor, a pile of broken chairs dominated one area of the room and the smell of damp was stronger than in the public spaces.

Peter Roy seemed amused. 'What's up?'

I faced him. He had the advantage in weight and height.

'Where's Labelle? What've you done with her?'

He stiffened. 'I really don't know what you mean.'

'Where's your daughter?'

He shook his head, faking confusion. 'With her mother. With Reba. Where do you think she is?'

He was amazing. If I hadn't known better I'd have believed him.

'I think she's dead. And I think you killed her.'

'What? Delaney ...'

'It was you Tom Donald recognised, so you ran.'

'Who? I don't know what you're talking about.'

'She isn't with Reba. She's dead. You killed her.'

He smiled and shook his head. His voice sounded stranger than ever. 'You clown. You fucking idiot.'

'She's dead. Labelle's dead.'

He stepped closer. I pulled out my gun. Faced with its authority, he stopped, and the persona of easy-going Peter Roy fell away like the mask it had always been. I brought the weapon level with his chest. He believed I'd shoot him. He was right.

'Over here. On your knees.'

The gun forced him to the floor. When he got down, I used the handcuffs Delaup had given me to chain him to a big cast-iron radiator anchored to a wall; the heating system was useful for something.

I read him his Miranda Rights.

'I'm arresting you on suspicion of murder. You have the right to remain silent. Anything you say can and will be used against you in a …'

Laughter interrupted me; he thought it was funny. Tears formed in the corners of his eyes. He grinned. 'Moron. The City of New Orleans is in big trouble, if you're the best they've got.'

The contempt and revulsion I felt for him won out. 'You're crazy. Pathetic. Inadequate and stark-raving mad.'

'You think?' He giggled and reminded me of Julian Boutte in the shotgun in Algiers. 'That your *professional* opinion?'

I took out my cell and called Fitzpatrick. He would take it from here. Tom Donald hadn't failed; he'd given us what we needed.

I waited for my friend to pick up. Deep in my stomach a bad feeling stirred.

'How did it begin, Peter? Was Labelle the first? What lie did you tell her mother?'

I heard myself and knew it couldn't be right. My thinking wasn't logical.

'You fucking halfwit. Can't you see it?'

'See what?' I tried to stay calm.

'She told me you were a fool. I was worried she underestimated you. I was wrong.'

He was enjoying himself. 'Labelle, Labelle, Labelle. You stupid cunt!'

A feeling too terrible to describe crawled through me. 'What're you saying? What're you telling me?'

'I didn't kill Labelle, Delaney. I haven't killed anybody.'

The noise in my ears was deafening; the sound of my own stupidity.

'How could I hurt Labelle? She doesn't exist. She never did. We made her up.' He shook his head at me. 'There is no Labelle.'

The phone fell to the dusty floor.

We made her up. There is no Labelle.

I raced from the room to find Reba Roy, with the sound of his insane cackle chasing after me. I doubted I'd ever outrun it.

Thirty-Eight

It happened so fast. One minute, she was singing, the next, they were announcing her name.

'And the winner is – Katie Renaldi!'

She was overwhelmed but not too carried away to forget her mom and dad, and Gran Russell. She owed it all to her gran. A man shook her hand. She bowed and glanced to where her folks had been. Their seats were empty.

In a small room to the side of the stage, her mother was fighting back tears, squeezing Emily Russell's hand and pleading, 'Come on, Mama. Please, Mama, come on'.

Her dad paced the floor, asking over and over where in hell the ambulance was. The older woman was unconscious. Eadie Renaldi returned from wherever fear had taken her. A new terror seized her.

'Where's Katie? We forgot about Katie.' Her voice was a frantic whisper, poised to become a scream. 'Find her, Bob.'

Bob Renaldi rushed into the hall. This couldn't be. How could they let this happen? After all they'd talked about.

Her safety is our responsibility, nobody else's.

How could they forget about Katie?

The lights were on. The audience was settling down for the next group. He scanned the crowd, his eyes darting from face to face. There was no sign of his daughter. Then everything went dark.

One unforeseen circumstance. Only the shortest time.

A couple of seconds, either way.

All it took.

* * *

I raced towards the main hall. Before I could get there, a man burst through the door running towards me, the look on his face told it all.

'Katie! Katie!' His voice rasped with emotion. 'Katie!'

I grabbed his arm. 'What's happened?'

'My little girl. I can't find her. She was in there.'

This was the nightmare so many parents had gone through, beginning with a missing child: their child. The rising terror, then the guilt and the unimaginable sorrow of identifying the broken body.

And it was about to happen.

We'd come from opposite ends of the building, without finding what we were searching for. That left only two choices: the entrance or the door to my left. I didn't hesitate; there wasn't time for that. I shouted over my shoulder to the distraught father to take the entrance and tried the door handle. It turned and opened. Inside was a broad corridor and a sign pointing to the stage.

I ran, conscious I'd been here before with Tom Donald, and remembering, all too clearly, how that had turned out. A hundred thoughts and a thousand images flashed through my mind, amongst them, Julian Boutte's giggling face.

Déjà vu, all over again.

The competition had restarted. Far away, I could hear an off-key voice. Another corner brought me to another. Reba Roy was at the far end in front of a fire door. 'Delaney.' She greeted me like an old friend, her head tilted in a gesture of pleasant surprise. Still the charmer. 'How are you? How's Molly doin'?'

What stopped my heart cold was the child holding her hand. Comfortable with her new friend: trusting. 'This little thing has lost her mommy.' Reba lifted their joined hands. 'We're off to find her, aren't we, honey? She won't be far.' She ruffled the child's hair with her free hand.

'Where's Labelle?'

She replied, without missing a beat. 'With her group, getting' ready to go on. You'll hear her soon.'

Like her husband, she was very convincing.

Our eyes locked. She knew.

'Let her go, Reba.'

'Who? Katie? Katie's fine with me.' Her hand tightened on the child's.

'Let her go. We know about Panama City and Fort Worth. Baton Rouge and the rest.'

She moved her head from side to side, deciding her next move. Her lips pursed. Her eyes narrowed, and she morphed from a captivating southern belle into a cornered snarling beast. 'Fuck you.'

'Peter told me all about it.'

The mask fell. 'Fuck you! Fuck you!'

She growled like an animal, through gritted teeth. Suddenly, a door to her right marked "Boiler Room" opened and a stagehand came through. Reba darted through it, dragging Katie Renaldi, and slammed it behind her. Precious seconds were lost trying to free whatever she'd used to bar it. Seconds – enough time to snuff out a young life. We put our shoulders against it. The door groaned and edged open. I ran into the bowels of the building; past pipes lagged with cloth, where the air smelled of oil and years of dust lay undisturbed, with Katie's father at my heels. At first, I couldn't see. But when my vision cleared, the horror her innocent victims must have known in their last moments – Timmy Donald, Mimi Valasquez; Pamela, Jolene, and all the others – washed over me.

In the semi-darkness, Reba knelt on the stone floor, whispering words I couldn't hear, looking deep into the girl's eyes. One hand stroked the child's blonde hair, while red-painted fingernails caressed the whiteness of her throat. Hands closed round the tiny neck, preparing to squeeze the life-force from the small body like she'd done more times than we'd ever know. In that hellish scene, the expression on Reba Roy's face was terrifying and awful; something I never wanted to witness again. The only word to describe it was rapture: the ecstasy of the insane.

'Reba! It's over. However, it goes, it's over.'

The murderess smiled and spoke to her captive. 'Is it over, Katie? Don't you want it to be over, honey?'

The child whimpered. Behind me, Katie's father was frozen with fear. Agent Diskins had said the killer's greatest thrill was being there when the end came. Maybe that's what saved her – I don't know. Reba Roy could have snapped the slender neck, and there would've been nothing anybody could have done to stop her. Instead, she kissed her forehead and threw her towards us.

It was so unexpected, it took me by surprise. The father caught his daughter and held her in his arms, crying. The distraction had lasted seconds: no more. When I turned to face her, Reba wasn't there. We'd had her. Now, she was gone. I moved forward, one careful step at a time, barely able to make anything out until I saw an illuminated EXIT sign above a door.

She was getting away; I couldn't let that happen.

The door brought me to the bottom of a flight of stairs. Somewhere, a child was singing. I climbed them and found myself in the wings. Movement to my left – a figure half-running towards the back of the stage – told me she hadn't escaped. I rushed after her, tripping over something on the floor, almost losing my balance but staying in pursuit. She pushed past a couple of people standing at the side. I followed at a run, with no idea where we were headed. Two stagehands drew apart as I charged between them behind the curtains. In the background, the tinny, tuneless vocals, jarring and surreal, added a discordant soundtrack.

All I could make out were shadows. Then, I saw her crouching behind one of the secondary curtains. I ran between hanging ropes, chairs and abandoned props. When I was almost on her, she saw me, broke cover and ran across the stage. I dived and caught her round the waist. We fell together on to the boards. The singing stopped, the backing tape played on. She clawed and scratched at me, her face ravaged by a hatred frightening to be near. It took all I had to keep her pinned down. Nobody rushed to help.

She caught me on the side of the head. My hold loosened. I reacted instinctively and grabbed her hair.

It came away in my hand.

Underneath, Reba Roy was bald. Writhing and spitting; rouged cheeks and red lipstick: a raging distortion. To be face to face with such insanity was sickening and disgusting. But I didn't let go.

I held on.

Thirty-Nine

Fitzpatrick arrived with three uniforms. The Metairie PD was happy to turn Peter and Reba Roy over. It was enough to have held them even for a short time. In the future, it would be hard to come across anyone who hadn't had a hand in their capture. That success-has-many-fathers thing again.

I watched a handcuffed Peter Roy placed in the back seat of the cruiser and remembered his contempt. The leather patches on the elbows of his jacket brought Tom Donald's face to my mind. This time, I felt no need to shrink from it.

Over by another cruiser, Reba Roy refused to look my way. She'd had me fooled; for months on end. A talented lady and a heartless killer.

Driving to the city was a strange experience. Like dreaming in black and white. I ought to have been elated. I wasn't. It had been a rough weekend – and it wasn't over yet.

The moment I went through the door, the applause began. Someone shouted, 'Wayta go, Delaney!'

It had been good work. I'd got there in the end. But it had taken too long. I flopped into Danny's chair and waited for him to appear. When he didn't, I got some paper and began to structure my report, then abandoned it and called Stella.

'Hi there,' she said. 'What's cooking?'

'Tell you later, if you can hang on 'til then.'

'I'm not going anywhere.'

'Good.'

'You all right?'

'I will be when I see you. Just don't know when that'll be.'

'Well, I'm around until whenever.'

'Thanks, baby.'

I replaced the telephone on its cradle just as Danny walked through the door. The energy coming off him crackled.

'Yeah! Yeah!' He slapped my hand in a high-five. 'You did it. You caught them.'

'Where are they?'

'Downstairs.'

'Have they said anything yet?'

'Not a word. Not one, and d'you know what? It doesn't matter. They're gone. Thanks to you.'

'When will McLaren get here?'

'He's on his way as we speak.'

'And Delaup?'

'Any minute. This is a load off for him.'

I remembered how beaten he'd looked. 'What happens next?'

Danny sat on the edge of the desk. 'The Bureau'll take over when they arrive. Our work is done.' He pointed a finger. 'You solved it for them. We could do with you back here. Full time.'

'Dream on. I've got a report to write and a debriefing to attend. Then, I return to my own life.'

Fitzpatrick didn't try to give me an argument. He knew better. Still, he couldn't resist taking a pitch. 'That's an awful lot of talent going to waste, my friend.'

'What makes you think it'll go to waste? I've a business to run, clients to help …'

'Wrongs to right?'

'Not my motivation. Not anymore.'

'No interest in righting wrongs?'

'What I'm interested in is writing a report.'

'Two reports.'

'Two reports, and I'm gone. For good this time.'

'Want to bet?'

'Save your money, Danny. You'd lose.'

He leaned on the desk. 'Delaney, take a second to let what you've done sink in. Two sick bastards are in our cells. It's over. And it didn't take years. Because of you.'

'It's a shitty business. I hate it.'

'No argument there. Right now, you're on a comedown. On a different day …'

I shook my head.

'It's a shitty business, Fitz. Even when we win, it's a shitty business.'

* * *

When Delaup arrived, he shook my hand. 'Well done, Delaney. Well done.'

His skin had florid splashes that made him look like a seasoned drinker, though I'd never seen him touch a drop.

'Thanks.'

'I knew you'd do it.'

'Thanks,' I said again, and let go of his hand. He spoke to Fitzpatrick. 'Update?'

They walked to Delaup's office and closed the door behind them. I settled in front of the PC I'd been given and booted it up. The sooner I produced my report and answered any questions, the sooner I'd be on my way to Stella. McLaren and a man I didn't recognise passed without acknowledging me and joined the others. Everyone's expression was serious. In reality, they must've been elated. Fitzy waved me in. I saved the work I'd done and joined the quartet.

Agent McLaren pushed out a hand. 'Fantastic work, Vince. Your colleagues always had faith in you. They were right.'

I found a half-smile from somewhere. Now, I was Vince. I was impossible to please – call me Mr Delaney, and I didn't like it. Change it to Vince, and I still bristled.

'This is Agent McWilliams. He's been on this thing from the beginning, working with the teams in other states. He's here to assist me.'

He introduced the new guy – Bureau standard issue: clean-featured, conservative suit, well aware of his federal status. We nodded to each other.

Delaup jockeyed himself back in charge. 'Tell us how it went down, Delaney.'

So, I told them. How the list I'd asked Mrs Sinclair to give me showed no mention of a Labelle Roy; Tom Donald's words crystallising into meaning; my face-off with Peter Roy, his sneering admissions, and his wife Reba: just about the last person I would've suspected. When I described the chase across the stage and the wig, Agent McWilliams broke his silence.

'Unbelievable.'

Soon after, I went back to the report. It was somebody else's job now. My part was done. Almost.

Three hours later, she opened the door. Stella took my hand; fed me, made love to me and after, she listened.

'He was a friend. Least, I thought he was.'

'I know.'

'They haven't found his body. Perhaps they never will.'

'One minute he was there, and we were talking, then he shouted and jumped. I didn't see him fall. I was only a few steps from the barrier. When I got there, he was already gone.'

She held my hand. We sat like that for a while.

'You need sleep. It's after two. Let's go to bed.'

I hadn't had any rest since Friday, and now, it was Sunday morning. Stella laced her body with mine. I closed my eyes and was almost asleep when she asked her question.

'Cal Moreland. You said he jumped and shouted.'

'Yeah?'

'Well, what did he shout?'

Forty

Fitzy grinned at me. 'Just can't stay away, can you?'

Delaup joined in. ''Course he can't. This is where he belongs. This is home.'

I let them have their fun.

'How's it going?'

'Don't know yet. McLaren and his buddy have been interviewing them all night. We found two pairs of latex gloves in Reba Roy's handbag. Premeditation. Narrows down the defence options.'

'Defence? What defence?' Delaup's disgust was undisguised. 'They're guilty as hell, and that's where they're going. What they did …' He tailed off, there were no words.

I spoke to Fitzpatrick. 'We need to talk.'

He heard me, though his expression didn't alter.

McLaren chose that moment to come through the door. McWilliams followed a pace or two behind. The FBI man took his time before including us, enjoying his seniority. He'd reverted to type. We'd been a team for as long as we were needed.

'Well?'

Delaup tried to hold on to a corner of the case, but the Bureau was running things now. McLaren wouldn't be bullied or rushed. To emphasise his control, he walked round the desk and sat in the Captain's chair: a symbolic gesture that escaped no one.

'Peter's the weak link. He's got plenty to say, starting with the first body.'

I asked an obvious question. 'Has he told us where Lucy Gilmour is buried?'

'Uh, uh.' McLaren shook his head. 'The first body, not Lucy. These two have been at work a long, long time. He credits – and that's the right word – his wife with planning the whole thing. She's the leader.'

'He actually said that?'

'He actually did. The way he tells it, she's the smartest person alive. Smarter and more daring than anybody. His story drips with admiration. She's what he wishes he could be.'

'Trophies?'

'We haven't found them yet. Peter Roy says they kept the certificates the kids got. Winners. It was all about snuffing out life at its unblemished peak, before the world could corrupt it. "In the perfect moment of innocent victory." His exact words.'

That did it. For a long time, nobody spoke.

Danny broke the silence. 'What was his involvement?'

'Peter Roy views himself more like a student, a fan, privileged to be able to watch a master at work.'

Delaup spat. 'Sick fuck.'

The agent's interest in Delaup's opinion was nil.

Danny said, 'So what did he do?'

'Watched. Just watched. Says he never touched a single child.'

My turn. 'Who invented Labelle?'

'That's one of the best parts for him. They needed to be able to move freely at the pageants. Reba conjured up a daughter for them, and Labelle was born.'

'Reba's inter-personal skills border on brilliant. Her daughter was always on her way, always somewhere else but never got registered. Her mother spoke to everyone, dropped Labelle's name like confetti. People believed she was real.'

'High-risk strategy.'

'Indeed,' McLaren agreed, 'but it was all high risk – their front, the abduction, the murders. Her husband's eyes shine when he talks about it. Thinks it's great.'

McWilliams surprised me by speaking. His boss indulged him. Bureau-boys together. He said, 'Latex gloves in her handbag.

No fingerprints. And the wig minimised the chances of hair. She must've removed it before she started on the kids.'

Red lipstick and a hairless head: the last thing the terrified victims would see. I remembered my scuffle with her on the stage: I'm no kid, and it had shaken me.

McLaren said, 'All of us assumed the attacks on children must be by a male. But it isn't exclusively a single-gender crime. Child abuse in its many ugly forms is committed by both sexes. These crimes are rare, but not unique. Reba Roy outguessed us on that one.'

Reba Roy was a mystery I needed somebody to explain. 'What about her? What's she saying?'

'Nothing. Nothing about the murders. She talks. For all the world, a refined southern woman. Hard to believe. If I didn't know better, I'd have to say she's charming.'

Delaup spoke and added nothing useful. 'Charming? She's a mutant. Needs to be put down.'

'Yes, charming. And quite insane. Probably never stand trial.'

He let the agent's judgement fill the room. We knew he was right.

I said, 'How long have they been doing this?'

The Captain couldn't let it go. 'But she planned it. The gloves. Labelle.'

McLaren struggled to bring order to the story. 'They claim they heard voices. Both of them. Lots of voices. Their heads are full of voices according to him. When a team of psychiatrists have had them for a while, my guess is the verdict will be they're both unfit to plead. They'll spend the rest of their lives in some secure hospital facility.'

'Your tax dollars at work.'

'Something like that, Delaney. Better than the alternative. They could still be out there, and they're not. Because of you.'

'What now?'

The agent made a business-as-usual face. 'We'll spend the next twenty-four hours grilling them before a public statement tomorrow evening. During that time, we'll revisit the crime scenes, talk to people there. We can be more specific about what we're looking for now. The Roys – especially Reba – are distinctive types. It won't be too hard to place them at the scenes.'

He paused. 'Even if that gives us nothing, Peter Roy will tell it like it is. He's a fan, remember. And then, there's your testimony, Mr Delaney.'

Goodbye, Vince. Hello, Mr Delaney.

'Anything else you need from me?'

'No, just your report. When I've read it, we can talk it through.'

I left and waited outside the door until Danny joined me.

'What?'

'You haven't given me a copy of the transcript from Friday night.'

It seemed like a month ago.

'It's on my desk. Forgot about it with all this going on.'

'Can I see it?'

'Sure. We'll check it again if you like.'

In his office, Fitzpatrick lifted a manila folder. 'Want to do this now?'

'Is this the only copy?'

'Apart from the one with my report to the Captain, yes. Have you written yours? What's got you all fired up?'

'Not yet, and something Stel said.'

My interest in his transcription only concerned the last page.

'Cal! Not this way!'

'Yeah, buddy! This way! The only way!'

'You can cut a deal!'

I heard him laugh; it was eerie.

'The people I work for don't make deals, Delaney! There are no deals with them!'

'Cal! Don't do it! Think!'

Reading through it, I remembered the look on his face at that moment.

'Cal! Give them up! Whoever they are! Whoever's behind this thing!'

The sound of footsteps.

'Cal! Let's talk!'

'Who knows where the road goes? Sorry, Delaney. It's gotta be!'

'Fuck's sake, Cal! Don't! Let's deal! Give me a name!'

I lifted my eyes from the last words on the page. 'This isn't it all, Danny.' The certainty on my face stopped him disputing it.

'I'll get the tape. It's in the evidence room.'

He came back. We listened again to how it ended.

'Whoever's behind this thing? Cal! Let's talk!'

'Who knows where the road goes? Sorry Delaney, it's gotta be!'

'God's sake, Cal! Don't! Let's deal! Give me a name!'

We played it, and played it again. Then, we heard it: not the anguished wail I'd mistaken it for, but a long cry that faded with his fall. Cal Moreland used the final moments of his life to answer me. I'd asked him to tell me who was behind the extortion. He had. With his last breath.

The night hadn't devoured that truth.

'Can't make it out.' Fitzy said.

Neither could I. Anxiety fuelled by lack of sleep pulsed in my temple.

'Play it again.'

Twenty minutes later, we were ready to quit. Danny said, 'We'll give it to Randolph. He'll clean this up in no time.'

Randolph was Randolph Todd. He was in Tupelo visiting his mother. Tomorrow, he'd be here. Danny smothered the phone with his hand. 'He wants to know how early you want him to start.'

'Early-early.'

Fitzpatrick finished the conversation and closed the cell. 'He'll meet us here at 6 a.m. That the early-early you had in mind?'

'No, that's just early, but it'll do.'

Forty-One

The journey that began with Cilla Bartholomew was coming to an end.

Along the way, people had died. Now, we had all the pieces of the puzzle apart from the last, and tomorrow, a guy called Randolph would sprinkle his magic over the tape and make it give up its secret. That was the hope.

I drove to Catherine's to collect my dog and see the family. When I rang the bell, I heard Lowell bark and the tread of approaching footsteps. Molly was usually first to the door; instead, it was Ray.

'Hi, Delaney. Not at the game?'

'Not today.'

It was all I had. Lowell bounded to me, wagging his tail, pleased to have me back. Seeing him made my day. I had to hold myself back from getting down and wrestling with him on the floor. Catherine sat with her feet curled up under her on the couch. In the corner, the television was on, loose pages from newspapers were scattered around, a typical Sunday scene.

'Hi. How're you?' She kissed my cheek.

No announcement about the capture of the killer. That would be tomorrow's news. Until then, ignorance was bliss. I wasn't going to drag it through Catherine's Sunday.

'Fine. Thanks for looking after Lowell.'

Lowell licked my hand. I patted him and changed the subject. 'Where's Molly?'

'Oh, Molly.' Catherine made a face.

'She all right?'

'You could say.'

'Upset about her singing career coming to an end?'

'Not at all. She's got a new ambition.'

The sound of someone coming down the stairs made me turn. When she came in, I saw the change. She held her hands together in front, her gaze cast down, not looking at her parents or me, or even the TV.

'Hi, baby.'

I bent, expecting her arms to go around my neck and hear a dozen questions I couldn't answer. It didn't happen. She left as she'd arrived, with her head bowed and her hands together.

'What's going on?'

'Nothing. She's fine.'

'Well, what was all that about?'

'Molly's made a decision.'

'Really? What would that be? She's five years old.'

Catherine's face was solemn as her daughter's, except for the flicker of a smile at the corners of her mouth. 'No more pageants. From now on, it's mass. Molly wants to be a nun.'

I said my goodbyes at the door.

'By the way, I'll be bringing someone from now on.'

My sister seemed relieved. She sighed and kissed me on the cheek. 'About time.'

* * *

Randolph was about twenty-two, tall and thin. He wore jeans and a tartan shirt over a grubby T-shirt with writing on it I couldn't make out. His hair was long and unwashed, which might have been a description of him. When Fitzpatrick introduced us, he grunted and nodded, blinking behind his glasses.

Danny produced the tape and handed it to him. This guy spent his life in a part of the building I'd never been in; a basement section of the east wing. Following him there was like going in search of the *Phantom of the Opera*, except instead of a cavern, we found a neat room crammed with equipment I'd struggle to turn on.

He sat in front of a bank of screens and machines, flicked some switches, leaned in and passed from this world to his own. Fitzpatrick and I hung around. Apart from answering a few initial questions about what we needed, there was no role for us to play; we left Randolph to it. Whenever he had something, he'd call Fitzpatrick.

Danny and I went our separate ways. I returned to my unfinished report – likely to remain unfinished until we heard from Randolph.

The clock on the wall showed ten-thirty. My cell rang.

'Conference Room. Five minutes.'

I took the elevator. Danny was running through the channels on the big-screen television at the end of the conference room. 'Press statement any minute now,' he said.

We watched, not speaking. What was there to say? This was a level above our humble toil – the land of PR, of square-jawed senior officials asleep in their beds while the real work got done. It was about promises and confidence and perception; most of all perception. And, of course, recognition, the more public the better.

Danny's cell rang. 'Ok. Good.'

I knew who he was speaking to.

In the basement, Randolph said, 'Think I have what you want. Not sure you're gonna like it.'

His longest sentences of the day. He touched a switch. I might have been listening to a different conversation. My voice and Cal Moreland's were clear as glass. When Randolph stopped the tape after the fourth or fifth play, the silence screamed.

Fitzpatrick said, 'How could we have missed it?'

'The phone call about Tom Donald interrupted us. We never got past that point again.'

'But how did you even know to look?'

It would've been nice to take the credit and add another layer of shine to my legend.

'Female curiosity. Never underestimate it.'

* * *

He was alone. We gave it a couple of minutes and joined him in his office. He was seated behind his desk engrossed in a case folder, the same one that was my current fascination, jacket off and hanging over the back of his chair. His concentration never wavered. Everything about him said business as usual.

Quite an act.

'Saw you on TV,' Fitzpatrick said. 'Good that the department gets some credit.'

'Saw it, did you?'

He put the case-notes down and leaned back, pretending a modest acceptance of the heights he was forced to climb on our behalf.

'Only what we deserve. Making sure we get ours. Those Bureau guys want it all. Always been the same. It was important to be there this morning. Even so, we won't get a quarter of the recognition we deserve.'

Fitzpatrick said, 'Still, quite a thing to be on the same successful team as the FBI, especially with the Cal Moreland shit-storm coming down the line.'

'Yeah.'

The mention of scandal changed his mood.

'You read the transcript?'

'I did. Can hardly believe it. And he was your friend, Delaney. You must be feeling it.'

Yes sir. Quite an act.

Fitzpatrick produced the tape machine and placed it on his desk.

'One more thing I think you might like to hear.'

'Oh yeah?'

The recording was primed. When Fitzy pressed the start button, Cal Moreland's voice cut through the air so clear, he might have been standing in the room.

'Cal! Not this way!'

'Yeah, buddy! This way! The only way!'

'You can cut a deal!'

'The people I work for don't make deals, Delaney! There are no deals with them!'

'Cal! Don't do it! Think!'

'Cal! Give them up! Whoever they are! Whoever's behind this thing!'

Those footsteps again.

'Cal! Let's talk!'

'Who knows where the road goes? Sorry, Delaney. It's gotta be!'

'Fuck's sake, Cal! Don't! Let's deal! Give me a name!'

In the moment of silence before Cal Moreland's last word, I watched the transformation on the senior policeman's face. Disbelief became horror.

'Delaaauuuppp!'

And the strangest thing. For the first time, I was able to hear the faint splash as his body plunged into the murky water of the Mississippi. Two uniformed cops appeared at the door. A piece of perfect choreography. I brushed past them on my way out. Behind me, I heard Danny Fitzpatrick.

'Anthony Delaup, I'm arresting you in connection with …'

I knew the rest. We all did.

I didn't use the elevator. I headed for the stairs. People rarely used the stairs. I'd nothing to say to anyone.

Not hello. Not goodbye.

I was exaggerating. If push came to shove, I could probably manage a goodbye.

Forty-Two

On Tuesday morning – surprise, surprise – things were just the same. The phones had gone quiet again. And it felt all right. I spent time catching up – reading the paper – because a man needed to know what was going on in the world, and messing with the Word Jumble. Today was a breeze and took me less than a minute.

LFROOITOP

PORTFOLIO. Sometimes, I'm good, or maybe sometimes, it's easy.

When I was done, I took the harmonica from my coat pocket, put my feet up on the desk and began to blow, while Lowell lay in the corner; digging it.

Later in the afternoon, I had a visitor: Danny Fitzpatrick. My first thought was something must have gone wrong, but no, he'd just stopped by to update me on the case and talk about the gig on Saturday.

'We found cash at Delaup's house and bank accounts. A lot of money. There's probably more. We'll find it. Whether we can make the murder charges stick is less certain. Easy for him to admit to extortion. Claim Cal Moreland was acting by himself in the killings. It doesn't matter. He's finished.'

'Have you interviewed the traders?'

'Yes. Mrs Bartholomew and a few others. Your name got mentioned. By me, if that's what you're asking?'

I guessed it was.

'What happened to the little girl, the one with Reba Roy?'

'Katie Renaldi? She's all right. I spoke with her father. Her grandmother collapsed; too much excitement. They thought she was going to die and took their eye off the ball. The old lady recovered. If you hadn't come along, it would've been a different story.'

'Who's in charge down there?'

He hesitated. 'I am. Temporarily, at least. You don't want to stay on and work for me, do you?'

'How did you know that?'

'Need time to think about it?'

'No, but it gives me quite an edge on the opposition, doesn't it?'

He leaned towards me, suddenly serious. 'How many Chuck Berry songs do you know?'

'Not sure. A couple. Two or three. Why?'

He made a that-could-be-a-problem face.

'Tony di Marco's got a big party in on Saturday night. They've asked if we can play Chuck Berry.'

'So?'

'It would be good if you could learn some more of his stuff.'

'How many more?'

He took a deep breath. 'Another twenty would be good.'

* * *

In the end, Stella did go to New York but for a good reason. Her brother called to tell her their dad had had a fall. He was all right; a bit shaken, though otherwise okay. She decided she had to see him, and I ran her out to the airport to catch an early-afternoon flight north. Part of her didn't want to leave. She must have asked me a dozen times to be careful. I flippantly brushed her concern away.

'Aren't I always?'

That got the look it deserved.

Lowell stayed in the car, and at the departure gate, we kissed for a long time, like teenagers. I waited until her plane had disappeared into a blue sky and headed back to the city. The atmosphere in the car was subdued. We didn't play the radio.

Nobody was in the mood. Lowell lay on the front seat with his paws over his eyes, and I knew he was missing Stella already. He could join the club.

The last few days had been as traumatic as any I could remember in my fifteen years with the NOPD. The Reba and Peter Roy horror show had been brought to a close, but only after eight innocent kids had died. Of course, the credit went elsewhere. It usually did. That didn't matter to me. I was glad to have been involved, even though I'd risked my relationship with my family.

Cal Moreland was a different story.

Most of my memories were of two young guys, well impressed with themselves and each other. Talking trash and dreaming big. Better days.

Then, the sad truths dragged me down: Moreland was a dirty cop who had sanctioned the hanging of Clyde Hays in his back shop and tried to kill me at the Algiers ferry terminal. In the end, it was just as he'd said: no quarter. All we'd had in common was the Saints.

I couldn't face the office, so I went home. The afternoon would be filled with mundane tasks that had been left behind; boring stuff Lowell had no use for. He settled himself in a corner and stared across at the door. My dog still had the blues. I ran my hand through his coat and stroked his head. 'She's coming back, boy. Don't worry, she's coming back.'

I toyed with the Word Jumble, without making much progress, then went next door and asked Mrs Santini to look in on Lowell, though in his current mood, she wouldn't get much of a welcome from him. Before leaving, I tuned the radio to Bayou 95.7 and cranked the volume up. If that didn't lift him, nothing would. When I closed the door, he didn't look at me.

My first stop was the tax assessor's office on Perdido Street before they closed, and an interview with an inspector who was having difficulty believing my records. He was in his early sixties, grey-haired and serious. In his time, he had probably seen it all.

I watched in silence while he reread the notes he'd made in my file. Once or twice, his eyes narrowed, and he glanced across – unable to credit what was on the page. Then, he fired questions at me for half an hour, while an overhead fan blew air around the room without making a difference to the temperature. The answers I gave tested his experience and puzzled him. Finally, he got to what he'd wanted to ask from the start.

'Are you sure you're in the right line of work? I mean, are you any good at this PI thing?' He struggled to simplify his thinking. 'Don't make much money, do you, Mr Delaney?'

What could I say? 'I try my best.'

'Then, can I suggest you start behaving in a business-like manner, beginning with invoicing your clients? All your clients.'

'What would be the point? Some of them can't afford me.'

He shook his head. Tax, he understood, dealing with an idiot was beyond him. But his point hit home. I'd speak to Harry Love about putting my name around some of his colleagues.

Back on Dauphine, the office was as quiet as ever I remembered. With little else to do, I sorted through the pile of bills in the bottom desk drawer, then strolled to the nearest ATM and got a statement. The statement confirmed the tax inspector was onto something. Not for the first time, the cheque I was expecting from Harry Love for not doing very much was going to keep the wolves from the door.

Good old Harry.

Around seven o'clock, I grabbed a fried shrimp and oyster po'boy in Verti on Royal, not far from the office, and got a knowing nod and a smile from a Creole waiter with brilliant white teeth when I told him to ask the kitchen to go heavy on the wow sauce. By the time I made it home, the light going out of the day. I opened the door and heard Willie Nelson singing about a good-hearted woman in love with a good-timing man. Country music.

Lowell hated Country. Normally, he'd howl the place down.

It was dark in the lounge. When my eyes adjusted, I saw Lowell lying on his side. Earlier, he'd been morose: on a downer.

Now, he whimpered as if he was injured. I moved across to him and took his head in my hands. He gazed up at me and over my shoulder with pain in his eyes. Even then, I didn't get it. So much had happened in the last few days, maybe my senses had dulled, or maybe I was losing it, but seconds passed before I was able to put it together.

The smoky, sweet smell hanging in the air should've been enough. And Bayou 95.7 was a rock station; they didn't play Country. Lowell whimpered and didn't move.

Because someone had hurt him.

In that moment, the realisation of how stupid I'd been overwhelmed me. I turned, slowly, fighting the fear gathering in my stomach.

Julian Boutte was sitting on a chair against the far wall, grinning at me. A half-full bottle of Jack sat at his feet surrounded by cigarette butts and roaches. Juli had been waiting a while. The pen and the newspaper I'd left open at the Word Jumble lay in his lap.

I hadn't seen him since the day he was sentenced. By then, Ellen was gone, and I'd left the NOPD. Seven years was a long time. I expected him to have changed. As far as I could tell, he hadn't: he was older, though on balance, wearing as well as anyone who had spent twenty-three hours out of every twenty-four in a locked box away from the sun. His voice was thick with alcohol and pleasure.

'Thought you weren't coming. Thought we were gonna be ships that pass.' He laughed. 'Would've been a shame.'

Boutte stabbed a dirty finger at the newspaper. 'Finished your puzzle for you. Hope you don't mind. Did it every day, near enough, in Angola.'

My eyes were on Lowell, still on the ground.

'Surprised you were having trouble with it. Smart guy like you.' He read the letters out. 'NADMDARIE. Wanna last guess?'

I ignored him.

'What did you do to the dog?'

Boutte coughed and spat on the floor. 'Feisty animal. Gotta give him that. Quieted down after I kicked him a couple of times. Probably cracked a rib or two. Won't count. He'll be dead, right after you.'

His words fell into the darkness between us. I didn't hear them. I wanted to tear Boutte's head from his shoulders: For Ellen; for Lowell; for the black woman he'd murdered. But most of all, for me.

He repeated the Word Jumble again and shook his head. 'NADMDARIE. Took less than a minute. MARINADED. Easy. For a chef.'

Julian was high. In control. The gun in his hand said it was so.

'You hurt my dog.'

The pages fell to the floor, and his expression hardened. 'Dry your eyes, Detective. Givin' you the same chance you gave my brother. Remember how that went down? You shot an unarmed man and didn't serve a day for it. Take out your piece and roll it over here.'

I ran my hand gently over Lowell. Dogs weren't like people. There were things they couldn't deal with. He needed to see a vet.

Boutte took a slug from the bottle of Jack, set it back down and wiped his mouth on his sleeve. He lit a Gitanes and added its acrid stench to the room. When he spoke, he sounded relaxed, almost mellow. This was panning exactly as he had planned. Juli was happy.

'Won't ask again,' he said. 'Do it. 'Less you want me to smoke you right now.'

I opened my jacket, lifted my gun with two fingers from the holster and placed it on the floor.

'Kick it away.'

The gun skidded across the floor and cracked against the skirting board. Beside me, Lowell growled and bared his teeth. His courage was admirable, but courage wouldn't be enough. Julian was losing patience.

'No sense stretching it, Detective. The cavalry won't be coming. It is what it is.' Boutte cocked the hammer. 'This is fucking sweet. Ced would've loved it.'

'You talk too much, Juli. Anybody ever tell you that?'

'Yeah, maybe I do at that.'

He tossed the cigarette away. It landed over at the window. The flimsy net curtains caught fire, and for an instant, the flames distracted his attention. I dived at him and caught him in a tackle the Saints would've been proud of. We fell, pawing at each other and staggered to our feet, locked together, too near to each other to land any meaningful blows, until I slammed his back against the wall next to the burning nets and held him there. Our faces were inches apart. His breath was sour, and his eyes stared hatred.

Suddenly, he screamed as his hair caught fire, and his scalp blistered in the heat. Julian went crazy, shook himself free, lashed out and caught me. I stumbled and hit my head off something solid on my way down. Maybe I blacked out; it was impossible to know. But when I was able to focus, Boutte had managed to put out the flames on his head, although most of his hair was gone, and the pain must've been incredible. He towered over me and steadied himself, savouring the final moments of what it had been about for him from the beginning. He raised the gun. 'Tell Cedric I said hello.'

Later, I couldn't decide if Lowell had always intended to attack, or if the fire – by this time licking the ceiling – spooked him into action. Either way, it worked.

From the corner of my eye, I saw him race between us. Boutte saw him too though not in time. The dog caught the killer's wrist and bit him, hard. Julian howled, dropped his weapon and aimed a kick at him, which missed.

Lowell ran to the opposite wall, picked up my gun in his teeth and brought it to me. Boutte was holding his piece when I fired, and by the look on his face, he was the most surprised guy in New Orleans when the bullet blew him away.

That is, if you didn't count me.

Lowell's trick with the harmonica saved my life. I had no doubts and no regrets: the world was a better place without the Boutte brothers. With Julian, like his brother Cedric, it had been him or me. Except I wouldn't be carrying the can this time. Not for anybody.

Him or me? Same as before. When you got right down to it, not much to think about. And I hadn't.

* * *

The neighbours came out to watch and got a good show. More excitement than the good folks were used to: two fire engines and a whole lot of water, as well as a couple of police cruisers with blue lights flashing, and a dozen uniforms waiting until it was safe to go into the building.

When the blaze was extinguished, the crowd fell silent and watched the black bag with the body inside being loaded into the coroner's wagon. It drove away. I followed it with my eyes until it was gone.

Julian Boutte was finally out of my life.

A TV news helicopter hovered in the night sky. On the ground, a camera crew moved through the crowd photographing the scene from different angles and interviewing people who knew nothing about what had happened.

Nobody asked me anything. I tried not to take offence.

They were able to save the house, though it would be some time before it was fit to live in. The worst of the damage was the lounge – a blackened shell – and part of the roof had caved in. Strangely, I was unmoved; this had been Ellen's home, never mine. Without her, I wouldn't have been here. Now the man who'd caused her so much pain was dead, it was just a pile of bricks and mortar for the insurance company to sort through.

Me and Lowell were in the street when Danny arrived. He took one look at the smoking mess and whistled through his teeth. I half-expected him to mention Chuck Berry but he didn't. Good decision, Fitzy.

I hadn't noticed Rosa Santini behind me. 'Yes sir,' she said. 'No shortage of excitement with you, Delaney.' She eyed me up and down, satisfying herself I was alright. Lowell licked her hand. 'Get a vet to take a swatch at this guy.'

Maybe he'd take a swatch at me while he was at it.

Technically, my dog and I were homeless. All I had were the clothes I was standing in, and it didn't matter. Lowell, on the other hand, knew his priorities; he gripped the harp in his teeth. That made me smile.

I turned away from what was left of my house and called Stella. 'Remember we talked about where we should stay?'

'Your place or mine. You wanted to think about it.'

'Well, I've come to a decision.'

Acknowledgements

I would like to thank Betsy and Fred at Bloodhound Books for their faith and support. They understand writing and writers; a rare thing. John Hodgman deserves much credit for the many hours he spent bringing his skill to the editing of the manuscript, and for his comments and observations on the journey.

Heather Osbourne for her eagle -eyed proofreading and steering me right on more than one occasion .

Sumaira Wilson , who pulled the whole thing together painlessly - for me at least .

Sarah Hardy , for her tireless efforts to push this book out into the world.

Also, the people I met in New Orleans, so generous with their support. I am indebted to you and your wonderful city.

And my wife Christine, the real brains of the outfit, whose powers of imagination and invention stretch to the horizon and beyond. Without her this book would not have been.

Lightning Source UK Ltd.
Milton Keynes UK
UKHW041121221118
332789UK00001B/72/P